# Clancy's Bulba

# Clancy's Bulba

## Michael O'Gormon

Hutchinson

London Melbourne Sydney Auckland Johannesburg

Hutchinson & Co. (Publishers) Ltd

An imprint of the Hutchinson Publishing Group

17–21 Conway Street, London WIP 6JD

Hutchinson Group (Australia) Pty Ltd
30–32 Cremorne Street, Richmond South, Victoria 3121
PO Box 151, Broadway, New South Wales 2007

Hutchinson Group (NZ) Ltd
32–34 View Road, PO Box 40–086, Glenfield, Auckland 10

Hutchinson Group (SA) Pty Ltd
PO Box 337, Bergvlei 2012, South Africa

First published 1983
© Michael O'Gormon 1983

Set in Linotron Plantin by
Rowland Phototypesetting Ltd
Bury St Edmunds, Suffolk

Printed in Great Britain by The Anchor Press Ltd
and Bound by Wm Brendon & Son Ltd,
both of Tiptree, Essex

British Library Cataloguing in Publication Data
O'Gorman, Michael
Clancy's Bulba.
I. Title
823'.914[F]      PR6065.G/

ISBN 0 09 153770 3

For Kenny

# I

When the silver light of dawn entered the hotel bedroom it found all four souls fast asleep. On the bed itself was the cockerel, Taurus Bulba. He was nestled right in the centre of the mattress and it looked very much as though he was not only going to let the dawn slip by without opening an eye and taking note of the new day, but the whole of the morning as well. On the floor on the right-hand side of the bed lay Bulba's three owners in sound slumber. All three were snuggled up close together with blankets from the bed wrapped around their bodies. The man nearest the window was Barra Duffy. He was in his mid-thirties and he had a quarter share in the cockerel that slept on the bed. Next to Duffy slept Pagannini O'Leary, a man in his early fifties, and he too had a quarter share in the cock. The man nearest the bed was Milo Clancy and he had the remaining 50 per cent interest in the feathered fighter. Clancy, like Duffy, was also in his mid-thirties, and when at home on his little patch of land in the county of Mayo on the west coast of Ireland there too would be found Taurus Bulba in Clancy's own back yard, living out his peaceful life, marshalling his dozen hens and taking it easy. . . . But all four souls were far from home now. They were in one of Aggie Carney's rooms in the White Willow Hotel and well over a hundred miles away from their own little village.

The dawn disappeared; following close on its heels came a fine sunny summer morning. When the first shaft of sunlight came through the window the cockerel, Taurus Bulba, awoke. A second after he had opened his eyes he crowed out, apologizing to the morning for not having witnessed its coming. Then he rose up out of his unnatural sleeping quarters and looked around at his strange surroundings. He crowed again, this time with anger and venom, his eyes in search of the nearest perch. With powerful wings at full stretch Bulba rose up, hovered for a moment, then swooped to the headboard and took note of the morning. He saw the shaft of sunlight slanting through the window to the mattress, and he saw the four walls that closed him in, keeping him from this grand morning. Bulba's heart became heavy with self-pity and he crowed out his misery to the ceiling above his head.

'For the love a Christ, will somebody shut that scutterin' cock up!' barked Pagannini O'Leary as he brought the blankets up over his head and chased after his sleep once more.

Milo Clancy was startled out of his dreamless sleep. He sat himself upright and his eyes went to the bed. There was a moment of panic in his eyes on seeing the empty mattress, but Bulba crowed out his presence and Clancy breathed a sigh of relief. 'Arrah, there ya're, me darlin',' cooed Clancy rising to his feet. 'Did ya sleep the sleep a the just, light a me life? Did ya not dream about what ya were goin' to do Matti Finn's fucker of a cock come t'is evenin'?'

'That's it!' snapped Pagannini, flinging off the blankets. 'There'll be no sleep for ne'er a one now seein' that ye two are awake and kickin'!'

'Mornin' Pagga,' greeted Milo, stroking Bulba's copper-coloured breast with the fingers of his left hand.

'What's good about it?' snapped Pagga as he rose painfully to his feet.

'Yar piles actin' up again?' asked Milo, seeing O'Leary's right hand scratching hard at the bouquet of sorrows that nestled between the cheeks of his arse.

'Aye, they're on fire. They've been blazin' away without ne'er a bita let up all through the fuckin' night. 'Tis a bad sign, is that. Somethin's in the air this day.'

'Now none a that shit! Positive thought, that's all I want from yarself t'is day. If ya have any feelin's at all at all of the negative kind then leave them unspoken. Bulba is not to be upset.'

'Well, me arse is on fire and that's a fact, and when me arse is on fire there's somethin' in the fuckin' air. It might be somethin' good ya know. It doesn't have to be bad.'

'Bad or good, Pagga, keep yar morbidosities to yarself.'

'I'll not say another fuckin' word on the subject,' said O'Leary. 'But if the scutterin' day should turn sour on the lot of us, don't say that me piles didn't shout out their forebodings loud and clear.'

2

'Give Duffy a shake, will ya, 'tis time the last of the dead came to life,' said Milo.

'The fucker'd sleep 'til doomsday.' O'Leary's left boot tapped gently on Barra's ribs. 'Up with yarself, Barra Duffy, before yar bones take root to the shaggin' carpet and yar arms start sproutin' branches!'

'What time is it?' mumbled a voice from under the mound of blankets.

' 'Tis time ya were up and kickin',' answered Clancy, who was now stretched out on the bed and looking up at the roosting cockerel just above his head.

'There's a fine breakfast waitin' for us down there in that dinin' room, Barra. Buckets of greasy bacon, mountains of eggs and Mrs Carney's own soda bread, pounded and baked with her own fair hands. But there's rules and regulations governin' the eatin' of it. If we're not all three of us down there in that dinin' room between eight and eight fifteen, then Mrs Carney'll be havin' the food off her tables and passin' it on to her army of pigs.'

'I'll skip breakfast, lads, if ya don't mind.'

'Ya'll get yar arse off that carpet straight away!' barked Milo Clancy. ' 'T'll be the first and probably the only time ya'll have breakfast served at ya without havin' to go and cook it yarself. We're payin' the bitch good money. We might as well take all her facilities and gat our fuckin' money's worth.'

'Another five minutes, lads, and I'll be with ye,' mumbled Duffy, burrowing even more deeply under the blankets.

'Pagga, make use of yar left boot,' ordered Clancy.

Duffy felt Pagga's boot on the crown of his arse and grudgingly brought the blankets away from his face.

'The grand Barra Duffy arose and appeared to many!' smiled O'Leary as he watched him get to his feet.

'Jasus, but me poor ol' back doesn't half ache,' groaned Duffy, with both hands cradling the small of his back.

'And whose idea was it that us three eegits should bed ourselves on the hard fuckin' floor and give the cock the bed?' snapped O'Leary.

'Never mind him, Barra,' replied Clancy. 'That was a sound and brainfilled idea ya had there. 'Tis only right and proper that Bulba gets the cream and we the milk.'

'The milk me fuckin' arse!' cursed O'Leary. 'Look where the

thing is! Perched on top a the fuckin' headboard! 'Tis the devil himself that can come an' fetch me if Bulba hasn't been roostin' there all night. There's us three daft amadáns lyin' on the rock-hard scutterin' floor all night and right in front of our eyes is a half acre of mattress lyin' idle and goin' to waste!'

'Arrah, whist with yar naggin', Pagga,' said Clancy. 'Ya're like an old woman with yar moanin' and groanin'.'

'Bulba comes first,' added Duffy.

'Ya're not gettin' me drift! Ya're not gettin' me fuckin' drift!' groaned Pagga, the crimson coming to his cheeks. 'The three of us could have been on that bed last night, gettin' ourselfs some dacent sleep. Bulba would have been okay roostin' on the fuckin' headboard or even better still out in the fuckin' shed where he belongs. Instead of which, we're all full of the cramp and God knows what else because of sleepin' on the fuckin' floor.'

'There's no way we could have put Bulba outside for the night,' said Duffy. 'He'd have been sabotaged.'

'Sabotaged?'

'He'd have been got at,' persisted Duffy, looking to Clancy for confirmation. 'Wouldn't he, Milo?'

'Aye. Ya can't be too careful, Pagga.'

'Okay! I grant to both ye brainless gombeens that our Bulba could have been sabotaged, but couldn't we have left him perchin' on the back of a chair for the night, or on top a the headboard? Did he have to take over all a the bed that we paid good money for? Doesn't it sound a little daft to yarselfs that we humans bedded ourselfs down on the bloody floor while a winged bird with a coatin' a warm feathers lays himself down to rest on a mattress that was made for God's first creatures to lie on?'

'I'm tellin' ya, Pagga, for the umpteenth time,' hissed Duffy, 'Taurus Bulba comes first!'

'An' if I hear that watery mouthfilled shit comin' from yar gobhole just one more time, Barra Duffy,' bellowed O'Leary, 'I'll put me shaggin' fist right though yar knopper!'

Clancy was off his back and between the two of them before knuckles could be bared and punches thrown. 'Back off the both of yees! Ya'll upset Bulba, for Christ's sake!' Clancy got himself a roomful of silence. He let all of five seconds pass as he gazed with wrathful eyes from Duffy to O'Leary and back again. Both men

4

looked down at the carpet, neither wanting to face Clancy's scorn.

'We're here to do battle!' said Clancy, knowing that peace and harmony would soon be restored. 'If ye two are spoilin' for a shaggin' fight ya're goin' to have to wait 'til this day is over and done with. We have to take on Finn's black devil tonight and beat it. Ye've both got jobs a work to do. How can yar pinhead brains be on yar work when ya're both hell bent on puttin' the knife inta each other, eh? Eh! Now take each other's paw in yar own and let's have no more fuckin' crap outa the pair a yees.'

Grudgingly Pagga extended his right hand and even more grudgingly Barra took it.

'That's better!' Clancy beamed, 'Now go tidy yarselfs up, for the love a Christ. Ye look like a pair a withered prunes. Did ya have to bed yarselfs down in yar best clothes?'

''Twas cold sleepin' on the floor, Milo,' protested Barra weakly.

'And 'twas yar grand and brainfilled idea that put us there,' snapped Pagga.

'Is it that ya're startin' up again, Pagga O'Leary?' asked Clancy in a dangerously low tone. 'Ya're not tryin' ta best me now, are ya?'

'Sorry, Milo.' O'Leary quickly stepped a pace backward.

'Okay, let's get this mornin' under way. Barra! Bulba's breakfast.'

'Who's got fags?' Pagga searched through the empty pockets of his Sunday suit.

'There's some in the coat pocket a me suit,' said Clancy, sitting himself down on the edge of the bed.

'Where is it?'

'In the fuckin' wardrobe hangin' on a hanger where yours should be.'

Pagga inspected himself in the dressing-table mirror. 'Jasus, but 'tisn't half creased. Has any of yees got a brush?'

'Yeah, hang on there 'til I pull down me pants and shit one specially for ya!' sneered Duffy, busy mixing up a concoction of cereal for the handsome bird still roosting on the headboard of the bed.

'Cunt of a fucker!' hissed Pagga under his breath as he tried to smooth out the creases on the lapels of his coat with the palms of his hands. There were acres of bad blood between Duffy and himself. Their feuding went back years. But they never let their tempers get out of control – except in the company of Milo Clancy. Both men were grateful for Clancy. Both felt secure in his presence, for they knew that either of them could throw down the gauntlet, and that Clancy would never allow it to be picked up.

Pagga retrieved both fags and Clancy's suit from the wardrobe. Clancy dressed and all three sat on the edge of the bed with Taurus Bulba at their feet, eating his breakfast. The mood was calm in the room now. All three cooed and praised as Bulba pecked away at his food. Duffy said that Bulba was looking well and was no worse for his travels and his strange surroundings, and Pagga wholeheartedly agreed with him. Milo reckoned that Bulba was looking a bit under the weather, but Barra and Pagga told him he was talking nonsense.

When the cock had finished it was Clancy himself that housed him in his cage, made out of slats of ash, and carried him to the window. Barra took the only chair and placed it in front of the window. Carefully Milo placed the cage on the chair, and both men stood vigilantly by until the cock settled down. When they saw him start to preen his rich coat both men sighed their contentment. Pagga was left to clean up the little mounds of shit which were to be found all over the mattress. Ten minutes later the three of them headed downstairs for breakfast, leaving Taurus Bulba to bask in the morning sunshine which was now pouring through the window.

That same morning Stallion O'Casey and his son arrived at the White Willow in time for breakfast. In the foyer they were greeted by the manager and owner of the hotel, Aggie Carney.

' 'Tis the two of yees at last!' Aggie cried. She was a big buxom woman with a hearty smile. 'Here was meself expectin' ta see yar two darlin' faces since suppertime last night.'

'Sure, 'tis glad we are to be here at all, Aggie,' smiled Stallion, a giant of a man. 'Sure, wasn't it all of last night we were on the road. Five miles from home and old Sarchfield's bad leg starts playin' him up again. We had to leave him and the cart at Pat Larkin's forge and set out in the middle of the flamin' night on

6

bloody foot! Now ya haven't gone and sold our beds, Aggie Carney, have ya?'

'As if I'd go and do such a thing, Stallion O'Casey?' The broad smile left Aggie's face. 'The O'Caseys can turn up at the White Willow at any time of the day or night and they'll always find a bed and meself waitin' to tend them, as well ya know, Stallion O'Casey.'

'Sure, 'tis well I know ya wouldn't sell our beds out from under us, Aggie,' soothed Stallion. ' 'Twas only the tiredness of our long and painful journey speakin'. Isn't that so, Colin?' He looked down at his son.

'Mrs Carney is as grand as they come, Da,' agreed the frail-looking boy. 'She'd no more sell our beds out from under us than she would leave her grand fat pigs to starve.'

'Now there's a son to be proud of, Stallion.' The smile came back to light up Aggie's ample cheeks. 'Ya've not got yar da's doubtin' ways, have ya, Colin?'

The lad, just into his teens, looked up at her with blushing cheeks. He was bowlegged, sparse of frame, with very little flesh to cover his frail bones, and his complexion was milky white. Something stirred deep within Aggie's heart every time she clapped eyes on the boy. The Lord Himself should have taken ya right from the cradle, for ya're far too delicate for this rough bog of a place, she thought, as she watched his pale blue eyes smile up at her. Out loud she said, 'Ya look like ya could do with a dacent feed, Colin, darlin'.'

'I could, ma'am. I'm starvin' somethin' awful.'

'He's been talkin' on that road all through the night of yar culinary prowess, Aggie. He's been lickin' his chops at the thought of yar fat and sweet rashers and the substance and thickness of yar sausages and the largeness of yar egg yolks,' Stallion said.

'Then off with ya to the dining room and tell Paggy to fill yar plate to the full, and mind that ya eat it all up now, for I'll be in there in fifteen minutes and I'll be expectin' ta see yar tummy three times bigger than yar own da's!'

Stallion and Aggie watched as Colin hurried off, with his awkward, drunk-like gait.

'He's not lookin' at all well, Stallion.'

'Well, he may not be lookin' well, Aggie, but last winter came and went and he never saw sight or sound of a cold, flu or the wheezes of the chest which usually pay him a visit every time the winds change direction.'

'Thanks be ta God for that!'

'If there was no such thing as bloody winter our Colin might be able to see a full span a life.'

'Well, how's yarself anyway?' Aggie changed the subject, seeing the heaviness in O'Casey's face.

'Well, I could complain, but I'll not. I'm here for the fights to cheer meself up. So ya can give me the lowdown as to who's here and what the competition's like.'

'Well, 'tis the same crowd except for three – three savages from the other side of Ireland.'

'From the other side of Ireland?' echoed Stallion, his interest sharpening.

'Aye, from Mayo. Mountain men if ever ya saw 'em. Wild as they come. In they came last night with their fighter under their arm. "Where ya goin'?" says I, as they walk inta me nice clean foyer with their prize cock gawkin' at me as if it were a human being. "We've booked a room with yar good self," they say. "Ya might have at that," says I back ta them. "But yar cock stays out back with the rest of his kind!" Well now, Stallion, they go on to offer me three times the price of the room they've booked for themselves, on top of which they offer to pay for any damage their cock might do to me mattress and sheets. Have ya ever heard of anythin' queerer than that in all yar born life?'

' 'Tis queer indeed, Aggie. By gad, it's queer! Ya didn't go and let them house their cock in one of yar best rooms, did ya?'

'Indeed I did not, Stallion O'Casey! I gave them that cold old draughty room on the very top a the house, but sure when they saw it they declared that they had never clapped eyes on anything finer.'

'Have they got the look a money about them?'

'Indeed they have not.' Aggie sniffed, raising her chin and looking fierce. 'I made them pay up before they laid their heads to the pillow. God only knows how they slept the night through with the three of 'em squashed and crushed into the one bed. They look ta me as if they'd have a heap a trouble tryin' to muster up the price of a pint. But that's on looks I'm goin' by. What's in the darkened corners of their pockets is another matter entirely.'

8

'Mayo men, you say?' asked Stallion, looking thoughtful.

'Aye. A hundred miles from their homes and loved ones, that is if they've got any.'

'Their cock must be somethin' special.'

'It doesn't have the look of a looker, if that's what ya mean.'

'Who are they down to fight? Anyone I know?'

'Randy Sheeba.'

'Matti Finn's pride and joy!'

'Aye. The Mayo men were given fourteen. The second cock to come outa the hat was fourteen B. That's Finn's own number.'

'How did Finn react?'

'Well, he wasn't too sure if he was receiving good news or bad. No one knows anything about these mountain men or their fighter. Finn'll have to bide his time and wait 'til he puts his up against theirs in the sawdust ring tonight.'

'Well, what about meself? Who have I got?'

'The Kelly brothers.'

'Blast!' swore Stallion. 'Twice in the one bloody year!'

'Aye, and they've got President Lincoln and Spanish Point with them.'

'Oh God! There goes me chances of makin' a few bob.'

'Who did ya bring?'

'Whiskey Maker.'

'That's all?'

'Aye. The rest are in need of time.'

'Well, ya can consider yarself lucky. Ya've only the one bird to lose.'

'Yeah. I suppose ya could say that's the bright side of me long journey.'

'Well, enjoy yar stay anyway. Into the dining room with yarself and I'll serve ya breakfast with me own fair hands.'


'Well, as I see it,' Barra was saying, as he pushed an empty cup and saucer away from him with his fingertips and sat back in his chair, 'to have a hotel such as this with all its paraphernalia an' all you'd have to be a right thorough-goin' bastard right from the start. Y'ad have to have made yar money dishonestly right from the word go. Now that one, Mrs Carney, I'm not sayin' she's

9

a bastard but she is a rap. A first-class bitch if ever I laid me eyes on one. How she came by this place only the devil and herself know.'

'She got it from her husband,' replied Clancy, as he brought the cup to his lips and drained it.

'Then the husband is the bastard, but that doesn't make her less of a rap,' stated Barra with finality.

Pagga O'Leary was taking no part in their conversation. His whole attention for the past ten minutes was focused on the other side of Aggie Carney's dining room. His eyes were on a table to the left of the dining-room doors. 'There he goes again,' said Pagga.

'Did ya say somethin'?' asked Clancy.

'I said there goes that bastard again.'

'What bastard?' asked Barra.

'That fellah over there by them doors.'

'What about him?'

'He's been starin' at us at this table ever since he sat himself down.'

'So? 'Tis a free country,' said Milo.

'He's a big fucker, isn't he,' said Duffy.

'He's got a kid with him,' added Milo.

'Have ya got a bad feelin' about him, Pagga?'

'Aye. 'Tis the way he's been lookin' at this table for the past half fuckin' hour. The way he's been gawkin' at us three as if he's about ready to take us to the cleaners.'

'He's harmless, Pagga. He's got a kid with him.'

'What's that got to do with the price of eggs?' Pagga snapped back, looking hard at Clancy. Or as hard as he dared.

'Jasus, he could be a sabotagist!' exclaimed Barra, glaring at the stranger.

'For Christ's sake,' sighed Clancy wearily, 'relax, will ya?'

Duffy got to his feet. 'You relax, Milo Clancy. I'm goin' to check on Taurus.'

'Put yar arse back on the chair, Barra.' Clancy waved him down.

'And what about Taurus? That fellah's gombeen men could be up in our room now whiskin' away our Taurus to God knows where!'

'Sit yar arse to that chair now!' ordered Clancy, glaring up at

Duffy. 'Sit and don't show us all up.'

Seeing the iron anger in Clancy's eyes, Barra relented.

'Ya read too many a them fuckin' comic books for your own good,' chastised Clancy. 'Yar fuckin' imagination is as large as yar fuckin' brain isn't!'

'Milo, Barra might have somethin' in what he said. That character over there has been gawkin' at us as if we were fat turkeys ready for the slaughter.'

'Maybe he's just musical!' sighed Milo.

'Musical?' Barra repeated, plainly perplexed. 'A singer, ya mean?'

'Oh Jasus!' said Clancy through clenched teeth. 'Why the fuck we didn't leave ya at home, I'll never know.'

'He means neither one way or the other,' said Pagga.

'What the fuck are ye talkin' about?' bawled Barra.

'Oh God!' sighed Pagga in exasperation. 'Will someone kindly educate this fuckin' fool before I blow me shaggin' top?'

'Barra,' said Clancy, holding on to his temper as best he could, 'the man over there, sitting across from us. Well, he just might be a bit a the fairy; he might have a bit a the fairy about him, about his manner.'

But Barra still gawked at Clancy, his mouth open and ignorance plastered all over his face.

'Okay!' Pagga butted in. 'What about this shyster, Clancy? What do we do about him?'

Clancy sat back in his chair, as though settling something. 'Forget him.'

'I doubt if we'll be forgettin' about him,' said Barra triumphantly.

'Here he comes now. He's headin' for our table, fellahs,' explained Duffy as he watched the giant of a stranger and the bandy-legged boy cross the carpeted floor.

'Good mornin', gentlemen,' said Stallion. Three pairs of eyes looked up at him but not one of them returned his greeting in kind. 'This here is my son, Colin. My name is Stallion, Stallion O'Casey.'

'What's wrong with ya mite's legs?' jibed Pagga, his voice harsh.

Clancy saw the flash of anger come into O'Casey's eyes, but before he could apologize for Pagga the boy answered for himself.

Colin stared at Pagga without expression. 'I was born like this, sir,' he said simply.

Pagga looked into the boy's clear blue eyes, then dropped his gaze. 'Sorry lad,' he nearly whispered. 'I didn't mean to ask such a question in such a forward and heartless manner.'

'No offence taken, sir,' replied Stallion, placing a gentle hand on his son's frail shoulder. 'Isn't that right, Colin?'

'That's right, Da.'

'Won't ya grab some chairs and sit yarselfs down?' invited Clancy, with relief if not friendliness.

'Thank you, sir. We will at that.' O'Casey pulled up two chairs. 'We have all of a mornin' to get through, and it's layin' heavy on our hands with naught to do.'

'Me name is Milo, Milo Clancy,' said Clancy. 'And this here is Barra Duffy, and this here is Pagannini O'Leary; Pagga to his friends.'

'Glad to know yees,' smiled O'Casey. 'Ye'd be quite a distance from yar homes and loved ones?'

'How would ya be knowin' that?' asked Barra Duffy with a smile on his lips but mistrust in his eyes.

'Yar speech. To me poor trained ears it sounds as if ye've come all the way from west of the Shannon.'

'Ya'd be right there, Stallion. We're Mayo men born and raised. We're here for the fights.'

' 'Tis a long journey ya've taken, Milo, just for the fights.'

'We intend to make it worth our while,' replied Barra significantly.

'The best cocks to be found anywhere are to be found in this area,' said O'Casey, as though there could be no dispute.

'That might and mightn't be true,' Duffy smiled. 'But the best cock in the whole world comes from Mayo, and we've got him.'

'Indeed?' grinned Stallion, looking suitably impressed.

'Indeed is right!' declared Barra.

'And what's yar own like, Stallion?' asked Clancy with a smile, showing no signs of the fury beginning to burn within him.

' 'Tis a poor ol' thing to be sure. I'm thinkin' now with hindsight in front a me that I should have stayed at home. I came here hopin' for a good draw and I just found out that my cock has to fight one of the Kellys' devils.'

'The Kellys?' asked Pagga.

'Aye, the Kellys. They've two grand cocks here for the fights, and so me cause is dead and me journey a wasted one. How about yarselfs, who've ye drawn?'

'Randy Sheeba, owned by a fellah called Finn. Da ya know him?' asked Clancy.

'Sure, that I do, much to me own regret. And I also know his Sheeba. That one cock of his, may it rot in the bowels of hell, has cost me dearly,' said Stallion gravely.

'How's that?' Barra's voice was anxious and strained.

'Let's see now,' replied Stallion, sitting back in his chair. 'There was Black Lightning, Basket Maker and me darlin' and lovely Poems from Heaven . . . he was my very best.'

'What about them?' whispered Barra.

'They're all dead, Mr Duffy!'

'Randy Sheeba?' Pagga's voice was barely audible.

'Aye, Pagga,' replied Stallion, looking straight into O'Leary's eyes, and seeing a mountain of worry quickly gather there.

Clancy was also worried, not at what the stranger was saying but at the raw fear on the faces of Duffy and O'Leary. He could visualize himself turning for home, tail between his legs, Bulba under his arm, and Pagga and Barra leading the way. Turning tail and running with shame crowning all four of us. Jasus, thought Milo, I'll not have it. Not this time. Turning his back on his own fear, Clancy looked straight at the stranger. 'Won't it be grand for yarself, Mr O'Casey, as you watch our fighter drive Finn's pride and joy right through the floor? Ya'd surely revel in our victory, after all the misfortune Finn's upstart has brought upon you.'

'Aye, I'll wallow in yar victory for sure. I'd dance on air to see such a fine sight, but that's if yar cock can do it.'

'He can and he will, Mr O'Casey,' Clancy stated, nothing but total confidence in his tone.

Stallion O'Casey smiled at each of the Mayo men in turn but said nothing in reply.

'You think he won't, don't ya?' shouted Barra, murder in his eyes.

'Mr Duffy, how can I say if your fighter'll win or lose? I've never seen him and I don't know his history.'

'The cock's name is Taurus Bulba,' explained Clancy firmly, staring hard at the other man. 'He's owned jointly by all three of

13

us. I, me, Milo Clancy, have the larger share of him; I own exactly half. I bred him meself. Up to now he's only fought local; that is within fifty square miles from where he roosts. He's three years old and he's had himself six fights. All have been over and done with within five minutes. He's fought the best cocks that west Mayo can offer. He's had only the one fight with an outsider. A tinker by the name of Mangie Sullivan came to Mayo six months back. He offered to put up his against ours and we accepted. Bulba buried him in less time than ya'd have to boil a soft-boiled egg. Sullivan offered us twenty pounds for ours. We turned him down. He didn't take it badly. In fact, he said that Bulba was surely a winner if ever he saw one. And now we're here, on his expert advice. We're here. We're here and we've drawn Finn's fucker and that is Finn's misfortune!' Clancy folded his arms, sat back in his chair, and stared at O'Casey as though no more need ever be said.

Stallion was trying his best to keep the excitement he was feeling off his face. 'Mr Clancy, what was Sullivan's cock called, the one your Bulba beat?'

'Widow Maker.'

Stallion O'Casey's heart missed a beat. He mustered what calm he had left and asked again, 'Who?'

'Widow Maker – black as they come except for his red stubbed comb.'

'Jasus, I don't believe it!' Stallion's voice became a mere whisper.

'Ya're callin' us a liar, Mr O'Casey?' inquired Pagga.

'Widow Maker! Ya're a thousand per cent sure 'twas Widow Maker?' O'Casey kept his eyes on Milo.

'Widow Maker!' said Clancy again.

'Than ya'll make no money here,' said O'Casey.

'Why's that?' asked Pagga.

'No one will take yar money. Ya'll not find as much as one fool who'll be willin' to take yar bets. If yar claim is true, if ye've beaten one of the best cocks in the whole of Ireland, then no one'll take ye on. No one'll put their cash on the line for ye to gobble up!'

Pagga leaned forward, his eyes not leaving Stallion's face. 'The Widow Maker was that good?'

'Good?' laughed O'Casey, drawing his chair right into the table and resting his elbows on its surface. 'The cock ya're about to fight tonight, Matti Finn's pride and joy . . . well, Sullivan, the same Sullivan, the tinker who came into yar lives in west Mayo – God bless the man – that tinker was in this very town a year ago. He was down to fight Finn's fucker. When Matti Finn heard of it he all but had a stroke. Finn refused to put Sheeba up, claimin' that his cock had not recovered from his last duel. The tinker headed for the next county and Finn's cock had a miraculous recovery and fought one of the Kellys' devils less than twenty-four hours after Sullivan hit the road. Finn knew he hadn't a hope in hell if he put Sheeba in against the tinker's. The Widow Maker has almost the same reputation as that of Satan the First.' He looked from face to face, waiting for a reaction. 'Surely to Christ ya heard of ol' Satan?'

'Who hasn't?' answered O'Leary. 'Owned by the tinker of tinkers, Tilla Kusthi. His cock is said to have had a thousand fights and won every one of them. Best bird in all of Ireland!'

'He's had forty-two to date,' said Stallion.

'Ya're sure 'twas forty-two and not forty-three?' smiled Clancy.

O'Casey shook his head. 'I've followed his career. I've actually seen him fight.'

'Ya seen him fight!' exclaimed the three Mayo men in unison, their faces open with disbelief.

'Aye. I had to take Colin here to see some doctors in Cork city. On the way back I stopped off in Limerick. I heard of the fight, just outside the city it was, so both Colin and meself went to see the cock of cocks, the one that the whole of Ireland has built legends around. Everything that has been said and will be said about that cock is true. We saw it kill a bird that was three times its own weight in a matter of twenty seconds flat. It skewered its challenger with both its steel spurs right in the chest before the unfortunate devil had time to climb into its soar!'

'Mother a God!' gasped Barra.

'Surely ya're paintin' the canvas a bit thick?' suggested Clancy.

'He's tellin' the truth, Milo,' said O'Leary. 'I can see it in his face.'

'I'm a man that tells only what he sees, Milo. I can't stand spoutin' mouths in others and I keep my own gob well disciplined and under control at all times.'

15

''Tis also I find meself thinkin' that ya're a wise man,' said Pagga, giving O'Casey a full broad smile.

'I'm not an eegit, let's put it that way,' said Stallion sharply, not liking Pagga's smile.

'Can ya carry on then, Stallion?'

'Carry on?'

'Aye, ya know the game in these parts, the ins and outs of things as far as the fightin' goes,' coaxed O'Leary, his smile even broader, and his eyes on O'Casey.

'Well, let me ask you one or two questions first.'

'Fire away.'

'Does any other creature within ten miles of here know that yar cock fought and beat Tinker Sullivan's champion?'

'No one knows.'

'Ya're sure?'

'I keep sayin' ta yar good self that we're not liars,' replied Pagga calmly.

'Okay then.' O'Casey sat back in his chair once more. 'Ye fellahs have come to the right place to fight yar cock. 'Tis the very best place in the southwest to display his nature and prowess. No doubt back where ye come from ye've had the law to deal with from time to time.'

'Aye,' said Barra. 'From time to time, just like most other places.'

'Yes. But not here. The law doesn't bother the men of the cock in this town. Once a year the law in the form of cops comes to a predestined place and knocks down a door, we all look suitably surprised and hand over one or two ol' cocks that are well past it. We select one of us to go before the magistrate to pay the customary fine and that's it for the year. They don't bother us again 'til the next year comes round. We keep the sergeant's pocket well greased and he looks the other way. So ya're safe from the law.' He grinned with satisfaction. 'There are other advantages all too numerous to mention, save for one – the surrounding countryside houses some of the best dairy farms there is, so naturally there's a few big, big-shot farmers to go with them. They've got bulgin' wallets and little of what matters between their ears. Now, to get down to the gist of it, if it ever got out that yar Bulba ate up Sullivan's darlin', then for sure it is that ye'd be travellin' home as poor as ye came. So keep that a secret at all

16

costs!' Certain that they were warming to him, O'Casey pressed his advantage. 'Now I didn't mean to prise yar secret from yees, honestly. Ye're strangers here and curiosity got the better of me. But ye've done Stallion O'Casey a favour whether ye know it or not, for I intend to lay every copper I've got on yar cock's head. But I can't do it with any notable gain for meself unless ye march along with me plan.'

'And the plan?' asked Clancy cautiously.

'Are ye open-hearted men?'

'As open as the next,' retorted Pagga. 'But we're not fools and don't take kindly to scoundrels and shysters.'

'Neither do I, Pagga. Now, are ya open-hearted enough to take a fellah in amongst yarselfs and treat him fair?'

'They'll be shiftin' us from this dinin' room soon, Mr O'Casey,' interrupted Clancy. 'How about givin' us the gist of what's on yar mind?'

'I've a hundred pounds to put on yar cock. I might even be able to manage a hundred and fifty. How much have ye?'

Pagga and Barra looked towards Clancy and Clancy kept his eyes on O'Casey. 'A hundred between us,' he said.

'It's not much for the three of yees, if ya don't mind me sayin' so.'

'We don't mind. It's all we could muster together, and to us it's a great deal.'

'Okay, Mr Clancy, I'll take yar word on that. Mine and yours comes to two hundred and fifty pounds maximum. We can't put all that down in the ring. Money like that is bound to be noticed. So a good deal of it will have to be spread throughout the pubs of this town hours before the fight takes place. I assume yar Bulba is quite a looker?'

'He is. He cuts a fine figure,' replied Pagga.

'Well, ya'll have to do a job on him then.'

'Now whist there a minute,' Duffy barged in. 'Ya're goin' a bit too fast for the likes a meself. I groom Bulba before every fight. 'Tis a matter of pride with meself that I . . .'

'Shut yar mouth, Barra!' barked Clancy, then turned back to O'Casey as pleasant as could be. 'Carry on Stallion, ya have our attention.'

'I don't want to destroy yar goldmine, just ruffle 'is coat, downgrade his appearance.'

17

'Done!' snapped Pagga, ignoring Barra's black looks. 'What's next?'

'Get yarselfs around the town this mornin' and put in an appearance at all the pubs. Show yarselfs as bein' a bit short a the grey matter. Describe yar Bulba's fights in confidential tones to the barmen, but make sure ye slant yer stories in the right direction and for Christ's sake don't go overboard with yar act!'

# 2

Turnpike Road ran along the back of the White Willow hotel. It ran as straight as a die for the first half mile before beginning its climb on to Patriot's Hill. The road on that fine summer's evening was choked with men on foot. Halfway up the hill on the right-hand side of the Pike stood a huge corregated barn. For the crowds on the road that balmy summer evening the barn was the only goal. By eight o'clock the Pike was clear of tramping feet and only a few abandoned cars were to be found scattered on its surface as twilight fell, brushing away the fading light of day.

In an outhouse behind the barn the thirty-two cocks that would fight that night were housed. Half of them would not see the morrow's dawn. Biding time with the thirty-two cocks were their handlers; anxious men, all appearing busy, strain showing clearly on their faces. The first pair of cocks to enter the ring were already spurred, their two-inch slits of spiked steel gaitered and fastened sound to the stubs of their natural spurs. But their handlers still fussed over them, checking and rechecking good work already done.

Barra Duffy and Bulba kept themselves well away from the rest of the handlers and cocks. Duffy found himself a quiet corner once he had entered the outhouse and sat himself down on the wooden floor, legs outstretched and back up against the wall. Bulba was safely housed in his cage on the floor beside him. The cock was at ease and oblivious to the sounds and movement around him, but Barra Duffy was not. Duffy's cheeks were crimson with rage, as they had been since breakfast that morning. He had protested throughout the day that Bulba's dignity should not be violated. He had tried to argue his protest with logic, just as Milo Clancy always did, but they wouldn't listen to him, so his well-renowned temper had taken over. 'But it'll damage him mentally! If ye bastards were to degrade a racehorse by slashing off its proud mane, the thing would die of shame right there on the racetrack and run the worst race of its life!' he'd screamed at them. 'Bullshit!' Clancy had retorted. ' 'Tisn't bullshit! Ya'll end up doin' him mental damage! He'll lose his fight from that vile treatment!' But for Barra it had been a battle lost right from the word go. Now, in the outhouse, with an hour to go before Bulba entered the ring, he was still fuming at his miserable day. Smart men, men with little dicks and heads full of horse shit. Put them all up against a fuckin' wall and shoot the fuckin' lot a 'em, that's what I say! raged Duffy to himself.

But when he watched the tranquil creature surveying his surroundings he had to smile. 'Look at yarself Taurus Bulba! Ya should be swearin' like a trooper after all I've done ta ya. Half yar lovely belly feathers are in one of Aggie Carney's dustbins. There's enough self-raisin' fuckin' flour on yar coat to take the sheen off a prize bull's arse! As for yar entire general appearance, well let's just say that even a sex-starved hen that hasn't seen a prick in a month of Sundays would run a mile on seein' ya comin'! It doesn't affect ya in the least, does it? Just as long as I don't fool around with yar ol' rang-doo-rum. Now if I was to fuck about with that ya'd have somethin' to say, wouldn't ya! Ya'd be mentally disturbed then, me bucco, wouldn't ya?'

The door to the outhouse opened and every handler in the place turned to look. 'Nice and Easy! Potato Merchant!' cried the figure at the open doorway. Two of the handlers got off their haunches with their fighters under their arms and followed the master of ceremonies. The door closed and everyone tried to relax again. But every now and again eyes turned and sneaked glances at the closed door. Conversations were in low and whispered tones and most of them were between man and cock. Each painful minute went slowly by.

Duffy checked his watch. He reckoned there was at least another hour to get through before Bulba's name was called. But he decided he had baby-sat long enough and so he took Bulba from his cage and proceeded to dress him for the fight. Slowly and with infinite care Duffy wrapped pads of dampened cotton wool around both of Bulba's legs, then he slipped the alloyed shoes over the stumps of the cock's natural spurs. Next came the weapons of death – two two-inch slits of steel. These he slipped into the slots in the shoes, and over the shoes he fixed the leather gaiters. Long strands of the softest leather bound Bulba's armoury together. He checked and rechecked his handiwork, testing the rigidity and grip of the steel spurs. Satisfied at last, he gloved the spiked armoury in two strong cotton bags, and settled back cooing over the bird. 'Ya've got to do it tonight me darlin'. Tonight's yar night, you have to eat the bastard right inta the ground because everything yar uncle Barra has is on yar back!'

Well over five hundred men were packed inside the barn that night. The platformed arena where the cocks would fight was in itself a perfect circle eight feet in diameter. It was surrounded by a grilled barrier high enough to prevent the combatants from jumping out. Above it was a big arc lamp pouring down light onto a sawdust ring. Just to the right of the ring was the judge's box, a plastic see-through hut which was also round. The spectators sat on wooden benches circling the ring. The wooden benches rose in tiers up and up, the topmost failing to make contact with the roof by a mere six feet.

The atmosphere was electric. Noise fairly bounced off the corrugated steel walls of the barn. Hundreds were on their feet shouting their bets and hundreds of takers shouted, eyeballed and nodded back at them. The air was already pungent with clouds of tobacco smoke, and the odours of whiskey, poteen and porter mingled and settled over the place like an unseen haze. Everyone was waiting for the master of ceremonies to come through the giant doorway bearing the first cocks of the evening. The fight was about to start.

Milo Clancy was right beside the ring. His hands were on the metal grille and his eyes were on the very surface where Bulba would do his fighting that night. He was impressed, to say the least. If there's a Mecca for bullfightin', then 'tis Madrid for sure, he thought. And for Gaelic football? Croke Park, in the heart of Dublin. And the place of the cock? Where the cock goes to seek out his destiny? His eyes didn't move from the ring, imagining the fights that had been fought there. Here, he told himself.

Surely this has to be the place. He turned his back on the ring and looked around him. My God! There must be ten thousand men here and all of 'em lookin' down at meself! Jasus! But 'tis a wonder that the cocks don't come over all embarrassed and walk away.

He glanced down at his left lapel, at the bright green badge that marked him out as a man of some importance. It had been given to him an hour earlier by no less a person than the judge himself, and it signified to all that he was a 'presenter of the cock'. This gave him additional rights: he could approach the judge's box, converse with the judge before and after the fight, and enter the ring and present his bird. But, most important of all, he, and only he, could pace the outskirts of the arena while his bird did combat and usher him on to victory. Everyone else had to remain by their seats. 'Tis civilization at work, thought Clancy to himself. To think of Pat Darcy's pigstye of a shack back there in the bogs of Mayo. With meself being shoved and hassled as I urge Bulba on to another victory, and Pagga standin' at the fuckin' broken doorway lookin' out for Sergeant O'Malley to come down on that crock of a bicycle of his and arrest us all. How the fuck can people live like that, I ask ya? Jasus, they won't believe us when we get back and tell 'em of the glories of this place.

'Milo!'

Clancy managed a smile as O'Casey drew level with him. 'How's it goin'? Did ya manage to get it all down?'

Stallion rubbed his hands with satisfaction. 'Everythin' is down except for the last hundred. I'll split that with Pagga just before Bulba makes his entrance. We'll lay it with the bookies proper if they'll give good odds.'

'What about the stuff laid already?'

'Well, since we started this mornin' and with what we've laid tonight, Pagga and I reckon it works out at about six to one over all.'

'That's good.'

'That's good? That's fuckin' marvellous, Milo. Have ya ever known the outsider of two cocks to fetch more than three to one?'

'Never.'

'Then we're in heaven,' Stallion smiled broadly. 'Right!'

'Right,' answered Clancy, his face straight as a poker.

'Worried about Bulba?' asked O'Casey, anxious himself.

'No,' said Clancy simply. 'Where's Pagga?'

'Checkin' up on Barra. Seein' if he needs a hand.' O'Casey noticed a harshness in Clancy's eyes. Those eyes had been on him all afternoon. But then, he knew that Clancy was a cautious man.

'Clancy?'

'Wha'?'

'I can be good for you. Real good.'

Milo looked at him closely. 'Oh . . . in what way would that be now?'

'I can make ya rich, richer than yar wildest dreams.'

' 'Tis a generous man ya are if ya could do it. But tell me, Mr O'Casey, why would ya be bestowin' such generosity in my direction?'

' 'Tis a two-way thing,' replied Stallion, ignoring the expression on Clancy's lips. 'For me to be good to you, you'd have to be good for me.'

'For you?'

'For me, and my son.'

'Ya've dreams to fulfil, Stallion O'Casey. I can see that. Ya're a man of ambition to be sure.'

'I have one dream,' said O'Casey flatly. 'I want to give my Colin a full expanse of life.'

Milo looked at O'Casey steadily for a moment, as though choosing his words. 'Only the Lord can do that, I'm afraid,' he said at last.

If Stallion wanted to reply he hadn't a chance, for just then a great wave of shouting went up as the master of ceremonies entered the barn.


The presenters of the first fight of the evening stood in the centre of the ring, their fighters nestled in the cradles of their arms. The judge, alone in his box, just ten feet away from them, blew his whistle and the presenters faced each other. He gave a second blast on his whistle. This was the cue for the grand challenge to be made. They thrust their birds forward and the statutory angry contact was made. Both birds were willing to do battle unto the death.

The whistle blew for the third time, killing momentarily the tense silence that hung over the barn. The two men walked the few paces to the opposite gates of the ring. Then they turned and looked across at one another, each awaiting the other's nod. The owner and presenter of Potato Merchant got the ball rolling with the wink of an eye; the presenter of Nice and Easy followed at once with a nod of the head. The cocks were lowered to the ground, pointed straight at each other, and their minders left the arena.

Potato Merchant was as black as midnight except for his stubbed red comb. Nice and Easy was a deep copper except for his neck, which was a mixture of copper and bright yellow. He carried himself well, had a champion's chest and the money was on him. But the Merchant was an old hand, a veteran of seven fights. He knew his trade and carried some heavy scars on both his wings. In appearance he didn't look a winner. His chest, what there was of it, was all on the bone. There was no meat to spare on this wily fighter.

Nice and Easy took the baton straight away and showed the old hand the terrain on which the battle would be fought. Easy shifted his way round the ring in a clockwise direction. The Merchant immediately went the other way, his eyes never off his opponent. But suddenly, without a hint of warning, Easy shot high into the air, wings blasting hard to gain maximum height. The Merchant followed a split second later. Easy reached the peak first, feet up and the glinting shafts of steel ready. He was already descending while Merchant was still in his climb. Merchant saw the mortal danger coming down and whirled in midair – but too late. There was an explosion of black, copper and orange feathers, and a second later both birds were back on the sawdust. There was a trickle of blood running down the Merchant's back as they started to manoeuvre for position once more. Outside the ring it was clear to all that Easy's spurs had not gone home. All he had done was to kiss a little of the Merchant's sparse flesh.

Thirty seconds passed with the birds just circling in opposite directions. But the width of that circle was decreasing rapidly. Finally their beaks met, and they pecked and stabbed and hacked away at each other, darting backwards and forwards as they tried to seek out the hidden flaws in each other's defence. It was soon clear to all that both birds were well matched. Then again without warning Easy was up off the ground and soaring, but Merchant went with him and, with a desperate effort of his scarred wings, got to his summit first, his legs positioned for a thrust at the oncoming Easy. His left spur caught Easy in the face. A squawk of piercing pain tore from Easy's throat as they exploded into each other. Feathers burst and splayed out over the arena, then both birds dropped like stones. Easy landed badly and staggered. His right eye had been plucked from his head. There was a black clotting hole where the eye had been and a fountain of blood was pouring out of the empty socket. Merchant's fall was a split second behind Easy's but his drop was true. He came down on his wounded prey with thunderous force, legs on point and slits of steel on target as they plunged deep into Easy's back. It was over without another squawk. Potato Merchant stayed put on the mound of bloody flesh and, head held high, crowed out his victory to the rafters.

Two hours later eight fights had been completed. Eight cocks were alive, cheered as the victors, and were being cradled away to have their wounds tended. The other eight were either being given a ceremonial burial by their grief-stricken owners, or were already being plucked and gutted and made ready for the stewing pot.

There was an hour's interval while spectators, owners and handlers got their breaths back and killed the rawness of their parched throats with bottles of stout, served up by the twenty-odd hawkers that now surrounded the ringside. It was the general opinion of all that the first and last fight of the eight were the ones that would be remembered for a long time to come. Potato Merchant had been sold straight after the fight to a publican for £60, a staggering sum to be sure. The publican reckoned that if Merchant could see off his next three challengers his reputation would be made. He could then retire the bird with honour, and put him on show in his establishment. He reckoned that would be good – very good – for business. The last fight of the set had turned out to be a marathon event. A fighter named Broadchest, which had been on the sawdust floor and apparently dead, came back to life, got to his feet and killed his aggressor, before an astounded audience.

The ninth fight of the night was under way and the crowd were on their feet. Bets and counter-bets were being screamed back and forth and the fight itself (inside the metal grille) was up for grabs.

Behind the judge's box, four men on their haunches surrounded their bird.

With a wet sponge Clancy was busy dousing the bindings that held Bulba's steel armoury in place. Barra Duffy was fanning the cock with a makeshift cardboard fan. O'Casey and O'Leary were dragging hard on their cigarettes, ready to help out if needed.

'Someone in this fuckin' place should go and open a fuckin' door!'

'Aye. I agree with yarself there, Barra,' replied O'Casey. ' 'Tis like an oven in here.'

'Not a good place for cocks at all,' fussed Duffy. 'Bulba'll sweat himself to death before he ever gets into the ring.'

'Fan the fuckin' bird, Barra Duffy, and shut yar shaggin' gob!' hissed Pagga, rising to his feet. 'Jasus, but the piles are playin' me up somethin' awful tonight.'

'Do ya suffer from the piles then, Pagga?'

'That I do, Stallion. An army of brimstones burnin' their ugly fires on the lips a me arse.'

'That can be a curse,' O'Casey sympathized. But his eyes were fixed on Clancy and Duffy, checking to see that they were doing their job well. He had watched all three Mayo men throughout the day, willing to give advice. But no advice was required. They really knew their job, and that irritated O'Casey, for it meant that he needed them more than they needed him.

'Well, that's that. He couldn't be readier than he is now,' said Clancy.

'Spurred, laced and all ready to go!' answered Barra, cradling Bulba in his arms.

'How's that pox of a fight goin', Pagga?' asked Clancy.

'They're still at it. They'll be at it for another hour or two the way they're carryin' on.'

'All the same,' continued Clancy, 'why doesn't yarself and Stallion here go and lay the rest of the green stuff down?'

'Good idea, Milo,' agreed O'Casey. 'How about it, Pagga?'

'Age before beauty!' smiled Pagga.

O'Casey was already into the crowd, Pagga following, when Clancy called out, 'Hey Pagga, just a minute!'

Pagga turned back. 'What is it?'

'Don't let that bastard outa yar sight.'

26

'Ya still don't trust him?'

'If he goes to the bog follow him. Wipe his arse if ya have to, but don't let him out a yar sight.'

'Gentlemen, your attention. The tenth fight of the evening. On my left – four years old, nine fights, owner, Matthew Charles Patrick Finn – Randy Sheeba!'

A roar went up from the crowd. Sheamus Collins waited for silence. 'Gentlemen! On my right – three years old, six fights, owner, Milo James Clancy – Taurus Bulba!'

A few scattered roars came back at Sheamus Collins's ears. He stepped down from his rostrum in front of the ring and turned towards Matti Finn. 'Yar cock, please.'

Matti Finn held his bird out for inspection. Collins checked Sheeba's spurs and beak and, satisfied, pointed towards the left gate of the arena. 'Yar cock, please.' He checked Bulba's armoury and sent Clancy and cock to the right gate.

The third blast of the judge's whistle signalled the end of the introductions. Milo Clancy bent down, got Finn's half nod, let Bulba go, and left the enclosure.

Taurus Bulba watched as the midnight cock began to make his circle, but refused to participate in the etiquette of cockmanship. All he did was shift his body and keep his eyes on the target. This baffled the well-mannered Sheeba, who stopped in his tracks, staring at this peculiar opponent. A roar of disapproval went up from the crowd. Randy Sheeba's eyes left Bulba for a second. It was his biggest mistake. Clancy's cock charged into a run, took off and climbed for the heights. Only when he heard the flapping of Bulba's wings did Sheeba take notice. Immediately he saw the mortal danger of the slanting soar and darted backwards. But Taurus Bulba had his legs at full stretch, and the steel spurs caught and bit deep into Sheeba's fleeing arse. Bulba crowed with rage as Finn's cock slipped from his grasp and took to the air in flight.

He did not follow, but stood his ground, looking up at the glinting spurs coming down at him. Swiftly he sidestepped out of harm's way, and when Sheeba met the sawdust he was on him like a shot. Sheeba's landing was heavy and Bulba's charge was true. Close-quarter fighting was his speciality and he did his work with great will and determination. He stabbed home time and time again with slashing beak, using it solely on his victim's head, while the spurs ripped and lanced at underbelly and wing. Sheeba had no chance of recovery, no chance of flight; the flaying wings of his aggressor blocked sight of all retreat. Sheeba's sap was ebbing away with the passing of each second. With one last, tremendous effort he managed to break free. But even while darting back he saw the beating wings of Bulba above him. Sheeba strained to climb and meet the challenge but his legs gave way. The cock keeled over, skidding in his own blood. Both of Bulba's two-inch spurs sank into Randy Sheeba's belly and scissored through the soft flesh. The dying cock's spilling guts tangled in Bulba's legs.

The gates opened and in came Sheamus Collins. Squatting on his haunches, he examined the stricken Sheeba while Bulba, in his frenzy, slashed and pecked away at his bloody, lifeless victim. Collins took a red handerchief from his pocket and waved it high in the air.


The bar at the White Willow Hotel was dead so far as trade was concerned throughout the early evening. But on the stroke of half ten the first trickle of pilgrims to the fight began returning. By eleven o'clock it was jam-packed. Stout kegs emptied and were replenished. Aggie Carney's well-renowned ham sandwiches were gobbled up as quickly as they appeared on her counter. There was a lot of money about for the two days devoted to the cock, and the White Willow would take a great deal of it.

Aggie Carney took the meaning of her title seriously – Manager/Owner. She managed, with whiplash tongue and the dour, threat-of-bodily-harm look on her face, to keep her little army of employees on the hop. But at the same time she also managed to mingle with guest and visitor alike, so that she always knew what was going on.

Aggie stood in front of the bar, her patrons all around her, most of them talking about the fight. But her eyes were on the figure standing under the clock, Sergeant Tim Hassit. In theory he was there to enforce the law, but the pub was still open and the clock over Hassit's bald head was ringing out the midnight hour. An hour over, she thought, with a smile playing on her lips. Keep

Hassit's gob open, pour the contents of your cellar down his gullet and ya bypass the magistrate and keep yar licence. An expensive investment, but 'tis worth it! She turned her eyes to the man Hassit was in deep conversation with. He was as big as the bulky sergeant but was dressed like a gentleman. 'Tis airs ya're gettin', Condour Kusthi, she thought to herself. The tinker is still written on yar ugly gob. The long roads ya've travelled are still to be seen in every wrinkle on yar ugly ol' mug. God, I'd give three of me pigs to know why ya're in this part a the country. Is it the king of the tinkers, Tilla Kusthi himself, that directed yar feet to me own doorway? Is it that yar old man, bad zest to him, may he rot in the fires of hell, is thinkin' of bringin' the cock of cocks up here? Well, if he is, he can think again for he'll not find fools here. Mind ya, if he did find one fool, and if the fight was staged in my barn, well, it wouldn't do my business ne'er a bit a harm. She was pondering over this last remark to herself when a gentle hand touched her shoulder. 'Stallion! I've had my eyes out for yarself all night!'

'I just got back.' O'Casey rested an elbow on the bar. 'How's Colin?'

'Tucked in, sleeping soundly.'

'Is there a chance of a drink?'

'Maggie!' bawled Aggie. 'One treble Irish for a gentleman.' Then, turning to O'Casey, 'I heard there was some fight up there tonight.'

'Ya're right there, Aggie. 'Twas some fight.'

'They're talkin' as if the thing is the best in the land.'

'He is the best, Aggie,' replied O'Casey solemnly, the excitement showing on his face.

'Better than Satan the First?'

'Yes. Better than Satan the First!'

'Come on, Stallion! It's Aggie Carney ya're talkin' to.'

'I'm tellin' yarself that the cock I saw tonight, Taurus Bulba, is better than the tinker's own.'

'It must have been some fight!'

'Oh, Jasus, Aggie, ya never saw the likes of it in all yar born days. That cock has a man's own brain inside of him!'

'One treble Irish,' interrupted the barmaid.

'Ta, my darlin',' grinned Stallion, grabbing the drink from her hand. 'Ya just gone and saved a life.'

O'Casey threw back his head and emptied the glass. 'Aggie,' he said softly, 'I've got to talk with yarself right now and in private.' There was a pleading tone in his voice and a desperate look on his face.

'Did ya manage to squeeze yarself inta their confidence, then?'

'I did, Aggie, to a certain degree,' said O'Casey. 'But they don't entirely trust me. I can handle two out a the three, but the fellah that matters, Clancy, him I know I can't handle. I've been open an' honest with them. Without me they'd be walkin' back to their bogs without a penny in their shaggin' pockets. And still they've got no warmth towards me.'

'But ya've made a few bob for yarself no doubt.' Aggie smiled mischievously.

'Aye, ya're right there. Close on nine hundred pounds.'

'Jesus, Mary and Joseph – as much as that!'

'Aye, but 'tis not enough.' Stallion wiped the palm of his right hand across a weary and sweaty forehead.

'What is enough, Stallion?' asked Aggie, her smile fading.

'Enough is a lot more; a lot, lot more. I've got to get off this fuckin' rain-drenched island and soon, or I'll lose my Colin.'

'You should leave Colin in God's hands.'

'Fuck God!' spat O'Casey with real venom.

'That's blasphemy, Stallion O'Casey.'

'And 'tis blasphemy He brought down on to me, makin' my grand Mary a sick woman and she on the point of givin' birth. 'Tis blasphemy that He takes my Mary from me and leaves me with a crooked child with a chest made outa paper. Fuck God, I say! Fuck God and up the devil!'

'God forgive ya, Stallion O'Casey,' said Aggie, her voice stern but gentle, 'for ya're most certainly out a yar mind.'

'He can keep His forgiveness. Now will ya come away with me to a quiet corner so as I can talk with yarself in private or what?'

'Before we go,' replied Aggie, pointing a finger across the bar to the wall opposite, 'take a look at that fellah standing next to Hassit.'

'Ya mean the fellah in the pinstripes?'

'That's the one.'

'Who is he?' Stallion asked, taking the stranger in from head to toe.

'Ya don't know him? Ya've never laid eyes on him before?'

'Never.'

'Well, his name is Condour Kusthi. He's the son of the king of all the tinkers, none other than Tilla Kusthi himself.'

'Jasus! What the hell is he doin' in these parts?'

'That I intend to find out later,' she said evenly, then turned and linked her arm in his. 'But first we'll have our little chat.'

Clancy sat by the bedroom window looking out onto the street, while Duffy and O'Leary bedded down Bulba for the night. Milo tried to close his ears to the racket as Pagga and Barra bitched over Bulba's sleeping arrangements. It had been a grand night for all of them. Not only had Bulba won his fight and come out of it without as much as a scratch, but Pagga, Barra and himself were £600 the richer.

He watched the patrons of Aggie Carney coming and going, and listened to the drunken, addled blather of those who had had one too many rising up through the night air. His thoughts turned to O'Casey. We're richer because of him, he told himself, so why can't ya put a tick after his name and give the fellah yar hand? But that he couldn't answer. Bide yar time, Clancy, he advised, wait and see what the fellah wants from yarself, and then ya'll be able to answer. Barra Duffy's voice brought him from his reverie.

'He stays on the fuckin' mattress. We sleep on the floor.'

'He does not! I'll not spend another night on t'em boards!'

'Ya will and ya'll fuckin' like it!'

'That's enough!' shouted Clancy, getting up off his chair.

'Listen, Milo!' pleaded Pagga. 'Ya've got to have a bit of understanding about me frail condition. Me shaggin' piles are on fire, for God's sake! They've been that way since we set out over a week back. I've got to have a soft mattress under me or I'll be dead before the shaggin' month is out!'

'Milo,' said Barra, 'Bulba needs his comforts. He's just had a fight; he's in alien country, surrounded by strangers and a million miles away from his own roost. He needs all the comfort we can offer him.'

'He can perch on the foot a the bed tonight. 'Tis about time the three of us got a dacent night's sleep. Now, no arguments, Barra,' warned Clancy. 'If Bulba decides halfway through the night that he wants the mattress then he's goin' to have to share it with us. But we're not goin' to shove over and get outa that fuckin' bed for him tonight! Is that clear and understood?'

Duffy shoved his hands deep into his trouser pockets and shook his head in exasperation, but he kept his mouth shut.

'Okay. Down to the bar with all three of us now and we'll water our gills before we turn in for the night.'

'I'll drink to that,' said Pagga.

'Meself as well!' said Duffy, picking up Bulba and cradling him in his arms.

'Where are ya goin' with that cock?' barked Clancy.

'Takin' him with us, of course.'

'Ya'll leave him here!'

He held Bulba a little more tightly. 'There's a thousand fuckers downstairs who'd give their eye tooth for him now and I'll bet that Stallion O'Casey is right to the fuckin' front of those thievin' bastards.'

'He might be a bastard,' answered Clancy calmly, 'and he could well be a murderer, but he's not a robber, at least not in that sense. Leave Bulba here. As ya said yarself, he needs his rest. Just make sure ya lock the door!'

There was a flicker of defiance in Duffy's eyes, which passed as Milo Clancy glared back at him. Duffy was about to return Bulba to the carpet when he caught Pagga O'Leary's sneering grin. 'A fuckin' brain I might not have in my head, Milo James Clancy!' he suddenly exploded. 'Stupid and witless, a man that can't be relied on I might appear to yarself. But would ya be kind enough to have charity on the daft and allow meself to put our fuckin' cock on the shaggin' mattress until we get back from our shaggin' drink?'

With all the dignity he could muster, Duffy placed Taurus Bulba in the centre of the mattress. Then, straightening himself to his full height, he showed Pagga O'Leary the whiteness of his teeth and smiled his hard-won victory at him. O'Leary replied with a murderous glance. Seconds later the room was in darkness, and Taurus Bulba, left in peace at last, settled into the softness of the mattress like a clucking hen.

★

Condour Kusthi walked into Aggie Carney's parlour with assurance in every step. ''Tis been a long time, Aggie darlin',' he smiled, giving her his outstretched hand.

'And how's the fine, upstanding son of Tilla Kusthi?' Aggie beckoned the tinker towards her best armchair on the left-hand side of the fireplace. But there was no smile on her face.

'Tilla's son is fine, Aggie. Doin' very nicely, ya'll be glad to hear.' Condour settled himself into Aggie's favourite chair.

'I must say ya're lookin' prosperous, Condour.'

''Tis the suit ya mean. Hand-made, Aggie darlin',' smiled Kusthi, smoothing the lapels of his immaculate jacket.

'Cost a bob or two, I bet.'

'Aye, that it did, but worth every penny. In my line a business a man's tools are his suit. Put a decent suit on a good man and he oozes confidence.'

'What line a business are ya in these days, then?' asked Aggie feigning innocence.

'The da's. Everything the da was into I do now. Everything except the cocks. The training is still in his hands, 'til his day a judgement comes. Age has finally caught up with the old blackguard. He's got the rheumatism bad, 'specially in the arms and hands.'

'He's still on the roads?'

'Aye. He'll not turn his agein' back on caravan and cart and walk into a four-waller and accept civilization.'

'But ya're willin' to go with the times?'

'I'm glad they finally arrived, Aggie. I was never keen for horse and trap. I've got a fine three-bedroom bungalow just outside Queenstown in the county of Cork, and I've got another in Dundrum in County Dublin.'

'Then ya have done well,' said Aggie, not able to hide the fact that she was impressed.

'Aye. Scrap metal, Aggie, that's what made me.'

'And the cocks?'

'Ah, the cocks are only for public relations.'

'Sounds like ya swallowed a dictionary,' smiled Aggie.

'New words are needed, Aggie darlin', for the new age. 'Tis 1927 after all. We're a nation now. The whole of Ireland is dressed up in their Sunday suits with places to go. And some of us tend to go far.'

'Then what brings ya back to the startin' point? What brings ya back here?' asked Aggie, glad that the pleasantries were over at last.

'The fights.'

'Ya saw the Mayo men's cock then?'

'I did.'

'Impressed?'

'Yes.'

'How impressed?' asked Aggie, trying to keep her tone casual.

'Very.'

'You reckon he could handle Satan?'

'Not that impressed,' said Condour. 'He put up a show maybe, but Satan'd see him off.'

'Out there in my bar there's a few hundred that'd be for disagreein' with ya.'

'And I bet not a one of 'em has ever seen Satan fight.'

'Are ya thinkin' of offerin' these Mayo men a chance?'

'No. Tilla is retirin' Satan the First.'

'Retirin' him, is he?' said Aggie, neither her face nor her voice giving anything away.

'Aye. The da reckons he has nuttin' left to prove. He's the best cock in Ireland. Ireland'll not see his likes again after he's gone. The da is goin' to do one grand tour with him. He's goin' to take him round the four provinces of Ireland. In each he'll have one fight. Two weeks from today he'll fight in Cork city itself. Three months later 'tis Dublin, three months after that it's Galway and then . . .' Kusthi stopped short, shrugging his shoulders, a shrewd smile lighting his face.

Aggie's smile matched his own. 'It's here.'

'On the nose, Aggie. But which particular spot? Now that's the question.'

'My barn, of course. It can hold three thousand if need be. Lipton's old shack can barely hold five hundred, as well ya know, Condour Kusthi.'

'But I'm sure Lipton would expand his place if need be. After all 'tis Satan the First that'll be trhoddin' his sawdust floor.'

'Okay, all right!' snapped Aggie, with fire in her cheeks. 'What are ya tellin' me?'

'Twenty-five per cent of the barn's takings and a hundred pounds travelling expenses.'

34

'That's daylight robbery, Condour Kusthi, as well you know.'

'The Kusthis don't bargain, Aggie, as well ya know.'

'They demand. Take it or leave it. Tinkers all of ye and ye're the ones with the upper hand.'

'Aye, 'cause we have to be, darlin',' drawled Condour icily, his smile now vanished. 'Take it or leave it.'

'Okay, it's a deal. Who's the cock?'

'Copper General.'

'Frank Logan's darlin'? That's the first I've heard of it.'

'He came up to Dublin two weeks back. Paid us four hundred for the privilege.'

'Logan must be losin' what little bit a sense he has. Satan'll chew him up and spit him out before the poor ol' thing has time to get off the ground.'

'He can afford to splash his money about, so I've been told.'

'Don't tell that to his wife or she'll march him to his grave. You do know the General is fightin' tomorrow afternoon, don't you?'

'Yeah. 'Tis Logan must be a stupid son of a bitch. If his cock loses it's bad news for him.'

'You get to keep the four hundred!'

'That's the agreement,' nodded Kusthi, regaining his smile.

'What happens then?'

'We offer to give the fight to the winner. That's how it works, you know that.'

'And if he refuses?'

'Then I'll look this Clancy fellah up and see if he's willin' to back the grand talk about his cock with a little of the green stuff. Don't worry, Aggie darlin', there's always someone.'

'Always some mug, ya mean.'

'Depends how ya look at it. Satan could have an off-day. He could be beaten.'

'And pigs might fly,' sneered Aggie.

'And pigs might fly,' smiled Condour, rising to his feet. 'Well, I'll not detain ya no longer, darlin'. I'll hit the sack while there's still some of the black light left.' Kusthi gave her his left hand.

'And the date?' asked Aggie, holding his large, rough hand in her own.

'For the fight? June the 26th. Twelve months from today. If Satan sees the Cork, Dublin and Galway cocks to their final resting places he'll be in yar barn this time next year.' He shook her hand again. 'I hope ya got a good mattress down for me, for I'm fair bushed out.'

'Room sixteen, second floor.'

Kusthi had no sooner closed the door behind him than Aggie bawled out, 'Kathleen! Kathleen! Where the devil are ya?'

'Do you see that chair?' snapped Aggie when the girl rushed in, pointing towards her best armchair.

'Yes, ma'am, I see it.'

'I want it scrubbed with water, soap and scrubbing brush.'

'Now, miss?'

'Yes!' shouted Aggie. 'Yes, this very minute, if not sooner.'

'But 'tis two o'clock in the mornin', ma'am.'

'I know the time, Kathleen Costello,' said Aggie, turning her back on the maid. 'And first thing tomorrow mornin' I want you and Kitty to springclean this room from top to bottom. Understood?'

'Understood, ma'am,' replied Kathleen, watching Aggie disappear through the open doorway.

'Fuckin' trollop, whore of a bitch!' cursed Kathleen, as soon as she was safely out of hearing.

# 3

Pagannini's piles were in a bad state as he sat down to breakfast that morning. Even Duffy's sympathy was aroused as O'Leary nursed his arse onto the chair.

'Ya'll have to see a doctor and that's that!' exclaimed Clancy as he watched Pagga's face screw up in pain.

'No doctor, Milo!'

'You see the doctor today!'

'Ya're overextendin' the bounds of yar authority, Milo Clancy,' warned Pagga. 'No doctor! I'll not see one!'

'Then suffer in silence, O'Leary. We want to hear no more descriptions about the topography and terrain of yar fuckin' hole. Understood?'

'Under-fuckin'-stood,' sulked Pagga. 'As long as yarself and Barra keep all talk of quacks outa the reach of me ears.'

'Good morning, gentlemen.'

The Mayo men looked up from their breakfast to see the dumpling shape of Aggie Carney standing over them.

'Mornin', missus,' greeted the three in unison. Clancy and Duffy rose as one from their chairs but O'Leary stayed put.

'Won't ya take the weight off yar feet and join us in a cup?' asked Barra.

'Thank you, I will at that, Mr Duffy.' Aggie beamed at him.

Clancy and Duffy stayed at attention as Aggie pulled up a chair. When she was seated they resumed their seats, and Duffy's manners came into play. He drained his own cup in one gulp, wiped it clean on one of Aggie's napkins, and poured the remainder of the pot into his cup. Aggie, a slight flush coming into her cheeks, trained her eyes away at once.

'Ya're not lookin' yarself this mornin', Mr O'Leary,' she said.

'No, missus, I'm not,' agreed O'Leary sadly.

'What's the problem?'

37

'Not allowed to say, missus,' said Pagga, casting a glance at the formidable Clancy.

'I don't understand.'

'I suffer.' He looked at her, his face filled with silent anguish. 'I suffer like the good Christ had to do on the sacred cross. I bleed, just like He did for all our sins.'

'Sweet heavens above, Mr O'Leary. What are ya on about?'

'Piles, missus,' sighed O'Leary. 'Piles. And 'tis me that has to suffer every hour of the workin' day in silence because my so-called friends won't give me their ears and listen awhile to my woes.'

'Take no notice of him, ma'am,' said Clancy quickly. 'He likes to suffer. All that man has to do is go off with himself to a doctor but he won't have it. Our ears have been bedevilled with painted descriptions of every nob that has ever taken up residence around the cheeks of his – if ya'll pardon the expression – arse. For the past twenty years it's been goin' on and we've just about come to the end of our tether with the man.'

'And why is it that ya won't take yarself off and go see a doctor, Mr O'Leary?'

'Because, missus,' answered Duffy, 'six years ago his grandda died in his bed an hour after Dr Flynn left him.'

'Aye he did die, missus,' sighed Pagga. 'And 'twasn't an hour after the quack had left. 'Twas a bare five minutes after he stepped away from our cottage.'

'His grandda was ninety-five years old, ma'am,' explained Clancy, seeing the concern on Aggie's face. 'And ever since then, ma'am, Pagga O'Leary keeps a long, long arm between himself and the doctors.'

' 'Tis sad, Mr O'Leary, that you should suffer needless pain. Are ya so dead set against doctors?'

'That I am, ma'am. They might be all right as regards yarself, but when they enter an O'Leary cottage they walk away with murder on their hands.'

'How about surgery? You could have them removed.'

'The good Lord placed a half dozen of His stigmatas on my rear, ma'am, and if they're to be removed then only His good self has the right to take them away. After all,' he concluded righteously, 'they're His property.'

'Perhaps I could help.'

'You, ma'am?'

'My husband, Danny, ten years gone now – the Lord have mercy on his departed soul – he had them.'

'Piles, missus?' asked Barra.

'Yes, he suffered them for twenty years of his life.' The shadow of a memory flickered in Aggie Carney's eyes. 'He was very much like Mr O'Leary here,' she went on, retaining her poise. 'He didn't trust doctors. So I had to bear his suffering and listen to his woes of pain night in and night out. Finally I upped and did something about it. Through trial and error I found a remedy by which I helped to give my poor Danny some measure of relief.'

'Did ya get rid of the itchiness by any chance?' There was a glimmer of hope in Pagga's eyes. ' 'Tis the itch that's the worst of it with me.'

'I cured the itch altogether, and as for the inflammation, well, I managed to check it a good deal.'

'Oh, Jasus, ma'am!' exclaimed O'Leary. 'But if what ya're sayin' is true, then bestow yar healin' and lovin' hands on my twenty-odd years of sorrow. Do it and I'll bless ya for the rest of me natural life.'

'I never lie, Mr O'Leary. I'm a God-fearin' woman.'

'That ya are, ma'am, that ya are. I never meant to doubt ya for a second.'

'Tell me first, Mr O'Leary. Have ya tried to treat yarself?'

'Aye. For ten years now, mornin', noon and night I washed bottle after bottle of surgical spirit on to me misfortunate rear.'

'Mother of God, Mr O'Leary!' Aggie winced at the very thought. 'Why, why that's like pouring oil on to a blazing fire. Who on earth was sadistic enough to recommend that line of treatment?'

'Peggy Shaw.'

'Then when ya get back to Mayo, Mr O'Leary, seek her out and burn her at the stake as a witch, for that is what she must truly be.'

'Ya'll not find a finer woman in all of Mayo than Peggy Shaw when it comes to curin' corns, Mrs Carney,' said Barra.

'Shut yar mouth, Barra!' snapped Pagga, but his eyes never left Aggie Carney's plump face. 'Ma'am, if it suits yarself, and if ya need to catch up on yar charitable deeds, then would ya turn yar Christlike eyes in my direction and see what ya can do for meself?

I'm not a man that'll give ya an empty hand in return for yar deed of mercy. I'll see ya right for yar time spent.'

'I'll do what I can for you, Mr O'Leary, and if I'm in any way responsible for relieving some a yar pain, God himself will reward me when I join up with me Danny.'

'Dacent is the word for yarself. Dacent should have been yar Christian name. Can ya tell me now what it is ya're goin' to do to meself to ease me twenty years of misery?' A picture suddenly flashed in front of Pagga's eyes of himself with his trousers down around his ankles and Aggie's eyes staring at his lower regions.

From the look on Aggie's face it was clear that she had guessed O'Leary's thunderbolt thought. 'Rest easy, Mr O'Leary. It'll not be all that painful or embarrassing to yarself. But we'll not discuss the ins and outs of the treatment here at the breakfast table, in case it puts yar two friends off their food.'

'Aye. I agree with ya there, missus,' said Barra, only too willing to change the subject. ' 'Tis not a topic I care to delve into in detail over breakfast, dinner or supper. As a matter a fact, talk of piles and arses afire is a subject that is very low on me list when I sit down and converse with complete strangers. Yar tea, missus,' said Barra, passing cup and saucer across to her.

'Thank you, Mr Duffy.' She took a delicate sip. 'I hear all three of ye are to be congratulated. Yar cock, I'm told, put up one hell of a show last night.'

'That he did, missus,' replied Duffy proudly.

'Mr O'Casey tells me ye made quite a lot of money.'

'Stallion O'Casey is a friend of yours, ma'am?' asked Clancy sharply.

'Yes he is, Mr Clancy. Stallion O'Casey is a very good friend indeed.' Aggie's smile remained on her lips as guileless as her eyes. I wonder why Stallion thinks he can't handle you? she wondered. Aloud, she went on, 'The Carneys and the O'Caseys have been friends right down the centuries. My Danny and Stallion's father were very close indeed. I'm the last of the Carneys, and only through marriage at that. I never had any children and I look on Stallion as a son. My Danny, may he rest in peace, would have wanted it that way.'

'Friendship is a great thing, ma'am. 'Tis hard to find but, once found, people will try their damnedest to hold on to it,' agreed Clancy.

'And so we should hold on, Mr Clancy. Don't you agree?'

'I do. But caution, ma'am; caution and a little bit a suspicion should be in the forefront of the mind before you grasp an open hand.'

'Aye, of course,' smiled Aggie. 'Many a hand has been bitten. But too much caution, Mr Clancy, too much and a man can be left friendless and alone. Friends gain from each other. Let's say, for instance, one has talent and the other brains, combinin' both gifts together, and what have ya got but a fruitful team? But if hands weren't grasped in the first place both gifts would go to waste and that would be a pity now, wouldn't it?'

'It might.'

'No two ways about it, Mr Clancy,' giving Milo a significant look.

'I'll hear him out, Mrs Carney. I'll hear him out and then I'll turn yar Mr O'Casey down flat.'

'That's entirely up to you, Mr Clancy,' said Aggie calmly. 'But a little bit of advice to ya good self – make sure and clean the shit out from between yar ears before ya hear Stallion. Leave yar bogman suspicion and the evil glare of yar eyes up in yar bedroom, and make sure to borrow someone else's brain and bring it with yar, for what Stallion has to say is at least worth listenin' to with a clear head. Once in a lifetime a chance comes along. A clear chance to kick yarself outa the pit. O'Casey is willin' to kick your arse outa there as well as his own.' She stood up abruptly. 'Good morning, gentlemen, I've work to do. Thank you, Mr Duffy, for the tea. And if ya still want to see me about that little problem of yours, Mr O'Leary, call into me parlour after lunch.' With which she swept from the room.

'A fine woman,' said Pagga to Clancy.

'A good talker, Pagga,' Clancy replied, placing an empty cup back on its saucer. 'What did you think of her, Barra?'

'I don't trust the woman.'

'Why?'

'Why what?' asked Barra, taken aback by the intensity of Milo's eyes.

'Why don't you trust her?'

'Because she's in collusion with that fellah.'

'What fellah?'

'Stallion O'Casey.'

'Go on, Barra. Just for this once let yar brain expand and

develop its train a thought! It'll be interestin' to see if it cracks up under the mighty strain of it all.'

'Well, fuck you, Milo Clancy!' bellowed Duffy, his cheeks reddening and his eyes ablaze. 'You work it out for yar fuckin' self. 'Tis O'Leary and meself that's for ever in yar fuckin' wake, thinkin' that 'tis glad we are to be behind ya, thinkin' that you yarself is the one with the grand brain. Well, 'tis daft we are the both of us, for here ya are now just sittin' there all confused and bothered, lookin' as if that ten-ton bitch of a whore had just shoved a red hot needle up ya. If that ol' bag can confuse ya so much and trick ya inta a quandary about fuck-all, then 'tis sure it is that yar ol' brain is as small and useless as that of a fuckin' cock!' Duffy folded his arms and sat back in his chair.

Milo's eyes softened, his face softened, and slowly a smile played about his lips. 'So as far as yarself is concerned, Barra, we've nothin' to worry about. The woman isn't worth a single one of our thoughts.'

'That's what I say, Milo Clancy,' replied Duffy.

'And this collusion bit? What's all that about?'

'Search me.' Barra shrugged his shoulders.

'Guess, go on, guess. What do ya think they want from us?'

'I think they want to buy our Bulba.'

Clancy sighed in despair. 'What do you think they want, Pagga?'

'Why bother even thinkin' about it? We meet the bastard soon enough.'

Clancy looked from one to the other and wished he had left them both at home. They were his lifetime friends. They were open men. Where they came from there was no need to be anything else. The opportunities for gain were limited. Everyone had his patch of land, and worked to get the best from it. No one would think of encroaching on another's few miserable acres. Without them the family would starve. Bad harvests meant a grinding winter of poverty, but even then men like O'Leary and Duffy would not reach inside and dig out the cunning that laid dormant within them since their birth; instead their eyes went to the heavens, and frightened voices rang up through the roofs of their cottages begging God for deliverance from the curse of their day-to-day existence.

Clancy had once believed that the outside world was all the

same, and made up of the same kind of men. His mistake was apparent to him as soon as he set foot outside his own little universe. And he realized that he must look inside himself for the strength that would protect his two friends and himself until he could steer a safe course for home once more.

As he sat there watching the both of them, he longed to be on the road heading west and homewards. But today was a day to get through. If he wasn't careful, the unknown would take him and turn him upside down, and life for all three would never be the same again. Looking at Pagga he asked, 'When we had our nightcap last night did ya not notice anythin' outa the ordinary?'

'Such as?'

'A fellah. A fellah dressed like a lord, pinstriped suit, with a look a money about him?'

'Naw.'

'Well, the fellah I'm referrin' to goes by the name a Kusthi. Does it not ring a bell with yarself at all?'

'Tilla Kusthi!' O'Leary's voice was filled with awe. 'Ya're tellin' me Tilla Kusthi is stayin' under Carney's roof?'

'No, I'm not sayin' 'tis Tilla Kusthi. I'm tellin' ya 'tis the son of Tilla. A fellah called Condour.'

'The name Condour does ring a bell. Tilla's number one son. How do you know it's him?'

'I kept my ears open.'

'What's he doin' here?' asked Barra.

'Here's a chance for ya, Barra, to speculate again,' teased Clancy.

'No, I'll not bother. You're the one with the brains. You tell us why Kusthi is in these parts.'

'Now that I don't know, Barra. But I'll tell you who does. Aggie Carney does. That bastard O'Casey, and O'Casey's bandy-legged son does. Every one of Aggie Carney's fat pigs knows. Every son of a cunt in this place knows. Everyone but us. Now doesn't that sound strange to yarself, Barra Duffy? Doesn't it sound a wee bit strange that we're in the dark and will remain so until Stallion O'Casey opens his gob and lets us in on the secret?'


The O'Caseys had breakfast in their room. Stallion had heard his lad cough once or twice during the night and decided to keep him

43

bedbound for the rest of the morning at least. Colin was sitting upright in the bed with a half dozen pillows between his frail shoulders and the backrest of the bed; he was browsing through a comic he had read half a dozen times before. Stallion was standing by the window looking out onto the street.

'Da, what time is it?'

'What?'

'What time is it?'

'Gone eleven,' said Stallion, without turning round.

'Then the morning is over. I can get up now,' replied Colin, slapping his comic down on the eiderdown between his knees, hoping Stallion in his absent-minded state would nod his agreement.

'Stay put, son. I'll tell ya when to get up.'

'But Da, 'tisn't fair! You didn't hear me cough during my sleep, 'twas yar imagination playin' ya tricks.'

With a sigh, Stallion came over to the bed and, dropping to his knees, beckoned his son's head towards his left ear. 'Open yar gob and breathe hard . . . .' He listened for the faintest wheeze but it was as clear as a bell. 'I still hear the black angels of Satan down there, Colin,' he lied. 'Stay put 'til lunchtime.'

' 'Tisn't fair, it just isn't fair.' Colin buried his face into the mound of pillows. 'I haven't had the devil's choir in my chest for well over a year now and you know it. I haven't had the wheezies or the colliwobbles; my chest is as clear as a bell.'

'All right! All right! All right! None a the waterworks now!' Stallion ran a hand through his hair. 'Ya can face yar da and tell him about the latest adventure of White Hat Sam that ya been readin'.'

'I'll not! You want to know what's in the comic; ya can go read it for yarself.'

'But what about the extra colourin', man? 'Tis easy enough for you to say read the damn comic. 'Tis only you that can give it the colourin' and depth.'

Colin turned around and looked up into his father's eyes. He looked for the whimsical smile at the corner of his lips, but it wasn't there. If he was being hoodwinked he could find no trace of it on his father's face. 'I give you the gist of the story and a little bita the colourin'. Then I can get up, right?'

'No deal. The story, start to finish and yar thickest coat of colourin' that ya can paint onto it.' But Stallion could not disguise the mischievous smile that began to spread across his face.

'You rotten schemer, Stallion!' shouted the boy, swinging his fist in the direction of his da's head.

Stallion parried the blow with his left arm, laughing out loud. 'Arrah, go on now, Colin. Give us the story and pour yar fine imaginings over it!'

'As soon as I'm finished I'm up?' smiled the boy.

'O'Casey's own honour,' replied Stallion, crossing his heart.

Colin was in good form that morning. He painted a grand canvas with words of the sweeping pasture lands that the bold sheriff White Hat Sam rode across in pursuit of two of the meanest rustlers that ever set foot on the sacred soil of Texas. Stallion could see the great mountains rising up to kiss the blazing sun in Colin's own eyes. He could feel the soft breeze brushing against his cheeks – the very same breeze that White Hat Sam felt as he rode out that morning to bring the two desperados to justice. It took an hour for the boy to tell the story, and when it was told both of them were emotionally drained. White Hat Sam had done it once more, but only just. If Black Brady's shot from his six shooter hadn't hit that fencing post, old Sam would have got it straight through the heart and ended up in Boot Hill for sure.

'Jasus, but 'twas close that time!'

'He was lucky, Da.'

'What's next month's story?'

'White Hat's shoot-out with the Rango brothers! Five of 'em this time. All of them with Winchesters and him with only his two six shooters!'

'Jasus, but that won't stop ol' White Hat. He'll see them off all right. The very minute that comic appears in Nora Cooney's shop we must have it. We'll tell Aggie Carney to send it post haste!'

'By pony express!'

'Texas, Colin! Just imagine it! Not long to go now, son, another year at the most and we'll be on a ship and headin' for that grand, grand place.'

'Where it never rains. Where the temperature never drops below eighty and where the grass is tall and the air is as clean as snow-white handkerchiefs,' interrupted Colin, repeating the words that came at him day in and day out from his father's lips.

'Aye son, that's the very truth. Ya'll not be standin' out from the rest of them either. Every cowboy out there has bandy legs. They have to because they're in the saddle every minute of the workin' day. The legs have to twist and bow themselves otherwise the grip and control of the horse would be bad, and they'd be for ever fallin' off. It'll not be long now, son. We need a few breaks. We need Mr Clancy's help and we're away this time next summer.'

When Stallion O'Casey stepped into Aggie's bar it was just after twelve o'clock. The place was full to overflowing with the cock-fighting fraternity, but O'Casey's sharp eyes spotted Clancy at once, sitting alone at a table at the far-off corner of the bar. Stallion went to the counter, ordered a round of drinks and, with his back to the counter, studied the man he was about to try and do business with. Clancy was half a head shorter than himself, but the Mayo man made up for this in weight, being about ten pounds heavier; and it seemed to Stallion that Clancy carried every single pound of his bulk like a prize fighter. He reckoned he was about the same age as himself. He studied his face. Ordinary. Fusspot women might say a bit on the plain side, he thought to himself. He had a straight-on view of the man's eyes. Nothin' there now! Just two green emeralds passin' over me shoulder. No suspicious fire, just bogman eyes starin' into fuckin' space with ne'er a bita malice about them. They'll change though, won't they, Milo Clancy, when I step into their firin' range!

'Two double Irish and twenty Woodbines, Mr O'Casey.'

'Thank you, Kathleen,' he replied, handing her a fiver. With glasses in hand he approached Clancy's table. 'Good mornin' to yarself, Milo Clancy.'

'Mornin',' said Clancy. 'I've saved ya a chair.' And he removed his outstretched left leg from the empty chair opposite.

'I didn't see yarself or yar son at breakfast t'is mornin'!' said Clancy.

'Colin wasn't well. We had breakfast in our room.' O'Casey's voice was calm.

'My heart bleeds for ye both,' smiled Clancy with sweet insincerity.

'No need. 'Twas nothing serious. Colin is up and about now.'

O'Casey watched as the Mayo man glared back at him. A mixture of confusion, suspicion and anger was plastered in bountiful abundance over Clancy's face. He waited for the next move.

'What kind of a fuckin' watery-shitted article are ya anyway?' roared Clancy.

O'Casey leaned forward to look Clancy directly in the eye. 'The kind of article that's goin' to take you out into Aggie Carney's back yard and beat the livin' fuck outa ya as soon as we settle this fuckin' deal!' He made his threat quietly, but with easy assurance.

'I'll hold ya to yar word, O'Casey.'

'Don't worry, Mr Clancy. I always keep my word!'

'Good, okay, talk to meself. Tell me what ya have to say!'

'A double Irish for yar good self, Mr Clancy.' With a smile, O'Casey passed him his drink.

Both of them tossed back their heads and drained their glasses.

'There's a man stayin' at this hotel who's a relative of Tilla Kusthi,' said O'Casey. 'He's here to make arrangements with Aggie Carney. This time next year Tilla Kusthi and his cock Satan the First will come here to Aggie's barn to fight one of our locals, Copper General. Copper General is owned, trained and presented in the ring by Frank Logan. He's one of the big-shot farmers round these parts. . . .'

Clancy didn't stir. 'Well?'

'Copper General is fightin' this afternoon. He's down to fight Pappagina's Cottage.'

'And if the General loses?'

'The tinker's son is prepared to take on the next best cock. That's if the money can be put up.'

'Okay, okay, O'Casey,' interrupted Clancy. 'Shorten it, for Christ's sake! Come to the fuckin' point! What do you want from us?'

'I want to see your cock in the ring with Satan the First.'

'That's the gist of yar proposal?'

'Yes.'

'Well, that's simple enough. The answer is no.' Clancy shifted impatiently in his chair. 'Is there anything else ya have to say to meself?'

'Bulba could beat Satan!'

'I took you for a real clever man. Streets smarter than meself!

47

There isn't a cock in the whole of Ireland that can match Kusthi's devil.' Clancy hesitated, glaring at O'Casey's impassive face. 'Okay. Tell me why you think Bulba could take Kusthi's beast and beat it.'

'If you were to put Bulba up against him right now 'tis true indeed that yar cock wouldn't last a half minute.' O'Casey chose his words carefully. 'But give me three months with your Bulba and the outcome of the fight would be a whole lot different. Satan the First would be drowning in his own blood on the sawdust floor and Bulba would be crowing out his victory call. I want to take over the training of Bulba.'

Clancy wiped a hand over his face in exasperation. 'Jasus, this is fuckin' madness!'

'For Christ's sake, man!' said O'Casey. 'Bear me out.'

'Okay,' groaned Clancy, seeing the desperation in O'Casey's eyes. 'Fire away!'

'Right!' said Stallion. 'Now, just one question. Give me, let's say . . . five cocks! Five cocks livin' or dead who were or are masters of the sawdust ring.'

'Satan the First, Iron Balls . . . Ringmaster, Coffin Maker and White Blood.'

'I'd agree with ya. Every one of them true masters. One more question, what have those five cocks in common?'

'Give up!' Impatience entered Clancy's voice once more.

'All of 'em are owned and trained by tinkers.'

'Sure I know that!'

'I know. The point is, only the tinkers raise the best cocks, train the best cocks and present the best cocks!'

'That's always been the case. They've got the secret.'

'And so have I!' said Stallion, thankful at last to get his point across.

Clancy paused for a moment. 'Ya're not a tinker. There isn't a drop of the open road about ya!'

'There isn't and that's true. My father got the secret from a tinker called MacDonagh, Batty MacDonagh. He got the secret because he did the man a great favour.'

'I'm to believe that! I'm to believe that tinkers spout out the sacred secret that has been developed and nourished deep inside their sly hearts for hundreds of years. They told your da what they wouldn't reveal to the English landlords even when they

48

were fastened to the rack and the flesh scourged off their bones?'

'One tinker did. Batty MacDonagh, ninety years old with a stomach full to the top with a murderous cancer, left on the roadside by his sadistic idiot son to die in his agony. . . . John Michael O'Casey, my father, took him in and put the man to rest for his last hours in his own bed. There is no cancer worse than cancer of the bowel. There is no sleep for the poor bastard that has the misfortune of gettin' it. After five days under my father's roof MacDonagh calls my father to his bedside and asks him to do him a great mercy. A night and a day MacDonagh pleads and finally my father consents to the old tinker's request. In return for such a favour Batty MacDonagh gives my father the secrets of the fightin' cock! My father pressed a pillow down on the old tinker's head and in a few seconds all the pain and all the agony leaves Batty MacDonagh's frail ol' body for good. . . . On my da's deathbed he passes the secret on to his only son, that bein' meself.'

Clancy's eyes dropped from O'Casey's face to his Sunday-best boots. He sighed a heavy sigh, then slapped the pockets of his jacket. 'Have ya got a fag on ya?' O'Casey gave him a cigarette, lit it for him and waited. After twenty more seconds had passed Clancy said, 'Ya're tellin' the truth.'

'I'm tellin' the truth,' stated O'Casey.

'I know ya are! I wasn't askin' a question, I was statin' a fuckin' fact.'

'Then we're agreed on something.'

'But if ya know the tinker's secret,' said Clancy thoughtfully, 'how come yar name and yar cocks hasn't been heard and hasn't been hailed in the village where I come from?'

'Because I've never managed to breed a champion. A man can know the secret of the cock but if he hasn't got the right cock from the start then the secret is no good. For fifteen years I've tried to breed a true bird and I never managed to do it. I never managed to get my paws on a champion.'

'But ya're tellin' me that I've done it?'

'I'm tellin' yarself, Milo Clancy, that you have managed to breed by accident or design the best fightin' cock that ever trod the sawdust floor. You bred a cock that has got a human brain. That cock of yours, Taurus Bulba, doesn't fight with his instinct, he fights with reason. He knows that he will die unless he brings

49

his brain into the ring with the rest of his armoury. Clancy, there is no other cock in the whole of the universe that is quite like yours.'

Clancy had known since rising from his bed that this was a day he would never forget for the rest of his life. 'Okay,' he said matter of factly, 'what's the deal?'

'Satan will fight yar cock in one year's time. I'll need Bulba for the last three months before the fight.'

'Right! But ya'll have to come back to Bulba's own back yard. Ya train him on my own ground, and as you do so ya'll reveal the secret of yar methods to me.'

'Done,' replied O'Casey. 'I've got to go back home. I've got a harvest to take in come the end of September. I'll let the winter and a good bit a the spring pass by, and I'll be in your own patch, let's say, by the middle of March.'

'Fine with me.'

'Ya'll put me and my boy up, of course?'

'Of course.' Then, with the devil's own smile appearing on his face, he asked, 'But aren't we forgetting about Logan and the General; doesn't the General have first call on Kusthi's grand whore?'

'You are a clever man, Clancy,' smiled Stallion. 'You've worked it out, haven't ya?'

'It doesn't take a professor of conology to work that one out! You and Aggie Carney, ya've set Logan up! Ya've doctored his cock, haven't ye?'

'It'll drop down dead a minute after entering the ring.'

'Aggie's a remarkable woman!'

'Remarkable.'

'And poor ol' Logan?'

'I told ya, he's a big shot. All big shots are bastards and cunts to boot! They deserve what they get.'

'I think I'll have to keep my eyes well open when yarself comes west. We country culshies are a bit simple, don't ya know. If we're not careful ya'll swipe the land of Mayo right out from under us.'

'I'll never cross ya, Milo O'Casey. We're partners now. You and I will be livin' and sharin' the same house for three months and more. We'll have to trust each other if we're goin' to survive that harrowin' time. All of Ireland will gather here to see Kusthi's devil play his game. They'll have their money and they'll put all of it on Satan and we will take their money and we'll be rich. But Jasus, Clancy, if we're stupid, if we behave like fools and start mistrustin' each other then we are done for!' Stallion O'Casey spat hard on the palm of his hand and presented it to the watchful Clancy.

Slowly Milo doused his fag end in the ashtray, and surveyed his own calloused hand. Stallion counted all of five seconds, but finally Clancy spat. Their hands slapped together, fastened and the deal was struck.

'Well, I can't linger about here all day. Best be up and doin', I suppose,' said Clancy, rising from his chair.

'Milo . . .'

Clancy looked down at the smiling O'Casey. 'Haven't ya forgotten somethin'?'

'Oh aye.' Clancy grinned. 'Aggie Carney's back yard . . . well, we'll forget about it. We're business partners now.'

'Sorry,' said Stallion. 'I gave my word. I never go back on my word, Clancy. Let's go on out there and get the thing over and done with.'

'Why not?' said Clancy. ''Tis been manys a day since me fists kissed another man's flesh.'


The yard was twenty foot square, the ground concrete. The walls that jailed it were six feet high and made out of red brick. There was plenty of room for a man to use his feet and swing his fist.

Stallion stood in the centre in shirt and pants, his sleeves rolled up, waiting for Clancy to make his move. Clancy looked back at him, eyes intent, and he too waited. 'Okay Milo! After the count of three: one, two, three!'

Clancy charged on 'three', making for O'Casey's stomach with a bear-hug. O'Casey sidestepped easily and as Milo went shooting by, delivered his left boot onto the Mayo man's fleeing arse. It was a hard and true kick and knocked Clancy to the ground. Stallion stayed where he was, legs spread and fists at the ready. 'Ya're on the ground, Milo,' he said. Clancy was up like a bat out of hell and charging again. But he ran right into a straight left jab.

The power of the punch felt like pure granite as Milo's chin took the brunt of it. It sent him toppling backwards onto the concrete. 'Ya're on the ground, Milo.' He stayed put awhile, nursing the chin and looking up at the unmarked O'Casey. When he rose to his feet, he kept his eyes firmly on O'Casey. Once again he charged for the stomach. This time, however, he was alert for O'Casey's sidestep and veered after him. An instant later Milo had engulfed his prey and they were on the floor. Entwined, they rolled from the centre of the yard to the back wall. Jammed against the red brick, arms unfolded and fist after fist was thrown. All punches very much on target. Neither tried to duck the other's blows. O'Casey felt two of his back teeth shatter, and tasted a mouthful of blood. Clancy saw the rainbow and polka-dot stars before his eyes as two blows buffeted him about the temple.

Fortunately sheer exhaustion claimed both of them at the same time, and fists that were halfway to their targets stopped in mid-flight. Arms as heavy as lead dropped downwards without instructions from their masters. They sat themselves up against the wall, eyes heavy in their heads, staring blankly across Aggie Carney's yard. It took all of two minutes before both got their breath back.

'Mr Stallion O'Casey!' said Clancy at last.

'Wha'?'

'Ya're on the ground! Ya're on the ground, Mr O'Casey.'

'So are you, Mr Clancy.'

'Ya know somethin'?' sighed Milo heavily. 'Ya're fuckin' well right!'

# 4

Pagannini O'Leary was face down on the bed, entirely naked from his waist to the tips of his toes. The upper part of his body was clothed with the shirt and waistcoat of his Sunday-best suit.

He was in a small room situated just behind Aggie Carney's scullery. It was a storeroom of sorts, housing a rickety old bed with a mattress, a few empty beer crates and a half dozen tea chests filled with books. The bed dominated the centre of the room, and the late afternoon sun that shafted through the small window high up on the back wall illuminated the rumpled old mattress and O'Leary's bare arse.

Pagga had been waiting for a good ten minutes now and still his nurse had not returned. He was not only getting impatient, but could feel the dying fires rekindling for another attack. He lifted his face out of the pillow and, turning his head to the closed door, shouted, 'Kathleen Costello! Kathleen Costello! Am I to fuckin' well lie here under the boilin' rays of the fuckin' sun 'til my arse ruptures and explodes into smithereens or what?' There was silence. He sighed a terrible sigh and buried his face back into the pillow. Ten seconds later Aggie Carney's parlour maid returned, clutching a bag of ice in her left hand.

'Where in God's name have ya been?' snapped Pagga, looking up at the slip of a girl that stood over him.

'The devil himself take ya, Pagga O'Leary!' spat Kathleen, her eyes blazing with anger. 'Ya're callin' and bawlin', rantin' and ravin' can be heard right throughout the scutterin' hotel. 'Tis patience, by Christ, that ya require, Pagga O'Leary, boxes and boxes of it. I've two hands and 'tis that bitch Aggie Carney that has the hirin' of them. I look after her personal needs, and the needs of her toffee-nosed parlour, scullery, kitchen and bedroom – and all for a lousy fifteen shillin's a week and now she burdens me with yarself.'

'So by rights,' snapped Pagga, 'I come before all yar other duties. I'm both guest and friend to Aggie Carney. Ya're attached to meself for the duration of me treatment here. So do yar duty and get that bag of blessed relief on to me sufferin' region.'

'Much good that it'll do ya. Ya're more than likely to up and die of pneumonia.' And Kathleen slapped the bag of ice on O'Leary's burning hole.

'Oh Jasus, but I do declare that's grand,' groaned Pagga. 'Oh Jasus, relief, what relief!' He let his face sink back blissfully into the pillow and closed his eyes.

'Does this friend and guest of Aggie Carney's require anything else?' asked Kathleen snidely. 'Or is it that ya want meself to stand here like an eegit for the rest of the evenin' 'till ya can think of somethin' else that ya want me to be doin'?'

'Yes! Ya can keep that gob of a cakehole of yours tight! Off with yarself outa here and keep those bags filled and comin' in my direction! No more slip-ups! When this bag turns to water I expect to feel the weight of a brand new one on those cheeks before ya've got time to fuckin' well blink!'

'There's been ten bags on yar poxed hole already, Pagga O'Leary! Aggie Carney's two ice boxes ya drained already. If ya keep demandin' more, the toffs of the parish'll have no ice to go in their scotch and sodas come this evenin'!'

'Oh, but me heart bleeds buckets a tears for the bastards!' mumbled Pagga.

'Bad zest ta yarself, Pagga O'Leary, and your scutterin' hole!' hissed Kathleen, turning her back on her patient. 'Make that bag last an hour. The'll be no more comin' in your direction 'til teatime.' The door slammed behind her.

'Ya'll keep it comin', do ya hear!' bawled O'Leary. 'Ya're under Aggie Carney's instructions. Useless trollop!'


It was just after eight o'clock that evening in Carney's bar when the trouble started.

Frank Logan's fighting cock had died of a heart attack thirty seconds after entering the sawdust ring. Thus, O'Hagen's cock had been declared the winner, even though neither of the birds had come into contact with each other – and Logan's blood was up. There was foul play somewhere along the line as far as he was concerned and he had no trouble pinning the blame on Tim O'Hagen. The tiny little farmer was supping his pint peacefully at a table by the stained-glass window that looked out onto the street. Coming up on him from behind, Logan grabbed O'Hagen by the collar and the seat of his pants, and with little effort sent the stunned farmer into orbit. Everyone in Aggie's packed house stood transfixed as the little man shot forward through the air. Hundreds of mouths gawked in disbelief as he smashed through Aggie's prized window. Then their eyes turned to the man who had shattered their quiet evening of drinking and talk. Big Frank Logan, tallest man in the parish, standing an inch off seven foot, was gazing with murderous hatred at the pavement where O'Hagen lay sprawled amidst the jewel-like broken glass. The little man was still, a patchy halo of crimson following the circumference of his head from cheekbone to cheekbone. Frank Logan's eyes stayed on the man until he heard him groan and saw the stricken unfortunate move. Then Logan turned to survey Aggie Carney's barful of silent souls. Eyes dropped away pair by pair as he challenged each man in turn.

'Is there a man in this bar by the name of Kusthi? Condour Kusthi?' he demanded, his voice just under control. A roomful of silence greeted his question. But directly to his front a wave of frightened bodies parted, and Logan found himself staring at a man with his back towards him, quietly drinking his pint as if the racket and the exploding glass had never reached his hearing. 'Condour Kusthi!'

The man at the bar drained his glass, placed it on the counter, and slowly turned to face Frank Logan.

Kusthi's face broke into the broadest of smiles. 'Well, I declare to the livin' God if 'tisn't Frank Logan himself!'

''Tis me, Condour Kusthi,' replied Logan, his eyes on fire.

'Then up with yarself here to the bar and ya can buy a man a drink.'

'I'll drink with no cunt of a tinker this evenin' or any evenin' come to that.'

'Well, it hasn't been yar day, so I gather,' said Kusthi mildly.

'Me cock, the General, died of a heart attack in the ring.'

'Yes. Yes, that I did hear. Terrible news. Terrible. Me sympathy goes right out to yarself.'

'Well, seein' as how yar sympathy is out, how about diggin' yar left hand in yar coat pocket and bringin' out that fat wallet of yours. There's four hundred pounds on yar person that rightfully belongs to me.' Logan spoke through clenched teeth.

'That, Frank Logan, ya know I can't do,' smiled the tinker. 'A bargain was struck. A bargain was made, and both of us are gentlemen enough to stick by it.'

'Ya're no fuckin' gentleman, Tinker Kusthi! Ya're a conman of the roads. Me grand cock is dead, there can be no shaggin' fight and I'm telling ya for the last time to hand over me four hundred quid.'

But Kusthi was unmoved. 'I'm sorry, that I can't do. But I'll tell ya what I will do. I'll fill yar belly with enough drink to make ya forget yar sad loss for a few hours at least. Now, I can't do fairer than that.'

'My money, ya bastard!' bellowed Logan, and charged.

Condour Kusthi hadn't time to get out of harm's way, so swift was the attack. The whole of Aggie Carney's thirty-foot counter shook violently as the two bodies slammed into its woodwork. Logan grasped the tinker's throat like a vice. The tinker's face was turning scarlet before he managed to knee his opponent where he knew it would hurt the most. Blinding pain dropped Logan's body to the ground like a felled tree. For good measure, Condour Kusthi swung his boot hard into Logan's spinning head. With a slight smile on his lips, Kusthi looked down at the defeated outstretched body. Two seconds later the smile vanished from the tinker's face as he saw the dead man come back to life, and sit up, the devil's wrath painted all over his maddened face. The tinker had enough presence of mind to aim another kick. It fairly flew to its target. But Frank Logan's shovel hands shot out and grasped the flying leg, propelling Kusthi back towards the counter.

He struck his head a ringing blow and, for all of ten seconds, the tinker left the living world. When he came to, Frank Logan was standing over him. Stupified eyes tried to focus on the giant and a numbed brain sensed the danger. Kusthi tried to move but couldn't. He saw a blurred left hand reach out to him and a second later felt as if Christ Himself was raising him up towards heaven. At last the tinker's head cleared, but too late.

The palm of Logan's right hand was already steadying its victim as it pressed the tinker's chest against the edge of the counter. Then he stepped back an inch or two to size up his target. Logan's left hand reached down to the counter and grabbed an empty beer bottle, crashing it down onto the tinker's head. The lights went out in Kusthi's eyes once more. He toppled forward, but Logan gripped hold of the pinstriped waistcoat and kept him on his jellied feet. A second later a half-full whiskey bottle blasted down on Condour's head. Once more Logan's victim had to be steadied. He reached out and grabbed another beer bottle, but before he could raise it, Frank Logan felt a stunning blow on the back of his skull, and a great mantle of black pitch fell down upon his senses . . . .

Aggie Carney stood over both men with a cast-iron frying pan grasped firmly in both hands. 'Can I have a bita help here, please, gentlemen?' she called.

Only after she had seen to the clearing up of the bodies did she rejoin her patrons.

'Jasus, Aggie, but ya swing a fine fryin' pan!' said Stallion with obvious admiration.

Aggie leaned against the bar. 'Ya'd have watched the two of them beat each other to death, wouldn't ya, Stallion O'Casey?'

'Now, 'twasn't for me to get involved,' purred O'Casey. 'That wasn't yar ordinary Saturday-night drunk rainin' bottles of yar best whiskey down on that tinker's head. That was Logan, the devil's own offspring.'

'Men!' Aggie snorted. 'The devil take the lot a ye for ya're all bloody useless!'

'Ya'll know my friend here, Milo Clancy.' O'Casey stepped back from the bar to bring the bogman into view.

'We've met.' Aggie's look was stern. 'How are ya, Mr Clancy?'

'I'm well,' replied Clancy, the shade of a smile on his bruised and swollen lips.

'I can see ya're well, with yar battered and pouched mug lookin' down at me as if it's danced the dance of its life with a steam roller.' Disgust was written all over Aggie's face.

'Now Aggie, love!' intervened Stallion, wrapping an arm round her ample waist. 'Don't go naggin' Mr Clancy here. Mayo men don't take too kindly to a woman's whiplash tongue.'

'Get yar drunken arm from around me waist, Stallion

O'Casey!' Aggie wrenched herself free, eyes ablaze. 'Go take a look at yar face in a mirror! Christ almighty! Is that how ye settled yar deal?'

'Don't blame Stallion, missus,' said Clancy, quickly intervening. ''Tis meself that has to take the entirety of it all.'

'Arrah, but 'twas only a friendly scrap!' O'Casey protested.

Aggie raised a clenched fist. 'I've a good mind to box yar ears, Stallion O'Casey. And yars too, Mr Clancy, for it seems to me yar mother hasn't half spared the rod with yarself.'

'If it makes ya feel any better, Aggie,' O'Casey said, pretending to duck back from her, 'ya can box away and we'll take yar chastisement without puttin' up resistance. Just as long as ya don't go and grab that murderous fryin' pan of yours,' grinned O'Casey.

'Men! Bastards the lot of yees!' spat Aggie. 'Oh Christ, will ya just look! My lovely stained-glass window! Thirty pounds won't be enough to replace it!'

'Arrah, never mind,' consoled O'Casey, gingerly putting an arm about her again. 'Let me get yarself a drink. It'll help ya to forget about it for a little while. Tomorrow mornin' ya can ask yar brain about how ya're goin' to get the thirty off Logan to replace it.'

'Frank Logan to pay for it!' roared Aggie, raising her eyes to heaven. 'Mother a Jasus, ya're not half daft, Stallion O'Casey. The man's just been done outa four hundred pounds. 'Tis more than likely that I've broken his childish brain in two, and you reckon I can just walk up to the bastard and ask him for compensation. Ya're daft for sure!'

'My wholehearted sympathies are with yarself, ma'am,' said Clancy with feeling.

'Much good that'll do, Mr Clancy!'

'Come on, Aggie, have a drink. What'll it be? The usual?'

'I'll not drink with yarself, Stallion O'Casey. There's a mess to be cleared up, and three dyin' men laid out in me front parlour, and all because the good Christ, in one of his daft moments, decided to put men upon this earth! The devil take the bloody lota yees!'

'Ya're leavin' us then?' said O'Casey with mischief in his eyes.

'Bastards!' Aggie turned her back on them and began to march away.

'Mrs Carney!' Clancy called after her. 'Have ya still got Pagga O'Leary in yar safe hands?'

'I have, Mr Clancy,' she replied over her shoulder. 'Ya can have him back in the mornin'.'

'And when can we see the tinker?' asked O'Casey.

She stopped in the doorway and turned around. 'If Dr Madden deems him to be alive and kickin', ya can all come to the parlour round midnight.'

Clancy nodded. 'We'll be there, Mrs Carney. Midnight on the dot.'

'A fine woman,' remarked Clancy.

'Grander ya couldn't get, Milo,' O'Casey agreed. 'When they made Aggie Carney, sure didn't they go and throw away the mould?'

'A good job too!' Clancy lifted his glass from the counter and drained it.

'Ah, ya're right there. Too many of Aggie's kind, and petticoats would have dominance over the trousers. What are ya havin'?'

'The same again.' Milo handed over his glass.

'Ya'll not have an Irish?'

'I'll stick to the porter if 'tis all the same to yarself. I think we'll have to have our wits about us when we see this fellah Kusthi.'

'Well now,' O'Casey said as he handed Clancy his fresh pint, 'I'll wager ya'll not see fights like that in the wilds of Mayo.'

'I'll be for agreein' with yarself there. God, but that Logan fellah must be the tallest fucker that ever set foot on the earth.'

'He is to be sure, Milo. And he's also the meanest fucker that ever drew the breath of life! A bad man, Milo, ya couldn't get badder!'

'I gather ya're not entirely in love with the man.'

'In confidence, Milo, I'll tell ya. I hate the bastard! I had a sister, lovely she was. Jasus, but she was an Irish rose if ever ya saw one. Well, to cut the balls off me story, that fucker Logan goes and ruins her. He flaunts his poxy hairy chest and his sixpenny smile at her and she falls for him like a ton a bricks. He takes her, deflowers her pure, young self and turns his back on her.' O'Casey's glass banged onto the table. 'Cunt! I hate the fuckin' ground he walks on!'

'He sounds like the devil's own.'

'She's in Canada now,' O'Casey went on after some seconds had passed. The angry flush had left his cheeks and his face broke into its customary smile. 'Married she is, two kids, both strong in mind and limb, and a husband who's pure Canadian and chops down trees for a livin'. A lumberjack.'

'There's lots of trees out there to be sure. Grand country for a man willin' to go.'

'Ah, ya can stick yar Canada! Texas! Texas, Milo! That's the place! That's where me boy and meself are headin'. The weather is in the seventies and eighties all the year round. Not a drop a fuckin' rain to speak of. No cold, no snow and no fuckin' wind.'

'So that's yar dream.' Smiling, Milo watched O'Casey lift his pint to his lips.

'Yeah, that's my dream.'

'And ya need a bob or two in yar pocket in order to get there,' Clancy suggested.

'Yeah. I plan to farm out there. Ranchin' they call it. If things were different, if life had given me a fair shake a the hand, I'd be as content as yarself. Ireland is doin' nicely now. She's free from her yoke, dressed up with places to go, but I can't tag along with her. I don't know why, but that bastard up there gave me a crooked son with a paper chest and a dickety heart. If Colin stays in this fuckin' country another two years, the Irish bogs'll claim his bandy little body. The Irish mist and damp'll have his chest, the winter's cold'll have his heart and the fuckin' winds'll fell the little gorsoon to the ground. That's what every quack in Ireland has told me.'

'And the cowboy country could be his salvation?'

'Warm weather, dry climate . . . .'

'I wish yarselfs a speedy departure, then,' said Clancy, and raised his glass.

Stallion O'Casey saw the pity in the Mayo man's eyes and swung the subject away from himself. 'And what about yarself? Everybody has dreams. What's yours?'

'To keep the roof over me head, I suppose. That and a full stomach – 'til the undertaker pays me a call and nails me inta his wooden box.'

'Come on, Clancy! What's yours? A year from now and ya'll have money in yar pocket. Ya're not goin' to sit yarself down for the rest of yar days and look at the stuff.'

'Well, God willin', if that fine day ever comes and I have a little bit ta spare, I might do a bita travellin' for meself.'

'No kiddin',' said Stallion. 'Where to? Australia? America?'

'Naw. Ireland. I'll see a bita me own country and while I'm travellin' the roads, I'll keep me eye open and see if there's another Taurus Bulba peckin' away in some farmer's back yard, or if there's a hen that looks like she could breed me a fighter.'

'So 'tis breedin'!' said O'Casey, the disappointment showing in his voice.

'Nothin' wrong with breedin',' said Milo. 'Me father and his father before him made it their life's work.' He looked over the bar as though it were the future itself he saw. 'Yeah, Stallion, that's what I'd do. Spend the money, breed the best and present them in the ring for all of Ireland to see.'

'Ya wouldn't be for raisin' yar sights a tiny bit higher now and try yar hand at breedin' racehorses? Ya never know, given time ya might breed the winner of the National.'

'That's for kings and princes. I'll stick ta what I know.'

'Aye,' sighed O'Casey. 'I suppose 'tis best ta play the fiddle ya've made yarself. Tell me about Bulba. How in God's name did ya manage a feat such as that?'

'Through trial and error. Fifteen years of it, as a matter a fact. Four winters ago I was on the point of givin' up. I had nothin' to show for half a lifetime's work, except a handful of mangy cocks. I was thinkin' just then that I'd go the way of me poor ol' da. The bastard gave the whole of sixty-two years to the cock and never had a one that lasted more than a couple a fights. I said to meself, quit, quit Clancy, or the rest of yar years'll fly by ya and see ya to yar grave with nothin' to show for yar time except a million failures. 'Twas Pagga O'Leary and Barra Duffy that took me outa me despairin' depths. It was the both a them that brought me along one day a fine-lookin' hen. I took it with gratitude, intendin' to pair it with one a me young cocks come the followin' mornin', but durin' the night, while I was asleep in me bed, the hen seeks out her own company – and Bulba was the result. No one saw anything much ta crow about on his arrival, no one that is except for Barra Duffy. Duffy may not have a brain in his head but the man is a prophet. He has eyes ta see into the future and he told us all that a champion had just been born. Time has proved Barra right.'

61

'And that's how three men own one cock.'

'Well, what else could I do but hand out shares to the fellahs who had given me that darlin' hen?'

'I suppose 'tis luck, pure luck, gettin' yarself a champion.'

'Yeah, 'tis that. Bulba came into this world by fluke. But if I hit the jackpot and Bulba sees Kusthi's pride and joy to his grave, I'll try my damnedest to prove me da's theory right. "Money to buy the best cocks and hens. Bring the best blood together, and ya got a champion worth havin'." That's what the da was forever sayin'. 'T'd be grand indeed to be able to scatter a bita money about to prove him right.'

'Then ya're a man with thorough ambition about yar person after all!' O'Casey grinned.

'Yeah, I suppose so. But I like to think of meself as bein' content with me lot. Anyways, that's in the future, if all our plans and schemin' comes off and Bulba does what he was bred to do.'

'He will, he will,' said O'Casey. 'I'm not a man that hangs his faith on the hanger of hope any more, Milo Clancy. Before ya stands a man that has total confidence in what he's about to do. He knows that the future for himself and his son is goin' to be a rosy one and I'm sure ya'll admit there isn't many men in the whole of Ireland that can say that about themselves. I fear nuttin' now!'

'Ya're talkin' daft, Stallion. Ya could step outside yar door tomorrow mornin' and a bolt a lightnin' could strike ya from right outa the blue.'

'Nothin'll touch me now! The hand of God can't touch Stallion O'Casey. If it gets in me way I'll chop if off at the fuckin' wrist!'

Clancy stared at O'Casey in shock. 'Now that kind a talk is just askin' for trouble!'

'I don't believe in yar gods or devils! A man's destiny lies in his own hands. I'll never fail from now on, for I've got all the cards of the deck in me back pocket.'

'Ya failed this afternoon. Yar cock died the death in Aggie Carney's barn. The Kelly brothers sent yar cock to hell. If that's not failure, what is?'

But there was no moving Stallion. 'Whiskey Maker's death was a foregone conclusion. That I knew before I ever put him into the ring.'

'Yes, but 'twas your failure. Whiskey Maker was yours, part of you. It failed and therefore you failed,' Clancy insisted.

'Okay, I'll admit that. But I regard Whiskey Maker as being me ace of spades. The ace of spades is now gone from that deck a cards I was talkin' about. No one wants that bedevilled card. Now it's gone and death can't touch me.'

Milo scrutinized O'Casey's face. 'Ya're langered, Stallion O'Casey,' he decided. 'Ya don't look langered but ya are.'

'I've never been drunk in me life, Milo. I can hold all the drink ya care to pour down me gullet.'

A quarter of an hour before midnight, Aggie Carney slipped away to the relative peace and quiet of her kitchen. She left behind in her parlour the three wounded warriors, alive and awake, their sap still drained from them but all on the road to recovery.

As Aggie came through the doorway, she found Kathleen sitting at the table, drinking a cup of tea. 'On yar feet, girl!' barked Aggie. 'Sandwiches and tea for six to be ready in fifteen minutes.'

But the maid stayed put.

'Did ya not hear what I said, Kathleen Costello?'

'That I did, Aggie Carney.' Kathleen turned her head around and looked her employer in the eye. 'Me butt stays put right here 'til I finish me tea. And when I finally do take it into me head to get up off this chair, 't'll be with the intention of goin' to me bed and nowhere else. Make yar own shaggin' sandwiches!'

For once in her life, Aggie Carney was lost for words. Her mouth opened and closed, she pulled up a chair, fell into it, and with a tired left hand poured herself a cup. She stared hard at the girl opposite, who looked back at her with undiminished defiance. It was Kathleen Costello that kept the bottom half of her great big house moving smoothly day and night. Parlour, kitchen, bedroom and scullery were Kathleen's department; but when the whole of the county descended on the White Willow for the fights, Kathleen became skivvy for Aggie's cook, dogsbody for Aggie's important guests, extra hand for Aggie's bar and, most importantly, whipping board for Aggie's sharp temper and lashing tongue. The girl had taken it all without complaint – up to now – and Aggie didn't want to lose her. 'Okay, Kathleen,' she said at last. 'Off to yar bed!'

Kathleen had been prepared for a showdown, and had all the right words and phrases stacked in her head ready to launch straight at Aggie's bossing tongue. She was going to tell her exactly where she could stick her job, and in no uncertain terms what she thought of her. But now Aggie Carney had taken the wind and guts out of her bravado.

''Tisn't that I don't want to make the sandwiches, Mrs Carney. 'Tisn't that at all. 'Tis that terrible man ya've got in that storeroom of yours, Mr O'Leary. Oh God, Mrs Carney, but he's had me on me feet solid since lunchtime.' Tears sprang to the young maid's eyes. 'I'm fair worn out by it all. I've ran to yar two fridges at least a thousand times this very day, stackin' the water inta yar ice boxes, takin' 'em out placin' them on his arse, goin' back again fillin' up the fridges again. Six o'clock tonight yar barmaid is ballin' me head clear off me shoulders 'cause there's no ice to put in the customers' drinks.' She buried her head in her hands and sobbed. 'If I have to look at Mr O'Leary's arse just one more time I'll die, I know I'll just lay down and die.'

'All right, all right, Kathleen, I'll get someone else to minister to him. Now off to bed with yarself.'

'No, no. I'll see to the sandwiches and tea. Where do ya want them?'

'It's not too much bother now?'

''Tis not,' replied Kathleen, wiping away the tears, draining her cup and getting to her feet.

'Well, if ya could bring them into the parlour in about twenty minutes . . . .' Aggie smiled. If only she could keep the young bucks away from Kathleen Costello's front door, she could hold on to the hardest working girl that had ever stepped foot inside her domain.


Tim O'Hagen sat in Aggie Carney's second-best chair on the left-hand side of the fireplace. The crown of the little man's head was smothered in a bandage which was fastened tight with half a dozen safety pins. O'Hagen sat bolt upright, afraid to move for fear of his stricken head falling off into his lap. In Aggie Carney's best chair sat Frank Logan, feeling and looking as sick as a dog. The upper half of his body was arched, elbows rested on his knees and the palms of his hands held the weight of his battered skull.

The metallic sounds of Aggie Carney's frying pan were still chiming away inside his brain.

Condour Kusthi sat at Aggie Carney's dainty little card table in the centre of the room. He was the only one of the three who had fully recovered. His face might have fooled anyone into thinking that he had not taken part in the brawl, if it weren't for the spattering of a plaster just over his left eyebrow where a fragment of a bottle had managed to fracture the skin. He had a bottle of Aggie's best whiskey and a fair share of its contents in a glass before him on the table. The room itself was as quiet as a church on a weekday afternoon.

The door opened. 'Have all the dead come back to life yet?' asked Aggie in her best and most cheery voice.

'Ah, Aggie darlin',' greeted the tinker, rising from his chair. 'Grub! Stacks of it! Get yar darlin' little girl to place it here before me and I'll rape it down to the last morsel. Those bastards by the fire are in no need of food for the next year or two, I'm thinkin'.' Smiling broadly, Kusthi took the tray from Kathleen's hands.

'Will there be anything else, Mrs Carney, before I head for me bed?' asked Kathleen.

'Yes, Kathleen. Ya can take that glass of whiskey and the rest of that bottle out to the bar. Condour Kusthi'll not be drinkin' any more this evening.'

'You touch that bottle, girl, and I'll chop yar hands off,' said Kusthi.

'Dr Madden said ya're not to have a drop for twenty-four hours. You don't know what damage them peltin' bottles did ta yar poor ol' brain,' said Aggie, pulling up a chair.

'Madden's a quack and me head never felt better. I'll keep the bottle and the glass if 'tis all the same with yarself.'

' 'Tis yar funeral, Condour Kusthi. . . . Well, don't just stand there girl,' she said to Kathleen. 'Off with yarself to bed.'

'Not a bad-lookin' thing, is she?' remarked the tinker as he watched Kathleen head out the door.

'Keep yar tinker's eyes off her! She's far too good for the likes a yarself.'

'And far too valuable to you.' Kusthi winked.

'Christ, for a man that has had his head all but bashed in, ya're in remarkable form!'

'Well, I thank the good Lord for a hard crown. Must be made a steel, I'm thinkin'.'

'Steel or not, it would have caved in eventually. If 'twasn't for me ya'd be dead.'

Kusthi smiled. 'Grateful I am, Aggie darlin', to you and your fryin' pan!'

'Grateful enough to knock a bit off the lump a money I'm to give ya for the pleasure of seein' ya da and his cock under me barn roof?' asked Aggie with a sly smile.

'Arrah, ya are a codger, Aggie Carney, and no two ways about it! All the money in the world can't pay back a debt like that. I wouldn't insult ya by offerin' filthy money for such a heroic act.'

'Insult me, I don't mind.'

'Ya're a terrible woman,' laughed Kusthi. 'If the deal is good tonight, I'll hand ya over twenty quid to help replace that fine stained-glass window. Can't say fairer than that.'

She knew when she'd been matched. 'I suppose 'tis better than nuttin',' sighed Aggie.

'They look like sleepin' angels, don't they,' remarked the tinker, gesturing towards the broken pair by the fireplace.

'Oh, leave them be. They'll come round soon enough.'

'Well, what and who are we waitin' for?' asked Kusthi, reaching out for one of his hostess's famous ham sandwiches.

Before she could reply, there was a knock on Aggie Carney's door and Stallion O'Casey, closely followed by Milo Clancy, stepped into the room. 'God bless all here!'

'And God bless you, too, Stallion O'Casey,' Aggie greeted them. 'Pull yarselfs up some chairs. There's a snack waitin' for ye.'

Aggie did the introductions, then poured the tea, waiting until her sandwiches were in the mouths of her guests before taking command. 'Now, Milo,' said Aggie with her best smile. 'There's no need to go into Condour's background, I hope. When ya get up from this table ya'll have to go away trustin' the man, for ya'll have made a deal that'll be bindin' to the both of yees. Is that understood?'

Clancy nodded. 'Understood, Aggie.'

'Good. Now the man that is sittin' over there on the left-hand side of the fireplace is Tim O'Hagen and by rights he has first claim on Tilla Kusthi's famous cock.'

66

'Have ya not asked him if he'll take up his claim?'

'The man's head is a fair bit addled, as I'm sure ya realize. I don't want him beatin' down me doors tomorrow mornin' sayin' that we tricked him out of the grandest of fights.'

'He's lookin' okay to me,' O'Casey said, looking over his shoulder to see the tiny little farmer still sitting bolt upright in his chair.

'Mr O'Hagen!' Aggie called.

'What's it ya're wantin', Aggie Carney?' The little man moved his mouth, but the rest of his face and his head remained rigid.

'Will ya not join us at the table and have a cup of tea?'

'I can't move; me neck's broken!'

'Dr Madden says ya're okay. Ya've got a few cuts and bruises on yar crown, that's all.'

'What does that quack know about anythin'? I tell ya, me neck is broken!'

It took a lot of coaxing before the nervous little farmer would join the group at the table. All four of them nursed and fussed O'Hagen into a chair and watched as he slowly and arduously brought a cup of tea to his lips.

'Arrah, Tim, but the flush is comin' back to yar cheeks. A blind man can see ya're well on yar way to recovery,' beamed O'Casey, watching the vanquished O'Hagen sip carefully at his tea.

'I'm half dead, and well ya know it, O'Casey.'

'It'll take ya a few days before ya're mended, that's for sure,' Clancy agreed.

The little man ignored Clancy's attempt at sympathy. 'Does any of ye know where Frank Logan is at this point in time?' he asked.

'God man, but yar brain is still addled!' exclaimed Aggie. 'He's been sittin' opposite you for the past three hours. Over there by the fire. And this here is Condour Kusthi,' she hurried on before O'Hagen's attention was lost on Logan for ever.

'I know him,' said O'Hagen shortly. 'He's the tinker fellah. So what?'

'Mr O'Hagen,' smiled Kusthi, inclining his head and ignoring the battered farmer's lack of good manners. 'My name is Condour Kusthi son of Tilla Kusthi. My da owns Satan the First. . . .'

'And I have first refusal on yar da's cock.'

'That's right,' replied the tinker smoothly. 'But if ya want to put yours up against Satan ya'll need to know the conditions, the terms.'

'Fuck yar conditions. Fuck yar terms!' The little man glared at Condour with all the hatred he could manage in his condition. 'I wouldn't put mine up against yars in a month a fuckin' Sundays! What do ya think I fuckin' well am, anyway? A fuckin' dope or somethin'?'

Condour Kusthi's smile never faltered nor faded. 'That's all I wanted to know. I just wanted to know if ya were goin' to take up the claim.'

'Whose bottle a whiskey is that?' asked O'Hagen.

'Ya can't drink, Tim!' warned Aggie. 'Madden gave ya some pills to swallow, no booze for forty-eight hours.'

'Don't tell me what I can and can't fuckin' well do!' O'Hagen bawled. His face was no longer milky white, but a full, rich crimson, and his voice had stunned all four of them with its power.

' 'Tis mine,' answered Kusthi eventually. 'But have it if ya want it. 'Tis a present from meself to yarself. But do take Aggie's advice and don't touch a drop till forty-eight hours has gone and passed ya by.'

'I don't take charity from anybody, least of all from fuckin' tinkers!' O'Hagen put a hand in his trouser pocket, pulled out two £1 notes and flung them at the other man's face. He staggered to his feet with a determined air. 'Thanks for the cup a tea, Aggie Carney. I'm off!'

'Ya're welcome, Tim, any time.' She watched O'Hagen take the bottle from the table, her eyes narrow with suspicion.

'Good night to ye all, and that goes for yarself as well, tinker Kusthi,' said O'Hagen, the iron leaving his voice for the first time. But Aggie Carney's heart skipped a beat when it dawned on her what was going to happen. Not one of them was even halfway out of his seat when O'Hagen smashed the bottle of whiskey down on the head of Frank Logan, who rolled off his chair without so much as a sound leaving his lips.


By ten o'clock the following morning, the three Mayo men and Taurus Bulba were on the outskirts of town, preparing for their

68

departure. Pagga O'Leary was in the process of guiding his horse and cart through Dillon Flannery's stable doors, Duffy was paying Flannery for the horse's accommodation, and Milo Clancy was having a last word with O'Casey and his unfortunate son who had come along to see them off. "'T'll be March then for definite,' he was saying.

'Aye. The middle of it. Just before Saint Patrick's Day, I reckon.'

'We don't get Texas weather up there at that time a year. Me house is right on the coast, ya know.'

'Aye, so ya said.'

'Make sure and bring plenty of woollens with ya for yar boy and yarself.'

'I'll do that.' O'Casey looked across the stable yard at Barra and Pagga who were standing by their cart, passing the time of day with Flannery's wife. 'Well, I'll not detain ya. Ya've got a fair-sized journey to make.'

'We've made a good deal. With Kusthi, I mean,' said Clancy, his left hobnail boot toying with the earth at his feet.

'Four hundred pounds for the privilege! 'T'd be daylight robbery if we were dealin' with anybody else. But I suppose 'tis a good enough arrangement seein' as how we're dealin' with that cunning tinker.'

'Aye,' Clancy sighed.

'We get it back though, when we beat his fucker into the ground. That's also part of the deal.' O'Casey studied the Mayo man's worried face, knowing there'd be bouts of despair before the year ran its course and they were ready to put Bulba into the ring against the greatest cock in all of Ireland.

'Tell me somethin', Stallion O'Casey,' said Clancy, taking a deep breath of courage before saying the one thing on his mind. 'What if we lose?'

'I told ya, I can't fail.'

'We all fail,' said Clancy, in an even voice. 'We're forever failin'. And most of us fail when we're at our cockiest, when we turn our backs on our gods and start to believe that we're somethin' more than mere mortals.'

But Stallion O'Casey was only interested in success. 'Clancy believe me. Before ya stands a man that can't fail. I can't afford to fail. For everythin' I am and hope to be depends on a victorious outcome.' He rested one hand on his son's frail shoulders. 'Yar persistent question is pointless, man! I can't give it an answer, for to do so would mean that I'm just another mortal like yarself. And I've made meself believe I'm different from other men.'

'Ya're a strange one to be sure, Stallion O'Casey.' Then Clancy turned to the boy. 'Well, I'm off, Colin,' said Milo. 'Look after yar da for me, for he's very precious to us all.'

Five minutes later the horse and cart clattered out of Flannery's yard and onto the main road. With a 'Giddy-up-outa-t'at!' and a whip of the reins across the animal's flanks, Barra Duffy broke the horse into a trot. O'Casey and Colin stood by the gateway watching until they were completely out of sight.

# 5

The wooden shed at the back of Milo Clancy's cottage moaned and groaned its doddering age as the devil of a wind coming over the clifftops smashed against its walls on that March night. Inside, Clancy's dozen hens crowded together, listening to the hellish spite of the tempest. Hinges creaked eerily in their fastenings and the rafters overhead strained the very foundations of the shack as they stretched and shifted in their joints.

Bulba, too, was awake and alert. He nestled high up near the roof, away from the rest of his clan, while below him, on a shelf that ran the length of the right-hand wall, his dozen cackling charges bitched at the storm and bitched at him. But Bulba remained silent and aloof.

An hour before dawn, however, an almighty gust of wind blasted at the door of Bulba's shelter. A thundrous noise erupted through the shed, followed by the snapping of metal. A split second later the storm had broken in upon them in full fury. Two of the youngest hens shot from their coops and flapped into the darkness. Squawking panic broke out all over. With wings beating hard in the darkness, Bulba flew to the ground. Whipping rain slammed into his plumage as he tried to stare his enemy into submission. The devil storm didn't turn from him, but swept through the broken doorway, mocking his defiant stance. Bulba's chest swelled with rage as he crowed his curses at the intruder.

At last the man appeared. The hens' panic died down almost at once, and they allowed themselves to be shooed back into their coops. Bulba stayed where he was on the floor of the shed until all his brood were safely back in their places. Then he soared back up to his place in the groaning rafters and stared down at the man who struggled against the still-raging storm, forcing the fallen door back into its frame and binding its hinges back into the woodwork. As soon as he had gone, the cackles and crowing started up again, but Bulba knew that the real danger had passed, and soon the storm was beyond his hearing and care.

Some time before morning, the shed was finally quiet. The dawn lingered awhile, squeezing its pale, silver light through the cracks in the old wooden slats, only to surrender eventually to a bleak, grey, rainsodden wintery morning. The storm itself petered out an hour after the morning took hold, leaving in its wake a soft clear rain that fell straight to the ground in the still and windless air. Another hour passed before Taurus Bulba opened his eyes. The storm had succeeded in blowing the rickety old door off its hinges again, and now it hung at a drunken slant. Through the gap, a shaft of watery sunlight came to rest on the floor of the shed.

Bulba crowed his hearty salutations to the morning, then stretched, shook off his nightmares and fluttered with easy grace to the ground. Lifting his head to its peak, he crowed once more. Everything was in order. His house still stood, his subjects were all in their coops, and calm had been restored.

Bulba looked out into the yard and liked what he saw. He filled his chest, shot his head and beak into the air and let forth a full-blooded cry of pure delight. In one of the coops behind him an old hen stirred and opened her sleepy eyes to see Bulba fly out into the morning.

Taurus Bulba radiated majesty as he stood there in the centre of his domain, taking in the whole of the new day. His proud fighting head lifted and lowered, jutted and pivoted from side to side as his piercing, all-seeing eyes looked out for danger. But his sparse pedigree chest was at ease, barely stirring. The powerful wings that rested tightly on his massive shoulders glistened and shone as the early light played on his rich, deep copper plumage. His menacing stance told every living thing to be wary, for a king resided here, a lord who had total control. Considering that a full and hard winter had just passed, the fighter Taurus Bulba was in excellent condition.

The fighter found the morning as it should be, tranquil and still, and so he strutted his way forward and on into the day. He pecked at a stony piece of ground beside the high, wire-mesh fencing at the far end of the yard. Above his head was an ocean of blue sky marred only by a few strands of slate-grey cloud. To his front, beyond the fence, was the last half acre of rocky land that sloped steeply to the cliff's edge. Beyond the cliff was the ocean itself, a bluish-green expanse of glass that stretched as far as the eye could see.

The air was cold and there was dampness to it, but the cock's rich copper plumage remained unruffled, for there wasn't a breath of wind coming in from the sea. Bulba heard a flutter of wings and turned to see the old hen peck and cackle her way towards him, but out of the corner of his eye he spotted a movement to his left. A worm was burrowing frantically, trying to get back to the earth. Bulba's swift beak shot out and seized it with ease. The old hen spotted his coup and darted towards him. She managed to swipe a wriggling quarter. But Bulba's temper was good that morning. He let her share his snack, and started to peck his way contentedly along the fencing. The old hen followed close at heel.

Half an hour later the rest of Bulba's brood were up and pecking, and clucked their way excitedly towards the gate at the far end of the yard. Bulba looked up to see the man, basket in hand, arriving on his domain. He crowed out to make his presence known, and ambled his way towards the clutter of hens who stood within inches of the man's feet. He caught the man's eye, crowed out once more, and watched as the man flung a shower of his favourite cereal at him. He breakfasted, oblivious of the man, who had his eyes on him and him alone.


Clancy was a worried man that morning. The morning was the morning of 20 March 1928. Two days had passed and another was in the passing since Saint Patrick's Day, and Stallion O'Casey had still not set foot on his doorstep.

Breakfast was a mug of black tea gulped down even without the aid of a cigarette. Then he was off; out the door of his cottage and away. With urgency in his step he headed for the road, and a little pebbled beach known by the locals as Michaelmas Bay.

Though there was no wind, the air around him smelled of winter; a depressing chill to it that seeped through his skin and straight into the heart. It was the kind of day that troubled the old and the sick, freezing their minds of all thoughts of the coming spring and the fields that would be put to the plough. Even

Clancy felt a shadow pass across his soul as he looked out to where the pale blue of the sky fused with the placid dark waters of Michaelmas Bay.

It took him a good two minutes to dig his half-buried currach from the sand and drag her into the waves. The only sounds for miles were the lap of his oars as they spliced through the chill water, and the cry of the gulls as they played, swooped, dived and soared along the cliffs. In the middle of the bay he brought his oars aboard and sat back, looking towards the land, his eyes searching the coastline from left to right. Where the cliffs were highest was his own patch of land: the summit of bleak grey rock called Devil's Nose that jutted into the bay away from the main body of the rising granite wall and the white speck of his cottage perched on the top of it.

'Tis a bleak enough place to be sure, he thought to himself, noting the barren scrubland that fringed the skull of the rock and the sparse vegetation surrounding his home. All of us hermits! Every Clancy that has ever been has shooed himself away outa sight and sound of his neighbour, taken himself off and built his dwellin' in god- and manforsaken places. 'Tis cursed we are to be sure! Well maybe 'twasn't intentional. Wasn't it ol' Mangan Clancy, yar own grand-uncle, lord have mercy on him, wasn't it him that used to say that the Clancys were the Lords of Ireland? Didn't he used to say that there was a time when all the Clancys resided to the east of the Shannon, in the lush fat pasture lands of Waterford and Wexford? Well fuck you, Mr Cromwell, thought Milo Clancy. This very day I hope Satan himself is fryin' yar balls, liver and gizzard for his breakfast! To hell or to the Devil's Nose with ya bastards! Wasn't that what ya used to say to us, ya black-hearted bastard? Ya done us proud, Mr Cromwell, real proud. Ya gave us the one patch of festered, decayin' rock, and told us to plant ourselves there, that one place on earth where 'tisn't possible for man or beast to get as much as a blighted bean from the barren soil!

Somewhere in the middle of the granite wall's run, a mile back from its top, was the village of Feacledown, a place where people lived. Barra Duffy lived there and so did Pagga O'Leary. Clancy sighed deeply as his eyes came to rest on the summit of those even cliffs which stood a good two miles to his right. A good five miles' walk between me and civilization, he thought. God, but I should have never made that fuckin' trip into the heart of Ireland. My eyes should never have seen Aggie Carney's hotel. Jasus, if that place was up here we'd be for askin' Father Dolan to move into it and he'd be willin' and only too glad to fuckin' well oblige. There was never a place so grand. Clancy remembered the White Willow in every detail. Ya're unsettled, Milo Clancy, thought Milo Clancy, and ya been that way since ya've come back from yar travels. I think ya've been infected, infected with a dose, a heavy dose of Stallion O'Casey's ambition.

And so he thought on as two more hours passed, and a light breeze coming in from a placid and calm Atlantic gently inched his boat towards the land. It was noon before he saddled his oars and helped his currach towards the sands and Michaelmas Bay.


It was noon, as well, when Pagga O'Leary opened his eyes to the day. He didn't linger but got himself out of bed and headed for the little shack behind his cottage. He pulled open the door, marched inside, did an about turn, halted, lifted the hem of his nightshirt up around his waist and exposed his bare arse to the bowl. With a look of pure determination on his face he sat himself down, and with a powerful grunt stretched the muscles of his stomach to their very limits. The veins on his forehead pulsated and his face became crimson. Beads of sweat formed on his brow, but he kept his stomach as tight as a drum. Only when an almighty fart broke free from between his nether lips did his muscles relax and his grunt of pain die. He gave himself a full minute's respite before launching the next attack. He gulped in the air around him like a greedy drinker, filling his lungs to their full capacity, and forced his stomach one more time. An agonizing cry for help slipped from between clenched teeth. Oh sufferin' sweet Jasus, help us now!

His prayer was answered. O'Leary's bowels moved. They moved with an explosive force, his great relief smashing into the muddy hole beneath him. Weariness shrouded him, so that he sat there a full five minutes before he could muster enough energy to get to his feet. Ten outa ten, Pagga, for the work ya put in, and ten outa ten for content and substance, he congratulated himself when he did turn around, his smile bursting with pride.

He was just about to make his way back into his cottage for a late breakfast when he spied Big Mary waddling her way along the coast road. She was a good five hundred yards away, but there was no mistaking the biggest woman in the parish, if not in the whole of the county as well. The joy of his victory in the little shack was swept from his face and a heavy sigh escaped his lips as he watched his sister labour her way towards him. She waved but O'Leary did not respond.

He was in the process of filling a teapot from the kettle when Big Mary walked through the doorway.

'God bless all here!' she cried, her voice cheery but very much out of breath.

'And blessin's on yarself as well,' greeted Pagga in turn.

''Tisn't breakfast ya're sittin' down to at this time a the day?' She plonked herself down on a chair. ''Tis fifteen minutes after twelve.'

'I'm aware a the time, Mary,' sighed Pagga with exaggerated patience, pouring himself a cup of tea. 'Ya want a cup?'

'No thanks. Ya haven't been in bed 'til this time surely?'

'Naw; I've been out sowin' five acres a spuds in me shaggin' nightshirt!'

'Language, Pagga. Have ya not been well then?'

'I was at Pat Barley's wake over in Mullach. Haven't seen sight a me house for the past four days and nights. Didn't reach me front door 'til three o'clock t'is mornin'. What brings yarself up here?' asked Pagga, his voice raw and sharp with ire.

'The reason I'm here is because of the ol' woman.'

Pagga sat upright in his chair and took note.

'Nuttin' to worry about, Pagga,' said Mary quickly as she saw the concern in her brother's face. 'She's not sick or anythin' like that.'

'Then what is it?'

'She's been actin' a bit queer that's all.' Her tone was casual, but there was worry in her eyes.

'Go on.'

'Well, this last week she's been talkin' of dyin' on us all. She reckons it's time for herself to go. Now she's all right, mind ya, so don't worry! She eats like a horse and has her eight hours' sleep and her naps in between without any fuss or bother at all at all. For a woman that'll be ninety-eight come July she's doin' fine. But, as I said, she's been actin' rather queer. She wants to see her

76

Timmy again. She says her and himself has been parted long enough. I told her that the Lord Himself would decide when her time was up. Now all a last week she's been goin' on like that, night and day talkin' about leavin' us all and packin' her bags for heaven. I finally get used to it and turn the deaf ear on her, and so she mumbles away to herself, talkin' to the wall and her ol' cat and the picture of Timmy in his Sunday best that hangs over the fireplace.' Mary could see the growing impatience in her brother's face. The disdain touching the corner of his lips told her she had best get to the crux of the matter. She was aware he had little time for her; that her very presence offended him. 'Then last night while we were sitting by the fireplace, just after supper it was, she goes and takes her pipe outa her mouth and puts it on top a the fireplace and sits herself back down in her chair. She looks at me and she says, "Mary," she says, "that's the very last time ya'll ever see me smoke me pipe." I looks back at her and asks, "And why is that, Granny Minno?" What comes outa her mouth next would have felled me to the floor if I hadn't been sittin' down. "Mary," she says, "I'm goin' to die on the 26th of March this year." I gawk at her like an eegit, thinkin' that either meself or herself is mad or maybe 'tis the both of us. I recover me wits given a half minute, and bawl the head off her for frightenin' the livin' daylights outa me. But the devil of a woman bawls back that she's tellin' me nuttin' but pure truth, and that I might as well accept it and start to make preparations for her wake. Well, the only thing I can think of doin' is to up off me chair and go out into a stormy night and fetch Dr Flynn. He gives her a good going over, tappin' her heart, takin' her pulse and feelin' her brow. Well, wouldn't ya know it, Pagga! Flynn turns on meself and curses me roundly for gettin' him outa his nice warm bed on such a cruel night. "Big Mary!" he shouts, "Grandma Minno'll outlive the fuckin' lota us. The next time ya want a docotor, go and fetch yarself Butler! The only thing wrong with yar grandmother is that she's goin' dotty just like the rest of us!"'

'Ya shouldn't have fetched no doctor to her!' reprimanded Pagga. ' 'Tis a wonder she didn't up and die the very minute the quack walked away from her front door.'

'I had to do somethin'.'

'What put the 26th a March into her head? Why stick her gamble on that particular date?'

''Cause Tipperary Tim died on that very day.'

'Ahh!' said Pagga with relief, the concern on his face easing. 'The poor ol' girl is only wishin', then! That quack Flynn was right for once. When ya're just two years off yar century some a yar senses are bound to leave ya. The poor old creature is pinin' and wishin', that's all. The good Lord'll not take her from us yet. She'll see her hundred – I'd put money on that!'

'Then there's nuttin' to worry about.'

'Nuttin' at all. All the same, I'll go down there and have tea with yarself tonight and help cheer her up.'

'Oh, that'll be grand, Pagga. She hasn't seen sight or hair a ya for a month now and she's always askin' for ya.'

'Well, don't dilly dally here all day, woman.' Pagga rose from his chair, a glint of hardness coming into his eye as he looked at his smiling sister. God, but she gets uglier with the passing of each new day, he thought to himself.

'Yes, I must be off.' Mary had long ago taught herself not to notice the disdain in her brother's eyes. With a smile still on her lips she said, 'We'll see yarself at six then?'

'If not before.'

Pagga knew the rest of the day would be a bad one. It was always that way every time that Big Mary crossed his path, every time he had to lift his head and look up at his sister's face. Shame and remorse at the way he treated her filled him now, and he knew he would carry them around for the rest of the day. When Grandma Minno dies, Big Mary, and you come knockin' at yar brother's door and askin' him if ya can keep house for him. . . . A trembling hand picked up a cup of lukewarm tea and brought it to his lips. He drained the contents and placed the cup back on the table, then shouted at the top of his voice, 'Lord God in heaven, if I didn't know ya better I'd be callin' ya one dumb stupid eegit of a fool. Did ya have to go and place two sexes down upon this earth? Why in the name of yar Holy Mother did ya have to invent women? Why? Wasn't us males grand enough for ya? Did ya have to plague us with that interferin', nosy, naggin' breed? Couldn't ya at least have the dacency to put them on another planet; eh? Well, couldn't ya? There hasn't been a woman that hasn't gone through life without sendin' a dozen of us and more right into our graves. Well, I'm tellin' ya; Big Mary is not comin' to live with meself when Minno goes home to her Tim. I'll have no woman drivin' me to me grave before me time!'


Stallion O'Casey and his son had crossed over the river Shannon and on into the west of Ireland at the end of their first day's journey. A soft drizzle had been with them from the start, and had stayed with them as their horse and cart took them on up through the lands of Galway, but on reaching the Mayo border the drizzle had thickened and begun to fall as hard, cold rain, coming down through the windless and deadened air. Just three miles from Ballinrobe, a stiff March breeze off the Atlantic caught up with them, and slanted the hard sheets of rain into their faces.

O'Casey and his son were jailed in the confines of a little pub in the centre of Ballinrobe for two whole days as the mother of storms tried to wash a good portion of Mayo right out into the sea. Now, with the storm gone and the little town thirty miles and more to their rear, O'Casey was doing his best to raise his dampened spirits. The skies above his head were clear, a very mild breeze with a hint of spring warmth to it was brushing against his face, and he was, at last, well into Clancy's territory; and yet he felt that his soul had sunk right through the floor of the cart. What he saw before him made him shake with fear; fear not for himself but for his son.

The landscape all about them was bitter and harsh, not only to the eye but to the spirit as well. He could smell from the air the ghosts and bones of a thousand storms. Everything around him was rock and shale and fields, so poor and starved of a decent coat of top soil that the smallest cow would have a hard time trying to fill its belly. And where in the name a Jasus are the trees, he kept asking himself as they left mile after mile of road behind them. But what worried Stallion O'Casey above all else was the damp. It was there all around him; he could feel it like the cold hands of death itself touching his skin. The little warmth that was to be found in the faint spring breeze couldn't kill it. His eyes scanned the landscape in front of him, searching out its source. He looked to the fields but it wasn't there; he lifted his eyes to the heavens, but the sky was void of cloud; he sniffed the air but it was clean and healthy and as dry as a bone; and then, because there was nowhere else to look, his eyes went back to the land.

''Tis in the fuckin' rocks. 'Tis comin' at ya from right outa the shaggin' ground. I declare to God but the shaggin' land yarself and yar horse is passin' over is pisoned!'

. 'What's pisoned, Da?'

Stallion quickly wiped the worry off his face before turning his head to look down at his boy. Oh Jasus, groaned O'Casey to himself as he watched Colin's pale, delicate head look up at him, waiting for an answer. Have I brought my son to his graveyard? A chill ran down the length of Stallion's spine and he shrugged his shoulders vigorously, trying to rid himself of his forebodings. He managed to muster a smile as he asked, 'Do ya smell anythin' comin' from the ground, son?'

''Tis the bogs, Da. 'Tis the turf in the air.'

'Aye.' Stallion sighed wearily. 'Turf it is. I thought me nose got hold of somethin'.'

''Tis been rainin' just as hard up here as it has been down in Ballinrobe,' explained Colin, seeing the concern in his father's eyes and trying, in his boy's way, to ease his father's mind, knowing that all that dread was on his behalf. 'Now that there's a fair share of heat in the air the water in the bogs is givin' off a lot of t'is moisture. 'Tis the bogs we're smellin' for sure 'cause of the heat.'

Fretful as he was, Stallion couldn't help but laugh. 'What heat, son? 'T'd take all the fires of the devil's own hell to put a smigeen a warmth down upon this soulless land. Anyway, how come ya're such an expert on bogs? When have you ever laid yar eyes upon a bog?'

But throughout the last few miles of their journey, O'Casey allowed himself to look at the landscape through his son's eyes, and the last few miles took on a strange and haunting beauty for him. The cold colour of the rocks softened, the fields were more lush than any he had ever seen before, and the harsh and never-ending changes to the contours of the land seemed suddenly exciting and inviting. From time to time he had to remind himself that he was only giving way to makebelieve; that he was seeing with his heart and not his eyes.

The first strands of a soft, early spring evening were appearing as the horse and cart and its two passengers passed through the tiny village of Feacledown.

★

Big Mary set a fine table for tea that night. The best china was taken down from the Welsh dresser and placed on the highly polished kitchen table. Above the fire a cast-iron pot suspended from its chains was bubbling away nicely. The steam rising from it like clouds scattered grand, mouth-watering smells throughout the room. The frail old lady sitting by the peat-based fire took a ladle to the pot from time to time, churning the contents and adding a pinch of salt from a saucer which she kept in the middle of her lap. Curled at the old woman's feet was a midnight-black cat, well advanced in years, staring blank-eyed into the flames. Outside the cottage, the winter twilight had come and gone and darkness was firmly established. The six o'clock bells from the village church had not yet struck.

The granddaughter of Minno O'Leary moved through the kitchen on tiptoe as she prepared the house for her brother's visit. Her ears were closed to the mumblings of the old woman who sat by the fire conversing with the cat and the stew that bubbled away in the pot. Everything that needed doing had been done, but she frowned to herself as she looked down at her neatly laid table. With a despairing shake of her head she gathered up all the knives and forks and polished the lot once more with the hem of the apron that was tied around her ample stomach. With meticulous care she laid them out once more. Then her eyes came away from the table and she scrutinized the rest of her kitchen. She looked into every nook and cranny and at last she was satisfied. She turned to look at the old woman in time to see her add yet another pinch of salt to the pot. Jasus, if ya don't get here soon, Pagga, ya'll end up sittin' down to the Dead Sea Stew, she thought to herself. But she was determined to keep a peaceful house and turned away from the old woman and tiptoed back across the floor.

In her bedroom, Big Mary splashed a few handfuls of water on her face from the basin that sat on the rickety wicker cupboard near her bed. Taking a towel, she sat in front of her dresser and patted her ample cheeks dry. A mortifying sigh left her lips as she regarded herself in the mottled mirror, and her shoulders sagged. Her eyes drooped to the area where her womanly chest should have been, but that was the one part of her that seemed flat. Her breasts rested on her ample lap. With both her hands she hoisted them up and regarded herself in the glass, sitting still and quiet, then let them fall again. Her eyes went back to scrutinize her face. As she had done so many times before, in the privacy of her bedroom, in front of her mirror, she smiled. Just a parting of the lips. Just a smile for her own eyes. The face she saw was not exactly the face of the Madonna, but it was an honest face, a caring face; and a smile that promised love.

She took the towel and covered the mirror.

The old woman was still nursing the stew and the old cat was still sitting by her feet when Big Mary came back into the kitchen. 'He's a bit late, isn't he?' she said, glancing at the clock on the mantelpiece.

'He'll be here,' said Minno O'Leary with certainty.

'He's twenty minutes late. 'T'll be a pickled stew he'll sit down to if he delays himself any longer.' Mary stooped down and deftly swiped the saucer of salt off the old woman's lap.

'Give us back that saucer!' snapped Minno. 'It gives it bite.'

'Bite, me arse! 'T'll be pisonin' him ya will with the way ya be splashin' that stuff around for the past half hour!' She turned her back on the old woman and placed Minno's saucer of salt on the table. Looking across it, she saw that the old woman was sitting back on her chair, mumbling to herself, well away into her private ramblings through things long since past. Leave her be, for Christ's sake, Mary warned herself. When Pagga sets foot in the house she'll be back and givin' him and meself the devil of a headache with her talk of death and her reunion with Timmy. The old black cat stirred and stretched, but Mary was on it before it had time to spring into the warmth of Minno's lap. She caught it by the scruff of the neck and threw it out into the night. 'And stay out, Shlabala O'Leary, 'til Pagga has come and gone!' she called after him. 'He'll not take kindly to yar mangy presence while he's sittin' down to me stew!'

The old woman was mumbling to herself, in a world of her own. Mary went to the fire and quietly ladled the stew. Then she lifted the big wooden spoon from the pot and tasted. Surreptitiously, she added a generous pinch of salt from Minno's saucer.

'Didn't I tell ya it needed saltin'!'

'Ya're back with us,' said Mary, startled for a moment.

'For a little while,' said Minno wearily. 'I'm back because the Lord Himself ordains it so. He must still believe I've penance to do, for every time I've opened me eyes this day 'tis meself that has had to stare at that scutterin' pot and yar stew that isn't fit for man or beast. But come the end of the month, my poor old eyes will not have to look on such sorry sights no more.'

'Arrah, give over, Granny, for Christ's sake,' begged Mary. 'I've given me ear to yar daftness all week.'

'Ah, the devil take yarself, Mary O'Leary! For when I'm gone 't'll be loneliness that'll come and surround yar life like a veil!'

'That I'm accustomed to. 'T'as been part and parcel with meself since I left the cradle.'

'And it doesn't bother yarself? It doesn't bother ya to think that when I'm gone the only thing ya'll have is me cottage and its four walls to talk to?'

'I'm past botherin'.'

'And past hope?'

'There was none to start with.'

'For every man in God's earth there's a woman. For every woman on God's earth there's a man.'

'Except for me.'

'There's a man for you.'

'If only ya were right, old woman. If only ya were right!'

'Mark my words, Mary,' prophesied Minno. 'There's one will come for you.'

'I'm forty in June,' smiled Mary. 'If he doesn't come soon he'll be marryin' me at me wake.'

Hobnail boots scraped on the stone flagging outside the cottage and Mary had the door opened before her brother had time to knock. 'Ya're late but welcome.'

'Stopped off for a quick one in Sullivan's,' said Pagga with an apologetic grin.

'Is it himself?' cried the old woman from her chair.

''Tis yar darlin' to be sure!' roared Pagga, coming into the kitchen like a homecoming hero.

Big Mary took his coat and cap and hung them on the back of the door, while he bent down to embrace the old woman affectionately.

'Now Minno, what's all this nonsense about you up and dyin' on the lot of us?' Pagga sat himself in the chair opposite. 'Sure ya look ten times better than meself.'

'Ya can stop spewin' out yar flattery with meself, Pagga O'Leary. We'll talk about me dyin' later. I've a crow ta pluck with yarself first!' said Minno, her eyes full of rebuke.

'And what would that be now?' asked Pagga innocently.

'Where have ya been since Christmas? And yer old granny all on her own?'

'Busy, my machushla,' soothed Pagga, holding the old wrinkled hand. 'Sure the days aren't long enough for me to get done all that there needs to be doin'.'

'Ya haven't even time to come down here and spend five minutes with Minno?'

'Now don't be like that,' chided Pagga. 'There's no place I'd rather be than here in this cottage talkin' over the old times with yar lovely self. It's just that I haven't had the time. As ya must have heard, the roof of me poor ol' cottage was all but blown off its rafters a month back. It was meself that had to replace it, and to do it, I might add, in foul weather the likes of which I'd never seen in all me born days. Then there was me poor old horse that came down with the most awful bout a the colic . . .'

'Enough! I get yar meanin'. Yar few miserable acres of land come before yar grandma. Now let me tell ya, I'll be requirin' yar company until 'tis time for meself to go.'

'Arrah, whist, woman!'

'Whist yarself, Pagga O'Leary. Don't ya dare whist me, or I'll take the strap to ya, and don't think I'm not able to either!' She waited for Pagga to answer back, but he had the good sense to keep his mouth shut.

'I'll be dead on the mornin' or the afternoon of March the 26th. I expect ya to give me a good wake; the full four days, and I expect ya to bury me on the mornin' of the 30th. . . .' She dug a knobbled old hand into the pocket of her bib and pulled out a little canvas sack. 'Here,' she said, her tone harsh. 'There's five guineas for me burial and me wake.'

'I wanted the privilege of payin' yar entrance fee into heaven meself,' replied Pagga, a twinkle in his eye, but a great deal of emotion in his voice.

'Ya'll not have that privilege, Pagga O'Leary. I'll pay me own way. All I expect from yarself is to see me off proper.'

'Done.'

'Good.'

'Can I ask just one question?' asked Pagga with caution.

'What's that?'

84

'What happens if March the 26th comes and goes and yarself is still alive and kickin'?'

'That day'll not pass without takin' me!' Minno repeated with finality.

'If God hasn't ordained that you should leave us on that day then ya won't be leavin'.'

'God has nuttin' to do with it,' snapped Minno. 'It's me that's tellin' Him the date of my departure.'

'And the Devil take Him if he lets yarself down?'

'He'll not let me down, come the 26th. 'Tis a grand date I've chosen to join up with my Timmy and God'll not let me down!'

'Well, if ya think I'm goin' to kneel down and pray that ya'll leave us all come the day, then ya're makin' a sad mistake!'

Minno's voice dropped to almost a whisper. 'I don't want yar prayers! What I would like though is ta ask yarself one great kindness.' Minno grasped his hands in hers.

'What's the kindness?' asked Pagga, fear coming into his eyes, certain that he knew what his grandmother's request would be.

'Big Mary. Take her in!'

O'Leary looked towards the table where Mary was dishing out her stew onto the three plates. He looked at Minno and saw the desperate pleading in her eyes. He looked into the future, and saw his peaceful life destroyed. 'I tell ya what I'll do. If she comes to me and asks . . . I'll take her in. But I'll not volunteer.'

'She's an O'Leary,' Minno whispered. 'She's proud like all our kind.'

'I hope her pride won't let her down.'

'She'll be alone for the rest of her days.'

'We're all alone,' said Pagga grandly. 'She's goin' to have to ask.' He freed his hands from the old woman's grasp.

'Supper is ready!' called Mary.


''T'd break every nerve in yar body to hear the bastard go on,' said Barra Duffy.

'Then ya shouldn't stop and listen,' replied Clancy, picking up the last bit of crockery from the basin and giving it to Duffy to dry.

''Twasn't me,' protested Barra. ''Twas me that was in Sullivan's an hour and more before the bastard stepped through the doors. 'Twas me that was drinkin' away quietly to meself and keepin' me own peace when the bastard comes in and starts to talk away at meself without seekin' out me permission first.'

'What was he goin' on about anyway?' Clancy took the basin of sudsy water and chucked the contents into the yard.

'I'll give yarself fifty million guesses.'

'Piles.'

'Got it in one,' grinned Duffy.

'I thought Aggie Carney had performed the miracle cure on him.' They sat down opposite each other by the fireplace.

'That's just it. Now instead of goin' on about his havin' them, he goes on about not havin' them. There's meself after a hard day's work with a pint of Sullivan's best stuck in me paw, and there's O'Leary describin' his mornin' shit! The whole fuckin' action of it. How he squeezed it through his poxy hole, and how the sweat dripped off his knopper with the effort of it all! Imagine it, Milo!'

'Well, I suppose we have to be thankful. 'T'was his talk of piles that used to drive us all around the fuckin' bend.'

'I think I preferred to hear about the piles. 'Tis hard to swallow a pint when someone's tellin' yarself about the colour of his shit!'

'That's the essence of the cure, isn't it?'

'So the fucker keeps sayin'. Two shits a day! He must be spendin' a fortune on castor oil.'

'What was he doin' in the village, then?' Clancy was keen to change the subject.

'Minno O'Leary is talkin' of dyin'. He's down in her cottage now tryin' to talk her outa it.'

'Is she not feelin' well?'

'Accordin' to O'Leary, she's as fit as a fiddle. No, the old thing is just goin' 'round the twist, that's all.'

'She's near her hundred.'

'Ninety-eight.'

'She can't live for ever.'

'Ah, she'll live a good while longer. There's been many an O'Leary that have seen their century come and go.'

''T'll be hard on Pagga when she finally does take off.'

'Big Mary, ya mean?'

'Aye. He'll have to take her in.'

'Naw. He'll find a way around that little responsibility,'

sneered Duffy. 'He's vile and wicked enough to bypass that little chore. He'll probably find some dumb bastard to marry her!'

'Marry her!' scoffed Clancy. 'Talk sense, Duffy! Marry Big Mary? Name one fool who'd go and do such a thing!'

Just then they heard the clatter of hoofs and the squeak of cartwheels on the flagstones outside the front door. Clancy went to the window.

'Who can that be at this hour?' asked Duffy from his chair.

''Tis Stallion O'Casey and his son,' said Milo, heading for the door.

Barra sighed. 'And here was me thinkin' that they'd decided to stay outa our lives after all. 'Tis goin' to be a long three months.'

# 6

It was not until the late afternoon of Monday, 26 March, that
Minno Mary O'Leary took her leave of the world. She slipped
away quietly, in her favourite armchair, sitting by the fireside and
surrounded by a haze of distant memories. Big Mary, who had
been by her side for most of the day, had only popped out to do
some essential shopping; and Pagga, who had been with her since
the dawn broke, had wandered off to Sullivan's about noon
promising to return in time for tea.

The first to know of the old woman's passing was her cat,
Shlabala, who had wandered into the kitchen after his late
afternoon stroll. He sensed death's presence as soon as he entered
the room. The cat's emerald eyes scrutinized the old woman's
face, tilted back onto the headrest of the chair, and a childlike cry
came from deep within his throat. Then he sprang onto his
mistress's lap, curled himself up into a ball, and meowed his grief
to the dying day, until finally Mary came home.

Her bundles dropped to the floor and she ran to her grandmother's side. Shlabala scurried off and Mary took Minno's hand
and searched for a pulse. She placed a hand on the old woman's
brow, but the touch of death made her draw back at once. Her cry
stifled in her throat, the shock felled her to her knees. 'Ya did it!
Ya did it!' she whispered, feeling her anger rise. Tears spilled
down her cheeks in a great stream. 'Ya heartless ol' hag! While
me back was turned ya upped and fled from me! 'Tis a cruel
woman ya are, Minno O'Leary.'


There was little or no time for the relatives of Minno O'Leary to
grieve after her departed soul – especially for Pagga, as it was his
responsibility to see her waked and buried with all the pomp and

honour due to her. After collecting Pagga from Mick Sullivan's pub, Mary let him grieve by the old woman's chair for ten minutes; then she had him up off his knees. She fortified him with two glasses of neat whiskey and then she sent him on his way to make the arrangements. 'The undertaker first, Pagga, and then get the poteen and straight back here,' she ordered as she escorted him through the open doorway.


When Pagga's horse and cart finally pulled up in the yard behind Minno's cottage four hours later it was a vexed Big Mary that was waiting for him.

'Where in the name a God have ya been?'

'Squattin' on me fuckin' haunches, pickin' lumps a hard shit from between the cheeks a me fuckin' arse!' shouted Pagga, turning to see his sister standing in the doorway.

'What kept ya? Ya've been gone the best part a four hours.'

'I see the wake is under way,' said Pagga, with a nod of his head to the brightly lit windows of the cottage, through which could be seen and heard a large and lively gathering.

'I opened the front door to all mourners at seven on the dot thinkin' ya'd not be long on arrivin' yarself.' Mary was tight-lipped with irritation.

'Well, if those bastards in there are wantin' a dry wake, let them stay put, but if they're wantin' Bridget O'Dea's finest they're goin' to have to get off their lazy arses and come out here and help me get these jars off the cart!'

'Ya went to O'Dea's? Ya went all the way to O'Dea's?'

'That's where the best and finest is made.'

'Ya're daft, Pagga! Twenty miles there and back and me with a hundred thirsty souls, offerin' them tea and soda bread this past hour.'

'Then get some a them out here to give us a hand, woman!' bawled Pagga, his temper, never that low to begin with, rising. He had turned to unshackle the horse from the cart when he heard Milo Clancy's voice call out, 'The water bearer at last!'

''Tis himself then,' said Pagga, managing to muster a smile of sorts.

''Tis,' replied Milo, placing both his hands on O'Leary's shoulders. 'And 'tis sorry I am. Sorry for this day that has come down so heavily on yarself. She was the finest woman that ever drew the breath a life. We'll miss her warm heart and her comfortin' ways, and her strong and forthright manner when it came to givin' advice. There's no such wisdom left alive. The last a the old ones have gone and by Jasus we're goin' to miss her sorely.'

Pagga was deeply touched. 'Thanks for yar condolences and yar fine words, Milo,' he said, almost gently.

'Aye,' said Clancy, his hands dropping away from his friend's shoulders and burying themselves deep in his trouser pockets. 'Aye. But they're only words, and when it comes to describin' Minno O'Leary's grand life I find words are very poor buildin' blocks. But then words are all we have.'

'We have a song, Milo. We can sing her praise as soon as we get Bridget O'Dea's jars a poteen down off this cart,' replied Pagga. At last he felt the real trauma of it all reaching him. He felt his emotion rising up within him and he prayed to God he could hold on just a little longer. He did not want to break down in front of another man, especially Clancy.

'Ya mean ya travelled all the way to O'Dea's!' exclaimed Clancy as he saw Pagga's inward struggle begin to crack at the seams. 'Jasus, but it'll be a grand wake; no doubts about that at all,' added Milo, averting his gaze, his eyes looking past O'Leary's shoulder to the cart. 'Colin!'

'Yes, Milo,' whispered the boy, who was hovering in the darkness.

'Into the house with yarself and drag four a the mourners out here, and get them to unload Pagga's precious cargo.'

O'Leary looked shagged out. His face was grey and the pain of his sad day was in his eyes.

'Away with yarself, Pagga, into the cottage,' said Clancy. 'And get some of Bridget's best down yar gullet. I'll take care a the horse.'

'Blessin's on ya, Milo,' said Pagga without any protest. 'I could use a drop.'

Clancy was busy unshackling the cart when he spied Big Mary coming back out from the cottage. 'Poor ol' Pagga is takin' it badly.'

'Aye. Oh, he'll be down in his boots until Minno is under the ground, but he'll rise. Ye men don't stay down for long. It'll be a foggy memory to him a week from now. 'Tis us women that do

the rememberin' and still waltz with our grief when ye have up
and forgotten all about it.'


The midnight hour struck its twelve mournful bongs on Minno
O'Leary's clock above the fireplace. There were seventy-two
mourners in the kitchen, and the cause of their grief was in their
very midst. Minno O'Leary lay in state on her brass bed in the
centre of the room. Around her an army of kneeling women were
sending up Hail Mary after Hail Mary to the heavens for the old
woman's departed soul. The men were in groups all around the
kitchen, glasses of poteen in hand, talking in subdued voices.
The few chairs were occupied by the old and frail, except for the
two armchairs near the fire's hearth. Pagga had Minno's throne,
and across from him sat Clancy, O'Casey and Duffy on the floor.
To the left of O'Casey and Duffy were two of Pagga's relatives,
distant cousins to him. Their names were Bango and Liam
Cronin. The Cronins were first cousins to each other. There was a
lot of bad blood between the two of them and only a funeral or
wake could get them together under the same roof. It was Bango
who had the ears of the little group gathered around the blazing
turf fire. 'Well, as far as meself is concerned, 'tis the strangest
thing that ever happened in this village. I've never known
anything stranger and that's a fact.'
    'Try and explain it, Bango. Tell us how she did it. For 'tis fair
drivin' me outa me head tryin' to apply a bita logic to it all,' said
Pagga.
    'Come on, Pagga, for the love a Mike.' Bango's round face
smiled up at him like a moon. 'Ya can't apply logic to it at all at all!
Minno O'Leary ups and dies on us. Nuttin' strange about that.
But she goes and tells us all that she's about to do it; she gives us
the month and the very day of her passin'. Ya can't do anything
but marvel when someone ups and does a trick like that!'
    'Then how would ya go about explainin' it?' pressed Pagga,
bent on having an answer.
    'Ya don't, Pagga! Ya don't! Ya leave the thing be!'
    Pagga's face was bright with drink and anger. 'Well, fuck it,
Bango,' he yelled back. 'Ya'll give it a stab, surely. After all, ya're
the one that's forever delvin' into the fuckin' impossible. Ya're
the one that's forever readin' the cards, lookin' up into the fuckin'

night heavens and buyin' every rag ever printed that has anything to do with the spooky. If reason could explain me grandmother's strange passin', 't'd be Milo Clancy I'd be talkin' to and not yarself!'

Cronin took a swig from his glass and placed it with great deliberation on the floor. 'What I'm goin' to give ya, Pagga, is a spiritual explanation. And ya're goin' to have to take what I give ya or lump it. A question to yarself first. Over the last few days did she have any conversations with yarself concernin' heaven?'

Pagga thought for a moment. ''Twas the last time I saw her alive. She was talkin' a bit daft really, ya know what I mean. Like the old ones always do. The conversation was really between herself and herself, if ya get me drift. I was sittin' there thinkin' about the wasted day I was spendin'. She was as healthy as meself and there was I sittin' on me arse wastin' away a day of me life when I could have been elsewhere. She was gabbin' on about heaven and how she was goin' to enter it. "There's big stairs," she says, "miles long, leadin' all the way up to Saint Peter's gates." 'And how the hell are you goin' to climb it with your bad feet?" I asked. She comes outa her half dream and looks at me with t'em condemnin' eyes of hers. She says, "Timmy'll be there. My Tipperary Tim'll be at the foot a t'em steps waitin' for me. He'll lift me on his strong back and carry me like the wind right to the top, right to the gates of Peter!" Those were her very words.'

'Interestin', Pagga. Very interestin',' said Bango, taking another swig from his glass. 'There must be somethin' there!'

'Get on with it, then, for fuck's sake!' snapped Liam Cronin, at his cousin's left elbow.

'It's exactly that I'm doin'!' Bango glared with murderous wrath at his cousin. 'I will when I'm fuckin' good and ready! Now get yar poxy arse off the floor and get us a refill before I put me fist through yar shaggin' gob!' And Bango shoved his empty glass to within an inch of his cousin's nose. 'Now lads, 'tis my opinion that our Minno had a vision some time before her death. She might have had it while she was asleep in her bed or while she was awake. Now if one has a vision, then there has to be a carrier; a heavenly carrier.'

'A saint, ya mean? An honest to God saint?' Barra's voice was hushed with awe. 'You mean Minno O'Leary saw a saint in her bedroom?'

Bango gazed at his audience with a face that radiated superior wisdom. 'No, not exactly.'

'Then what did she see?' barked Pagga, hanging on to every word.

'Not a saint, Pagga. Not a saint. In the Bible when carriers come down from heaven they usually have great big wings on their backs. There was Raphael who came down to taxi the prophet Elijah up to that grand place. There was Gabriel who came down to tell Holy Mary she was pregnant. . . .'

'So 'twas an angel,' interrupted Barra eagerly.

'No, not an angel, Barra,' corrected Bango. 'An archangel! That's a different kettle of fish altogether.' Turning his head, he gave his full attention to Pagga and continued, 'There's me explanation, Pagga. As simple as that. An archangel was sent down from above to tell Minno O'Leary that her time had come.'

'Are ya sure 'twasn't the good Christ Himself that came through Minno's door with the news?' jibed Clancy, who had been sitting quietly in his chair, just listening.

'Maybe 'twas a whole bloody band of angels! Maybe a whole tribe of archangels squeezed into Minno's bedroom to give her the news of her passing!' sniggered Liam, raising his glass.

'Now ya can see, Pagga, why I was so backward in comin' forward in tryin' to work out an explanation,' said Bango.

'Ya did yar best, Bango,' said Pagga consolingly. 'They might all be for sneerin' at yar good self but ya'll see no smirk come to my face. That doesn't mean to say that I accept what ya say. But ya've gone a dacent length in tryin' to solve the unsolvable. If anyone was holy enough to hear the spoken word of God, to hear voices from heaven, then 'twas our Minno. The answer lies somewhere inside that fact. So I'll not spend me nights tryin' to figure out God's ways and the workin's of me grandmother's mind. I'll leave things be. I'll accept Minno's prophecy of her own end as a miracle worked by God and Him alone.'

'Aye, 'tis best to leave it that way,' said Milo Clancy. 'Who are we to ponder into the workin's of the Almighty?'

'Little men,' sighed Pagga.

'Aye,' agreed Liam Cronin. 'We're nuttin' but drops a watery shit in the great big wide world.'

Eight jars of Bridget O'Dea's best brew had vanished down the throats of the mourners and three more were being uncorked and distributed as the clock on the mantelpiece struck the hour of two. Only half a dozen old crones were still at their watch beside Minno's bier; the rest of the women were on their feet, glasses in hand, and mingling with the menfolk. The odd mournful ballad was beginning to rise from the well-oiled throats of the old and practised crooners. As the poteen continued to flow, Minno O'Leary's wake took shape and form.

Four young girls well into their teens were dancing a reel and holding everybody's attention. Dimpna Murphy, the best of the quartet, was trying her damnedest to raise her dancing kicks all the way up to Minno O'Leary's rafters so as Pascal O'Mara could have an even broader view of her angel-white knickers.

At the same moment in time the finest fiddler in the whole of the county, Patsi Liddy, was getting the very sounds of heaven itself from his strings, but the saliva that was dripping from the fiddler's mouth had nothing to do with the miracles that he was obtaining from his musical instrument. No, it was the sight of Dimpna Murphy's bloomers that was making the poor man drool. But much good was the sixty-year-old fool to the likes of Dimpna. Her lasso was out and swinging for the young Buck O'Mara, but O'Mara at that moment in time was having none of it.

The wives of Bango and Liam Cronin were taking a lot of the burden of the wake out of Big Mary's hands. They saw to the replenishing of glasses, they fed the hungry and conjured up extra chairs from out of nowhere when more of the frail and ancient came in off the roads after their long and distant journeys. Big Mary was left to welcome the latecomers, to put them at their ease and listen to their condolences. The half glass of O'Dea's liquor that Pagga had poured for her several hours before was still sitting in her glass as she mingled with the crowd. From time to time through the night she found her eyes wandering in the direction of the fireplace and to the stranger that squatted on the floor next to Milo Clancy's chair. She took note of his gait, observed his quiet manner, never saying a word, and noticed how his eyes took in everything around him. She also noted the boy that sat beside him on the floor. Surely that can't be his son. Pagga must have got it wrong!

Pagga O'Leary did not have to bring the wake to life; the best poteen in the whole of Ireland had seen to that. All he had to do

94

was sit on Minno's throne and watch the proceedings take hold. The pride was filling up in his heart as the night went on. Patsi Liddy was coming into his own. The bow that ran over the strings of his fiddle had been blessed by God Himself and O'Dea's poteen was putting pure magic power into the man's fiddling arm. The four young girls that danced before the music of the maestro Liddy were heaping honour and glory onto Minno's sad passing. A fine wake was growing, taking hold and coming down over all.

Liddy was pumping out the 'Bride's Arrival', the liveliest reel in his repertoire, and the gallant four lassies were kicking for the heights, when the music came to an absolute stop. All eyes turned towards the fiddler.

Patsi's arse was on a chair in the middle of the room facing the front door. The fiddle was on his chin, the bow was resting on the strings, but the fiddler's body was rock-still; his bow arm, frozen, was held in midair. The fear of God was in his eyes. Their heads turned away from him and went to the door; Dimpna Murphy shrieked in fright.

The man that filled Minno O'Leary's doorway was old. Whoever it was that stood before them had seen a century of life and more. The man was an inch over six feet in height. A ragged cape the colour of pitch fell from his shoulders in great thick folds down to the floor. The blazing lights of the oil lamps picked up the whole of his mass while the backdrop of the dense black night behind him gave all there the uncomfortable feeling that the Angel of Death had come in person to claim the soul of Minno O'Leary. Everyone's eyes were fixed on the stranger's face. They stared with opened mouths and stifled breaths. Some eyes showed fear, some awe, others foreboding, and still others uncertain reverence. For the face before them told a thousand different stories. It showed every God-cursed bog road that scarred the landscape of Ireland. It showed the rain and the winds that howled and lamented as they swept over bog and marsh on black winter nights. It presented to the young men that cared to look deeply the futility of life, the knowledge that age brought nothing but the certainty of a bad and undignified death. It told the dreamer to divorce himself from hope, that there was no hope. It announced to the dullard, the fool and the insane that they had it all, that theirs was the perfect world, that they were the lucky ones. And yet the two eyes that looked out from those deep sockets could barely see the light given off from Minno O'Leary's lamps. The left eye, in particular, was almost dead, the grey haze that stood in front of it darkening with the passing of each and every day. The right eye still looked out upon the world but it, too, was dying, only at a slower rate. Dozens of fine tiny red lines snaking their ways across both of the pupils betrayed the stranger's infirmity.

Not one soul in that place could jolt itself out of its shock. Every last one of them stood as rock waiting for the stranger to release them. . . .

'Have the times become so quare and so feckless that the last of the seanachies is ordained to stay still in this doorway 'til death claims him? Will not the head of the house come forward and greet me with the hand of friendship?' The voice was deep and strong and carried with it the pitch and purity of a bell well struck. At last the spell had been broken. At once all of them knew that standing before them was none other than Gikitey O'Dowd.

''Tis yourself!' cried Pagga, pushing his way through the crowd.

'None other, Pagannini O'Leary.'

'Jasus to God, Gikitey, but ya're unrecognizable,' choked O'Leary.

'I'm a hundred and two, Pagga. The body begins to fall to pieces after it's kissed its eighties goodbye.'

'Yar eyes, Gikitey, yar eyes!'

'Me left? Dead in its socket these past five years. The other? Only a matter a time, Pagga, before the last of the blackness covers me completely. I'm dyin' in bits.' O'Dowd smiled as he saw the expression in O'Leary's eyes, then opened his arms and Pagga walked into the old man's embrace. He rested his head on the seanachie's shoulder and quietly wept.

Big Mary worked her way through the crowd towards the two men.

'Is it my little princess?'

''Tis herself, Gikitey.' Mary's eyes began to mist as she basked in the warmth of his smile.

'Ya've been eatin' more than yar fare share of potatoes, I'm thinkin', Big Mary,' smiled O'Dowd as he took in the whole of her mass. Here standing before him was the granddaughter of his friend and comrade, Tipp O'Leary. He could see where Tipp's great strength had been inherited. He could sense the vitality of Mary's personality and the stamp of the man's great tenacity was there for all to see in the outline and sculpture of her jaw.

'Eatin' is me one and only passion, Gikitey, as well ya know. I'm afraid I've been spoilin' meself of late.' Big Mary blushed like a shy young girl.

'Aye, I can see that,' grinned O'Dowd back at her. Silently he wondered why the two sons of Tipperary Tim had come into the world without the great man's fire – and Pagga, Tipp's only grandson – well, it was common knowledge that not even a spark of the great man's passion kindled in his tender breast. But as the seanachie basked in the warmth of Big Mary's heart-embracing smile he knew that the flame and a great deal of the passion of his great friend still glowed in one O'Leary heart at least.

'Well, 'tis glad we are to see ya,' said Mary. 'But ya've come on the saddest of nights, I'm afraid.'

'I was in Westport when the sad tidin's reached me. I came as quick as I could.'

'Then yar journey has been a long one,' said Mary. 'Come sit yarself by the fire and thaw yarself out.'

'Let's pay our respects to yar grandmother first. What do ya say, Pagga?'

Pagga straightened himself up, dried his tearstained face with the palms of his hands and, with his voice steady and clear, said, 'Gikitey O'Dowd, ya do my grandmother and my grandmother's house great honour. My sister and myself bid ya welcome and hope ya'll stay long enough to fill the passin' of the wife of Tipperary Tim with much glory.'

Escorted by the two O'Learys, the seanachie approached Minno's bier. The three of them went down on their knees; the rest of the house followed, and De De Mulcahey, the oldest of the women, led the friends of Minno O'Leary in yet another Rosary.

Gikitey O'Dowd took over Minno's throne on the right-hand side of the fireplace, while the women administered to his needs. And the house watched as the seanachie received a decent measure of Bridget O'Dea's best from the hand of Big Mary herself, and drained it in one gulp. Gikitey O'Dowd, a man they had not clapped eyes on for five years and more, was in their midst. All were aware that he was the last of his kind, and all had thought him long since dead. The atmosphere was electric, but no one spoke a word. They sipped, they watched and they waited, all eyes on the remarkable figure that had materialized from out of the night.

The seanachie's face was turned away from everyone's gaze towards the fire in the hearth. Though the crowd was tightly packed around him, the old man seemed neither to notice nor to care. Pagga stood guard behind the seanachie's chair and, while he ate and drank, made sure the old man's peace was not disturbed. Ten minutes O'Dowd sat there, sipping from his glass and staring into the flames, and only when he reached the bottom of his drink did he slowly turn and face them.

'Ya're rested then, Gikitey,' said Pagga.

'I am. A little bita food and a few glasses can still work wonders, even for the likes of me poor ol' self.'

'There's me sister's bed vacant and waitin' for ya. Why don't ya take it and rest some more,' suggested Pagga, still seeing the weariness of the roads in the seanachie's one good eye.

'Much as I'd like to take up yar generous offer, Pagga, I'm afraid I'll have to refuse it, if 'tis all the same with yar good self. As ya well know, only the major participant of any wake has the God-given right to rest her head and seek out the sleep she's pined and prayed for. The rest of us must stay vigilant and watch as that soul passes from us. We being mere mortals will watch with jealous eyes, envying her no doubt, envying that last grand and eternal sleep.' A mischievous grin crossed Gikitey's face. 'And will the only grandson of Minno O'Leary condescend to stay on this earth for the same length of time as her lovely self?'

'If the good Lord ordains it so,' said Pagga sombrely. Then added quickly, 'I'm in no great hurry to go, however.'

'None of us are, Pagga,' laughed the seanachie. 'Not even meself. Come sit down here at me feet, Pagga, and we'll get what's left of this night under way. The last of the seanachies is rested up now and is ready to pour glory on Minno O'Leary's ninety-eight years of living.'

The buzz of pent-up excitement reverberated throughout the kitchen, and another two jars of O'Dea's poteen were quickly opened. Everyone topped their glasses to the brim and sat themselves down in an arc round the seanachie, their chatter gradually subsiding. They watched Big Mary fill the old man's pipe, light it, and present it to him. They watched the light grey smoke drift from between pursed lips and veil the bearded face of Gikitey O'Dowd in a ghostly aura.

'Great men who have done great deeds are for ever remembered. They die and the flesh rots off their bones and their skeletons fill the churchyards and very few come to pay their bones homage. But their deeds live on; they live in our hearts and memories. No one can forget a great deed for we need it to uplift our spirits and bolster our courage in times of peril. In this house, this very night, a woman has laid herself down in her bed never again to rise. She's a tired old woman who has seen the best part of a hundred years. . . . How many pints a sweat have fallen from her brow in her lifetime? How many barrels a tears has she shed for the sorrows and trials that came to her day in and day out? How many aches and pains have racked her body, how many clouds of grief have passed over her heart and soul? Questions . . . questions that the wisest of the wise wouldn't dare attempt to answer and neither shall I.

'There's a hundred of yees and more gathered here under this roof to pay yar last respects to a woman ya loved and admired, but isn't it strange, isn't it strange I say. . . . Here before yar eyes lies Minno O'Leary. A woman! Where are her grand deeds that will sustain and keep the memory of her alive in our hearts?' The old seanachie stopped, brought his pipe to his lips, and the grey sweet-smelling smoke clouded his bearded face once more. 'Because of her sex, Minno O'Leary could not perform those feats that we praise so highly. 'Tis God's own law that the mountains shall melt only at the command of the Davids of this world. The Davids are few, and all of them that have ever come amongst us have been of the male sex.' Gikitey paused, and was glad to see he had his audience completely in his grasp. 'So ten years from now,' he continued, 'who'll remember the old woman that died in this cottage this very day? Who? Everyone. Everyone. Every man, woman and child in this room will. Your children's children and theirs as well. The very stones of Mayo will remember her until they are pounded into dust by the sea, wind and rains! Why? Why will this woman linger in our minds and our children's minds? Because she was the wife of Tipperary Tim! As long as the giant is remembered, so too will the apple of his eye remain in our hearts. Cast yar eyes away from me own humble self, and look at the picture that adorns that spot just over the mantelpiece there.'

Boxed in a simple frame and behind a sheet of glass, a dour-faced, black-bearded man in his middle years gazed down at them all. However, as the face itself did not merit too much contemplation, their eyes came back and rested on Gikitey O'Dowd's ancient features once more.

The ancient seanachie broke the silence. 'For every county in Ireland there is a Tipperary Tim, or at least that's what we're led to believe. Our own Tipperary Tim came here to this barren county from the lush lands across the river Shannon while he was still in his teens. The lad had no intention of stayin'. He had merely come to see what he could see and then turn round and head for home. There wasn't much, for our land is harsh and cruel to the eye. But he stayed, and we all know why, don't we? Our darlin' Minno, Minno Cronin, the most beautiful colleen in the whole of Ireland, fluttered her eyelids in his direction and manacled him to the lands of north Mayo for the rest of his natural life. Blessings and all honour be on the soul of Minno O'Leary for capturing him for us. . . . Bog-runner, avenging angel on the poxed body of our greatest aggressor, the bastard Milky Hawkins, runted son of the syphilitic Hawkins Senior himself! Poacher of a mountain a quail from Hawkins's own estates! Puddin'-maker extraordinary, using the blood of one of Hawkins's own thoroughbred horses to make fine fat sausages to feed and push down the gullet of sweet little Hawkins Junior! Pick one out, gentlemen! Pick any of Tipp's great titles and I'll give ya a bit a history that ya'll not find in the books!'

'Oh, for the love a God!' cried Barra Duffy, jumping in on the seanachie's invitation before the rest of them had time to open their mouths. 'Do tell us about the night of the avenging angel. The death a the bastard, Milky Hawkins!'

'Fuck Milky Hawkins!' snapped Liam Cronin. 'We've heard that a thousand times. Tell us about the raid on Hawkins's private chapel.'

'No! The night a the fire,' cried Bango. 'When he burned all four of the barns right into the ground!'

'Whist! Will ya whist all a yees!' cried the seanachie, waving his hands as a hundred requests fell on his ears. 'Little princess.' He smiled at Big Mary. 'Ya've fed my belly and tended to me needs, and succeeded in wiping the weariness of the roads from me poor ol' carcass. What is your command? What shall it be?'

Mary O'Leary's cheeks burned crimson as all eyes turned to her, but she kept her eyes on the old man, and without the slightest hesitation in her voice demanded, 'His last deed, Gikitey. His very last deed.'

A mutter of disapproval ran through the crowd of mourners, but she kept her gaze steady on Gikitey, waiting for the rebuke to fall from his lips. The best part of half a minute went by, the seanachie and Big Mary locked firmly in what appeared to all to be a battle of nerves, until finally the flicker of a smile caught the corner of Gikitey's lips and spread to light up his ancient, time-scarred face. 'I'm thinkin', Big Mary, that ya're the one that has the darin' of Tipp O'Leary inside of ya.'

'I mean yar good self no disrespect, Seanachie O'Dowd,' stated Mary solemnly. 'You asked for my request and I gave it to ya. Ya have the right to refuse or grant it. Correct me if I'm wrong, but isn't it a fact that ya've never told to a livin' soul the story of his last day?'

'The last day,' sighed the old man, looking down at the flagstone floor between his feet. 'The last day was a day of defeat for him, for him and for all of us.' His heavy tones filled the kitchen with dread, and strong, rounded curses were mouthed at Big Mary. 'Don't throw yar scorn in Big Mary's direction!' The old man's voice was harsh. 'No one 'til this very night has ever asked me to relate the last chapter in Tipp's own grand saga. No one has had the balls or guts to look me in the eye and ask it. It took a woman to gather up her courage, the courage ye lack, and face me. . . . Pagga O'Leary!'

Pagga lifted his head and looked up at O'Dowd's bearded face. 'Yes, Gikitey?'

'How come you never asked?'

'I know the gist of my grandfather's passin',' replied Pagga, his eyes avoiding O'Dowd's face.

'The gist, but not all of it. Ya're weak. Ya're weak as yar father was, Pagga. Tipp never passed on his strength. His blood watered itself down before it entered the veins of his sons. 'Tis not yar fault, Pagga,' allowed the seanachie in a more kindly tone. ''Tis not yar fault. Besides, Ireland no longer needs giants. The bad times are passed, the tyrants are long gone.'

'Tell us the passin', then, the grand passin' of my granddad,' urged Pagga, and looked deep into his glass.

'Last deeds, be they small or large affairs, never do credit to their doers.' Gikitey settled himself back in his chair. 'When death finally comes, 'tis very few that face it with honour. We beseech our gods to let us linger a little while longer, not wantin' to pass into death's dark embrace. . . . The family that owned our villages, our farms and our towns owned them by the rights given to them by the crown of England. Not only did they own all we had, but they also owned us too. They owned our bodies and our souls. A man couldn't as much as fart without first going to the Big House and askin' permission from Stewart Hawkins himself. He was our master, our lord, and the sword that hung for ever over our heads should we dare to bat an eyelid in protest. Yet there was a time when the men of north Mayo were made of sterner stuff. That time is buried now in ancient history. The French came to these shores in three fine big ships under the command of that darlin' man, General Humbert. With the help he got from our ancestors he lit a furnace of a fire across the lands of Mayo and Leitrim. The true sons of Ireland and France burned and pillaged every estate that met their marching eyes. English landlords kissed Irish pikes, English squireens, toffs, gentry and noblemen saw what their bellies were made of as our forebears opened them up with French bayonets. . . . But then Cornwallis came down upon us. Humbert and his soldiers retreated to the safe shores of France, and our poor forefathers faced the might of the redcoat army. So bloody was Cornwallis's butchery that the Mayo men never rose again to take arms against the robbers of our lovely land. Mayo men kowtowed to the English and their rule over us until Independence came.

'Our finest hour was in the year of 1798. All fight was gone from us after that. The men of Cork, Dublin and Wexford fought on, and tore us away from the English yoke. The Mayo men slept and licked the wounds that the bastard Cornwallis had inflicted. The spirit of Ninety-Eight was well dead when the Tipperary man came among us. He walked into a warm cottage and a lovin' wife named Minno. He was a quiet man, askin' nuttin' of nobody. All he wanted was peace and the basic human right to bring up his family and tend to his land as he saw fit. But the land wasn't his. It belonged to the great Lord Hawkins. The crops that he sowed with the sweat and toil of his body, they were Stewart Hawkins's as well. There was taxes and rents to be paid. . . . We all thought him mad when he walked up to the Big House and tried to pow-wow with the master himself. And weren't we right to think him mad? Tipp's own confidence in the art of persuasion got him a boot up the arse and the laughter and scorn from ourselves. But O'Leary soon wiped the smiles off our faces. That he did! His night raids on Hawkins's cattle, the burnin' of acres of Hawkins's barley and wheat did the trick! Not one copper did O'Leary have to pay to Hawkins in rent! His scorn and hatred for Hawkins became well known to us all. His deeds filled us with hope, and a little of his darin' and bravado slipped inside of us, and we too paid the Hawkins's estates many a midnight visit. But when it came to the rifling of the great lord's coffers, and the stampedin' of Hawkins's cattle over the cliffs of Michaelmas, it was Tipp, and him alone, who could claim those deeds for himself.

'Stewart Hawkins came to fear our Tipp and the time actually came when it was the lord of the manor who paid the peasant tribute! He put gold sovereigns into Tipp's calloused hands in order to gain some measure of peace and quiet for himself. Those were the golden days when victories and coups came easy to our champion, Tipperary Tim. . . . But then Hawkins's bastard son took over his father's grand estates and no more tribute or leniency came the peasant's way. Milky Hawkins enforced the law in the same vile vein as that fucker Oliver Cromwell had done centuries before. Twice the bastard came on to Tipp's own patch and set his torch to the O'Leary cottage and crops. It was then that Tipp made up his mind to rid the lands of Mayo of the cursed family that had plagued our lives for three long centuries.

'It was on the filthiest and dirtiest of nights that he kissed his young wife goodbye and headed for the Big House. He got there while there was still some night left in the skies, and laid himself low waiting for the dawn. When it did come up, it found the drunken, pox-ridden son of Stewart Hawkins on his fine steed riding up the grand walkway towards the manor. He had been out on the town with the rest of his kind, and was headed for his bed, or so he thought. When he came to the grand stables, little did our Milky think how short and fickle life sometimes is. There wasn't a single thought in his drunken brain as he dismounted from his prized and lovely horse. He opened the stable doors and let his treasure inside. Tipp wasn't lurkin' or hidin' like some Judas; he was there to face his enemy, standin' feet apart just inside the doors. Milky was so far gone with drink that he mistook our Tipp for one of the stablehands, and ordered him to unsaddle his charge and bed him down. Tipp touched his forelock to the master and said in his grand soft voice, "Very good, sir." He took the reins from Milky's hands, and at the same time slipped out his dagger. Before another second had time to pass, Tipp's sweet blade was travelling across the surface of the horse's throat! What was there for poor ol' Milky to do? Nuttin'! Nuttin' at all, except faint. The blood gushed from the animal's great jugular and the unfortunate beast hit the ground like a ton a spuds, Milky Hawkins followin' him but a split second later.

'When our darlin' Milky finally came round he found himself starin' up into the cold grey eyes of Tipperary Tim himself. It is said that all men see clearly the condition of their souls just before death draws its cold cloak over them. Did our darlin' Milky catch a peek at that soul of his? Did he see every one of his black, cruel deeds? Did he see the faces of the poor Mayo families that he sent onto the roads, drivin' them from their cottages in the dead a winter? Did he see what happened to them? Did it not enter his head to ask himself the question, whatever happened to the O'Fallon clan, those two darlin' families that lived out on the Michaelmas road? Well, I'll tell ya somethin'. That poxed cunt had very little time in which to read the book of his twenty-five years of black livin'. Tipp had him up off the stable floor, and for a full half hour he beat the livin' shit outa him!'

A murmur of approval went round the room.

'Only when Tipperary had tired himself out did he do his unfortunate victim a favour. But what a favour! What a brain it was to devise such a *coup de grâce* for one of the biggest bastards that ever walked the earth. He drove the scutterin' cunt onto his knees and, grasping Hawkins by his scrawny neck, he pushed his head into a horse's feed bucket wherein was a gleamin' gallon of the dead horse's blood. They say that Hawkins, in a vain attempt to save his miserable life, tried to drink the bucket dry. I for one don't believe that. The devil died without much of a struggle.'

Gikitey paused for a moment to survey his rapt audience.

'O'Leary knew that the killin' of Milky Hawkins was to be the very last of his legendary deeds. The mark of death was on him now. It wouldn't be the local sergeant that would be after his tail now, but the might of the British army! And so Tipperary Tim disappeared. Six months passed and no one so much as saw hide nor hair of him. But then, on a sad March morning, word came whistling through this village that the rebel had been sighted. Tipp had been spotted on the outskirts of Ballinrobe down near the Mayo–Galway border. He was starvin' and half dead and tryin' with one last supreme effort to get back to us; back to his darlin' wife, Minno, wishin' to die in the warmth and grandness of her gentle arms. Thirty redcoats had picked up his trail and they followed and chased him the length of Mayo. Three days later and he was less than ten miles from this cottage, but the murderous redcoats were fast moving in on their prey. They finally caught up with him on the outskirts of Yellow Man's Bog.

'If pure tiredness, six months of starvation and open roads hadn't sapped all of Tipp's strength, then surely he must have managed a smile, for before his very eyes was the place that he knew and loved so well! Wasn't he the man of the bogs where in his younger days he had taken on the best runners that Mayo could muster? Here is where he beat the greatest bog-runners that the whole of Connaught could produce. Renewed life entered Tipp's tired legs as they touched the bog's marshy surface, and renewed hope entered his weary heart. Away he went across its vast and treacherous expanse. Twelve very foolish and brainless lads in their red jackets followed. He led them on and on right into the centre. There he stopped and waited for his struggling pursuers to catch up. When they were within a hundred yards, Tipp turned his back on them and continued on his way. Not until he had crossed the entirety of the Yellow Man did Tipp turn round. And there was nuttin' to see! There was no one on the surface of the bog but himself! The sly and cunnin' Yellow Man had eaten up another twelve foreign bastards. Tipp was into the home stretch now. His feet were on the coast road and his village of Feacledown was before him. But his wornout boots never set foot inside his village again. The ambush was ready and waiting at John Dumphy's forge. Two dozen British rifles ripped open the still March day with their fire and brought Tipperary Tim to the ground. But he wasn't dead. Their aim had been intentionally low. The murderin' bullets had killed his fine, stout legs and that was all. The rest of Tipp was still alive. They dragged his bloody body towards the forge and lashed his dying remains to the giant cartwheel that leaned against the wall of Dumphy's building, and a line of soldiers surrounded him. We, his friends, Minno, his darlin' wife and his two wee sons, were allowed to come and watch. It took him two days and two nights to pass into the arms of his Christ. Yes, 'tis true that towards the end Tipperary Tim did cry out, did beg and plead with his murderers to put one of their bullets through his pain-crazed skull. But even the gods of heaven would cry out and beg if they had been through that six months of runnin' over mountains and bogs and had a couple a dozen army bullets embedded in their legs. There's no shame attached to Tipp's last few hours, but there is a justifiable amount of shame to be attached to ourselves for lowering our heads and closing our mouths for fear of relating the story of the last day in the life of the finest man that ever came into our lives.'

Minno O'Leary's kitchen was still as a churchyard. Heads were bowed, and the few who had their eyes on the old seanachie showed him their tears. O'Dowd knew that he had no right to tell that story. His being there in Minno O'Leary's house was for the purpose of giving succour and comfort, for uplifting their spirits, and guiding the wake into a grand occasion that would bring glory to the O'Leary name and honour to the house of the deceased. He had failed in his duty by the telling of his tale. He had murdered their spirits and clouded their hearts in sorrow. He had also taken a little of the sheen away from Tipperary O'Leary's grand life. But it was the granddaughter of the great man himself that had asked for the truth. He had granted her wish because it seemed to him that Ireland was at last changing. The young ones, growing up in a free country, were willing to ask for the truth, willing to hear the weaknesses as well as the strengths of the land that the British had ruled for well nigh seven hundred years.

As he looked at their tear-stained faces now, Gikitey knew that change had still a job to do in this backward and uncivilized place. Glory and grand deeds, lies and fairytales; nuttin' else'll get past yar hearin'. Ya're a simple people, he thought to himself. And a weary sigh left his lips. But he quickly shook off his disgust at the pettiness and weakness of their tiny, closed minds. He sat upright in his chair and, with a large smile on his lips, called out, 'Is the fiddler about at all at all?'

'I'm right here, Gikitey!' cried Liddy, jumping to his feet.

'Did yar father, Sheamus Liddy, not compose a tune just before he passed on, concernin' the good Tipp?'

'That he did, Gikitey. "King a the Bogs" 'tis called.'

'And can the grandson of Sheamus bring out its beauty and grace from that fiddle of his?'

'That he can!'

'Then on yar feet, man, and do yar stuff!'

The first dozen notes hadn't left Liddy's old fiddle before O'Dowd noticed the change that had come over Minno O'Leary's roof. Every man and woman was on their feet with the exception of himself and the dead Minno. The rousing strains of a grand jig filled the kitchen, and Gikitey's tale of the sad passing of Tipperary Tim had been washed clear out of their minds. Even the seanachie began to tap his boots on the flagstone floor in time to the fiddler's beat. 'Dance, ye bastards!' cried Gikitey as the music swept him away. 'Dance yar dance, ye sons and daughters, for Tipperary Tim has driven the English from our shores!'

# 7

On the morning of Friday, 30 March 1928, the friends of Minno O'Leary took her body and laid it to rest in Drumcliff cemetery on the outskirts of the village of Feacledown. The early morning was cold and grey with a fine, drizzling rain falling all around them as they watched the coffin being given to the earth. The service was short and simple and when it was over the hundred odd gathered there scattered back to their farms and cottages.

The clock on the mantelpiece rang in the hour of nine as Pagga and his sister came through the doorway and into their grandmother's kitchen.

'Sit yarself down, Pagga, and I'll have breakfast ready before ya know it,' said Big Mary with more cheerfulness than the situation demanded.

'Jasus, but 'tis like a morgue in here,' complained Pagga.

'The fire needs tendin' to, that's all,' said Mary, going onto her knees with an armful of turf.

Pagga looked around him gloomily. 'This cottage is dead now that Minno is gone. No amount of burnin' turf'll bring it back to life.' Then Pagga's eyes fell on the expanse of his sister's arse. 'Don't bother makin' breakfast for meself. A mug a tea'll do me, then I've got to be on my way.'

Mary clambered to her feet. 'I thought ya might stay a day or two longer.'

'What for, for Christ's sake?'

'I don't know.' Mary turned away from his scorn-filled face and knelt down again to tend to the kettle. 'Don't just stand there in the middle of the floor like a stranger, go sit yarself down at the table. The tea'll be ready in a minute.'

Pagga, seated at the table, nursed his mug of black tea in the palms of both his hands and allowed himself to wallow in the sweet aromas of the gristly bacon and black pudding that Big

Mary was preparing for herself. He was hungry but he was determined to breakfast at home. He cursed himself for coming back with her, but he knew he could not have escaped that duty even if he had really wanted to. Minno's house was hers now; both its contents and its loneliness. If only I could get her a fuckin' man, he thought to himself, watching her bent over the fire, frying pan in hand. If only one bastard would be dacent enough to take her off me hands.

'The day's paper is there if ya want a read,' she called over her shoulder. 'Are ya sure ya won't have a bita bacon with me?'

'No,' snapped the determined O'Leary. 'Where's the paper?'

Big Mary didn't even turn around. 'On the chair; ya're sittin' on it.'

He could hear her teeth munching away on well-done bacon. He could visualize the delicate mug being gripped in her massive hand as she brought it to her lips, and he could feel her eyes trying to bore through the pages of his paper to see his face. With pent-up irritation, he flicked through the pages, found the sporting section and tried to lose himself in the day's racing.

'Pagga?'

'Wha'?'

'That man, Mr O'Casey.'

'What about him?'

'He's nice, don't ya think?'

'Lovely. Absolutely lovely.'

'Milo Clancy says he's here to train Bulba.'

'Yeah. To do a job. Then he's on his way back to where he came from.'

'Pity 'bout his son.'

'Whist, will ya, Mary. I'm tryin' to catch up on events.'

Big Mary ate the rest of her breakfast in silence while Pagga hid behind his paper.

'Jasus, Mary and Holy Saint Joseph!' he exclaimed suddenly, dropping the paper on to the table.

'What's the matter? Ya look as if ya've just met up with a ghost.'

'Do ya know what day 'tis?'

'Friday,' Mary answered, blankly. 'What the hell is the matter, Pagga?'

Pagga's voice had dried to a mere whisper. 'The National is on today!'

'So?' She stared at him uncomprehendingly. 'There hasn't been a newspaper in this house for four days. We had a wake, ya know! Ya've plenty a time to pop into town and put on a bet. Take it easy, Pagga, they'll not run the race without ya!'

But Pagga was not to be easily comforted. 'Listen to me, woman! The last conversation I had with Minno, just before she upped and died . . .'

'What about it?'

'Oh sufferin' sweet Jasus!' Pagga's voice was hoarse with emotion. 'Tell me what Minno said to meself just before I left to go to Sullivan's pub.'

Big Mary could see her brother was about to explode. 'She was talkin' daft wasn't she? She was talkin' about Tipperary Tim. About how he was goin' to come down from heaven and take her up the grand staircase on his back.'

A sigh of relief left Pagga's lips. 'Yeah, that's what I wanted to know! In fact her very words to meself was, "Tim will be at the foot a them steps. He'll put me on his strong back and carry me like the wind all the way up to the top, right to the gates a Peter!" Minno was buried this mornin'. At this very minute in time Tipperary Tim has his wife on his back and he's running up them steps, runnin' with his darlin' and loved one!'

Confusion was written all over Big Mary's face. 'So?'

'Tipperary Tim is also running in the three o'clock at Aintree today!'

Big Mary looked at him as though he must be mad. 'Ya're not well, Pagga. Go lie down on me bed and I'll fetch Dr Flynn.'

'I don't need that fuckin' quack,' he shouted, leaping from his chair. 'What I need is every penny I can lay me fuckin' hands on.'

At last Mary's own O'Leary temper overcame her fear. 'For the love a Christ, Pagga!' she bellowed. 'What the fuck are ya on about?'

A strange, crazed rasping sound exploded from Pagga's throat. 'Pick that fuckin' paper up off the floor and turn it to the sportin' section.'

While Big Mary retrieved the paper, Pagga O'Leary counted out a few crumpled notes and some loose change into his hand. 'Two fuckin' pounds, eight and a penny ha'penny! Fuck it!'

Now it was Mary who was hidden by the day's news. 'What the hell am I supposed to be lookin' at, Pagga?'

'The runners in the fuckin' National!'

'There must be a hundred horses here.'

'Forty-two to be precise.'

Mary's eyes scanned the column from top to bottom. 'Surely it's anybody's race, Pagga. The nag that stays on its feet and is stupid enough to keep the jockey on its back for four and a half miles'll win.'

'Look for the one that stands out a fuckin' mile!' barked Pagga, rubbing his hands in glorious anticipation.

At last Mary found what she was looking for. 'Tipperary Tim,' she shouted triumphantly, pleased in spite of her own reservations. 'Jockey: Mr Dutton.'

'Information from heaven! Information received!' Pagga was ecstatic.

"Tis a sign then?' asked Mary. 'Ya're linkin' it to the passin' a Minno?'

'It's been a strange week, Mary. Our grandmother gives us the very hour of her passin'. And ya recall her very words to us before she embraced her time a darkness. "He'll carry me on his back," she says. "He'll carry me all the way up there to the gates a Peter!" Everything that Tipperary did, every feat he performed was done with the aid and the support of his lovely grand broad legs. He ran the bogs with those legs. He ran the length of Ireland with those legs and kept fifty regiments of British redcoats at bay for the best part of a year. Now there's a horse on the other side of the Irish Sea and it has the good fortune to bear the same name as our grandfather. That nag has a bog to run over. The best part a five miles lies in front of him and he has forty odd fuckers to beat. By Jasus, Mary, I'm tellin' ya he's goin' to leave the rest of his kind standin' still! They don't stand the ghost of a chance. The outcome is a foregone conclusion. That horse'll have the spirit of Tipperary on his back, and the both of them together can't fail!'

'And how much a yar life's savin's are ya goin' to invest this time?' asked Mary, seeing the gambler's glint returned to her brother's eye.

'Five or ten pounds.'

'Is that all?'

'Cast yar eyes at that paper again.'

III

'Jasus, Pagga! He's a hundred to one. He's the donkey a the pack!'

'Aye, he's the fool! Everybody in Ireland and England will regard him to be that. But not me! That four-legged beast is the spirit of our Tim come back to life, I don't have the smallest doubt. Minno O'Leary has been four days' waked now. Today she lies in her grave. Today her darlin' Tim'll come down from Paradise to retrieve her darlin' soul from outa the grave. He'll mount her on his own strong back and race with her up them steps to the gates a Peter. And when he reaches the gates a Peter so too will his spirit cross the finishin' post on the outskirts a Liverpool and win the English Grand National for us!'

There was a moment in which Big Mary weighed her brother's words. 'Keep yarself on that chair, Pagga O'Leary,' she ordered at last.

Pagga watched her as she crossed to the Welsh dresser and took down Minno's old tea caddy. 'Ya're the devil's own, Big Mary!' he laughed. 'Minno's not an hour in her grave, and there ya are as bold as brass rifling her nest egg.'

''Tis little use she'll have for it now,' said Mary, reaching inside the tin. 'And by rights everything in this cottage is mine.' She gave the caddy a half-hearted shake.

'How much?'

'Five pounds on his nose.'

'On his nose. A hundred to one, and ya're puttin' it on his nose?'

'Ya're the one that states it's goin' to romp home,' snapped Mary, handing him the faded fiver.

'An' 'tis true. I'll stake me life on that.'

'I'll be after yarself with the cleaver if yar donkey doesn't win by at least six lengths.'

But Pagga was preparing to leave. 'Don't ya worry yarself none. It'll be just fine.'

'Ya're off already then?' asked Mary, the smile fading from her face.

'To Clancy's. He's got every penny I possess. Not only has he got mine, but Barra's as well.'

'The money ya won on Bulba's last fight?'

'Five hundred pounds between the three of us. Clancy's mindin' it, keepin' it safe. When Bulba meets Kusthi's devil it's all to go on Bulba's back.'

'So I've heard.' Mary looked at her brother with a mixture of pride and amazement. 'Ya're daft, the lot a yees.'

'But if our daftness brings us victory we're millionaires.'

'Will Clancy give ya a tenner for yar miracle horse?'

'When he hears me out he will.' Pagga took his coat and cap from the back of the door. 'The thing is, I want to persuade the rest of them to lay some money down as well. That way we'll gather a small fortune together to put on the fight of fights.'

'Christ, but ye are mad, the whole lot a yees.'

'An' what will ya do with yar five hundred when Tipperary Tim comes in?' asked Pagga, opening the door.

'Put it in Minno's caddy,' smiled Mary.

'Ya'll not try to buy a husband with it?' Pagga asked, already yards from the cottage.

'Five hundred wouldn't be enough,' answered Mary. But so softly that he didn't hear.


Breakfast was over and done with, and Milo Clancy was sitting by the fire, thinking about taking himself off to bed for a few hours' sleep. The last night of the wake had been hard on him. Large quantities of Bridget O'Dea's poteen had disappeared down his throat and he was now sporting a very tender head. O'Casey, his son and Barra Duffy were out in the back yard, their hammers banging away as they did a quick repair job on the henhouse which had been all but demolished the previous night by another March storm. The hammering continued with no let up, and Milo decided that bed was definitely the best place for him. He was just about to crawl out of his chair when the back door opened and in walked Stallion.

'Ye couldn't by any chance use rubber hammers, could ye?' asked Milo.

'God,' grinned Stallion, taking a seat by the fire. 'A big fellah like you, and ya can't hold yar liquor.'

'I've no problem holdin' it, Stallion, as ya well know. 'Tis the day after with me.'

'Jasus, but ya look a right sight,' said O'Casey, not unkindly. 'Take yarself off to bed, man. It's the best thing for ye.'

'Naw, I'll stay put after all. I prefer to die sittin' up.'

113

"'Twas some fuckin' wake, wasn't it?' asked Stallion, smiling at the memory.

Clancy managed a half-hearted smile. 'The best I've been to in many a year.'

'You know they're dyin' out quick and fast on the other side of the Shannon. The undertakers take care of the dead now. They charge into the houses, grab the corpses and have them under the fuckin' ground before ya have time to recite a Hail Mary over them. They say it's more civilized that way. Well, if that's civilization they can shove it up their arses, that's what I say.'

'I'd hate to die and not be waked.'

They sat in silence for some seconds, thinking about the injustice that can happen to a person even after he's dead. The grating rumble of cartwheels on the flagstones outside Clancy's front door interrupted their reverie. Stallion got to his feet and went to investigate. ''Tis Pagga,' he announced a moment later.

Clancy rested his aching head in his hands. 'Well, if the fucker isn't carryin' a shaggin' hammer, tell him to fuck off back to where he came from!'

There was the scrape of hobnail boots on the doorstep, and a second later Pagga O'Leary walked in with the smile of a summer morning lighting up his face. 'God bless all here!'

'And you too, Pagga,' greeted O'Casey, closing the door.

'How's the patient?' O'Leary peered at Clancy cautiously. 'God! But as ya stood by my grandmother's grave this mornin', I was as sure as hell that ya were goin' to jump right down onto the coffin and join her.'

'You're in a fuckin' good mood, Pagga,' said Clancy, squinting at his cheery face. 'Yar bowels must have really gone forth this mornin'!'

O'Leary was not to be discouraged. 'I come bearin' good news,' he exclaimed, parking himself in O'Casey's chair.

'I could do with a bita that,' replied Clancy without enthusiasm.

'I'll come straight to the point, Milo.'

'Take yar coat off first, Pagga,' interrupted Stallion, pulling up another chair.

'I'll not be doin' that, if 'tis all the same with yarself, Stallion. As I said, straight to the point. 'Tis yourself that manages Bulba. 'Tis Barra that grooms and spurs him for his fights. The job that

114

you yarself gave to me is to devise ways and means of gettin' extra cash together, findin' out ways and means of addin' to the winnin's we already have. "All the cash we can get together to lay on Bulba's back when he fights the Devil's own." Those were yar very words. Well I've found a way of doin' it. A sure fire way of makin' a whole lot extra for very little expense.'

'How?' asked Stallion.

'How?' asked Clancy.

O'Leary pulled an unread newspaper from his coat pocket and presented it to Clancy. 'If this is the same newspaper I've been readin' in Minno's cottage at breakfast this mornin', then ya'll find what I'm talkin' about on the sportin' page. You know I was halfway here when I had to turn me fuckin' horse and cart around and head back to Feacledown and fork out tuppence for another in Jilly Doyle's newsagents.'

O'Casey got out of his chair to peer over Milo's shoulder. 'What are we supposed to be lookin' at?' he asked.

'The runners in today's National.'

Pagga sat back, watching in silence while the other two men scanned the page. A minute passed before Clancy lifted his head out of the paper. 'I know what ya're on about, Pagga,' said Clancy slowly, but the glint that O'Leary had expected to come into Milo's eyes was missing.

'Ya have looked, haven't ya?' he asked, disconcerted.

'I've looked.'

'And?'

Clancy folded the paper on his lap. 'It carries a fine name, Pagga, a very fine name. But it doesn't carry Tipp's breeding. Ya're talkin' about a fuckin' hundred to one shot!'

'But the signs, Milo. The signs are all there, for Christ's sake!'

'It is queer, Milo,' suggested Stallion. 'Ya must admit, 'tis awful queer. I mean, what Pagga told us on the first night a the wake. Remember, Milo? Tipp comin' down from heaven, takin' his wife on to his back and chargin' up those steps. That and other things. Tipp's life's been painted and brought to life by the old seanachie that the whole lot a yees thought dead and buried. Minno's been put down into her grave on the very day that this horse with the man's own name plastered all over it decides to go and run himself in the Grand National. 'Tis mighty queer,

Clancy. Ya could say 'twas Minno's partin' gift to her grandson and his friends.'

'Come on, Milo! Stallion is right. 'Tis a sign from heaven.'

Clancy's face remained unmoved. 'I'm sayin' nuttin', Pagga, except that all this crazy speculation is nuttin' but coincidence. If ya want to believe different, go and do so. 'Tis a free country. But I know what ya're askin', Pagga, and the answer is no! No one touches the fuckin' pot!'

'There's four of us now that has Bulba's interests at heart,' said Pagga coolly, carefully finding his words. 'If the majority of us goes against ya, ya have to back down.'

'I'll go along with that,' agreed Milo.

'Then let's get Barra in here. All I'm askin' is that we take forty quid outa the fuckin' pot. Ten apiece.'

Slowly and with a great amount of care, Clancy shook his head. 'We made a deal, Pagga. No one touches the pot unless the idea is a sure-fire thing. Backin' forty quid on a hundred to one longshot isn't sure fire in a sane man's book a things. If Barra says no, and the vote is split down the middle, ya don't have a deal. Is that clear with yarself?'

'A deal,' sighed O'Leary, bowing his head. 'And if the fuckin' thing romps home all I'll have had on his back is a lousy two quid. For 'tis all I've got in the world.'

The door opened and in walked Barra, followed by O'Casey's son. Clancy handed Duffy the paper without a word and Barra sat himself down at the table. All of thirty seconds went by. As soon as Barra lifted his head, Milo knew that the vote had gone against him. He got up from his chair, went to the cupboard beside the fireplace, and took out his portable safe – a battered biscuit tin. Wordlessly, he opened it, counted out £40, crossed the floor and handed the notes to Pagga.

'No hard feelings?' Pagga asked, looking into the stony face.

'I'm a democrat, Pagga,' replied Clancy evenly, the look in his eyes softening. 'I'll always abide by the decision of the majority, even though I believe majorities are made largely of fools.' He permitted himself the smallest smile. 'Cheer up, for Christ's sake, Pagga! Hundred to one shots have come in before.'

O'Leary grinned weakly as he pocketed the money. 'Thanks, Clancy. Ya're a rare and fine specimen of goodness itself.'

'I'm daft, ya mean. Daft like the rest of yees,' he answered, but his mood had changed. 'Okay, now where and with who are we goin' to lay our forty quid?'

'In town with Jack Dillon, a course.'

'With Dillon!' roared Clancy. 'Come on, Pagga, use the brain that God gave ya. If our longshot does his stuff, can ya truly see Dillon handin' over four thousand quid to yourself? He'd have to live five lifetimes before he got his hands on that kind a money.'

'The race isn't 'til three o'clock,' suggested Pagga hopefully. 'He can lay it off.'

'Who with, for Christ's sake? Dillon is a bog farmer like the rest of us. He takes the odd half crown from the housewives, and goes onto bended knees and prays they don't clean him out.' Milo was facing the room, his hangover forgotten. 'Dillon is wind and shit. We'll have to go all the way to Westport.'

'That's forty miles away!' cried Pagga.

Milo turned to Stallion. 'What time is it?'

'Comin' up to eleven,' said O'Casey.

'Barra! Go shackle up yar horse and cart.'

'Won't take more than a tick!' Duffy jumped to his feet and made for the front door.

'Why can't we take mine?' asked Pagga. ''Tis ready and waitin' to go.'

Clancy waved him away. 'Because we need an animal with a bita get up and go. Yars don't exactly qualify in that respect.'

'We're all goin', are we?' asked Stallion, marvelling as he saw Clancy come to life.

'Why not? The bookie that's about to fleece us of forty quid is called Ding Dong Brennan. He's got an honest-to-God wireless right in the middle of his joint. We can listen to the race and at the same time figure out what's to be done with O'Leary here as we watch our hard-earned money float down the drain.'

'If 'tis all the same with yarself, Clancy, I'll stay behind. I don't want to take my Colin along. 'T'd be a bit too much of an ordeal for him, what with his bad chest an' all.'

'Take him into Feacledown. We'll have to go that way anyway. We can leave him at Big Mary's,' said Pagga.

'She won't mind?'

'Naw, she'll be glad a the company.'

'That's settled then. Get yar coat on, Stallion.'

'Clancy! Do us a favour. Get a bottle out from yar cupboard

and we'll have a small measure each for good luck.'

'For the love a Christ, Pagga. 'Tis gone eleven. The shaggin' race is at three o'clock and we have forty miles a travellin' to do.'

'I'd like to do this proper,' pleaded Pagga.

'Jasus, Pagga, ya're slowly but surely flippin' yar top. Get the fuckin' bottle out but be quick about it!'

The four of them and O'Casey's son stood in the centre of Clancy's kitchen and charged their glasses. All eyes were on Pagga O'Leary.

'Men! The lot of us gathered here are desperate fellows indeed. My grandfather would have been proud of us, proud of the deeds that we're doin'. The path we've chosen is a dangerous one. A few months from now we fight the best cock in Ireland and with the grace a the Almighty we'll beat the fucker right into the earth. Money we're short. Money to adorn our Bulba's back as he steps into the ring to fight the fight of his life. We have aims to take that gold right out a the pockets of Ding Dong Brennan himself. And Tipperary Tim must be smilin' down on us now, the grand man's heart must be burstin' at the seams with overwhelming bouts a joy, for he must surely know that his children have the same stout hearts to take the biggest of risks in order to take all that life has to offer, and not be contented with halves or less. I give ya the two Tipperaries! The one that stands on the right-hand side of the throne of the Christ Himself, and the one that stands on the course at Aintree ready to run the race of its life for us!' Pagga's glass was in the air. 'The two of them!'

'The two of them!' cried Barra, Milo, Stallion and little Colin.


Lightning was the last name with which a sane man would have burdened Duffy's ten-year-old mare. A more appropriate name would have been Endurance or Stayer, for these were the inbred traits that had helped her to survive the hard graft required of her, year in and year out, as she toiled in front of her master to keep his few acres from going under. But Barra Duffy believed in the name he had given her, and never would admit to Lightning's lack of pace.

As soon as all five had mounted the cart, Barra brought the reins smartly down on the mare's flanks, and Lightning did what she thought was required of her and settled herself into a sensible trot. When she felt the second slap, she willingly took off with a fair amount of speed. But after six hundred yards her batteries started to run low and she resumed her trot until another niggling slap on her flanks suggested she should try again and, having a gentle and willing nature, Lightning tried again. She managed the best part of three hundred yards in top gear, then fell back into her trot, this time making it clear that the town of Westport would never be reached if her master persisted in bringing the reins into play. Duffy cursed her and his passengers cursed him.

With a gentle but sustained trot, Lightning had them outside Big Mary's cottage on the dot of 11.30. O'Casey waved his son goodbye and they were off again, with thirty-five miles of travelling in front of them. The drizzling rain had vanished by the time they came in sight of Lough Conn.

His heart singing with excitement, O'Casey pointed out that the signs were good. Over the brackish grey waters of the lake arched a magnificent rainbow.

'Jasus, but 'tis like the Madonna's own crown!' said Pagga, with awe in his voice. 'Ya're right, Stallion. Ya couldn't be righter. 'Tis a good sign from Tipp himself!'

It took an almost unendurable hour and a quarter over a bog of a road that was in dire need of repair before they left the shores of Lough Conn behind. But just as the lough ran out of sight they came to the Crossing, and on turning right their hearts lifted again. The last stretch was in front of them, ten miles to go and the road was fair and straight. There was no more talk of sending Lightning to the knacker's yard.

Pagga took his pipe from his coat pocket and cast his mind back over the week's events. On Monday Minno had died. On Tuesday the seanachie everyone had thought long since dead had returned. The old man had talked through all of Wednesday and Thursday, making their history live for them again. We'll not forget now, thought Pagga, his eyes watching the road. Ya came back, Gikitey, just in time, just when our minds were beginnin' to dim, when those tales, those grand grand deeds were beginnin' to fade. But don't worry old man, Pagga promised silently, we'll remember yar tellin's and we'll pass them on so they won't be forgotten. And now today, Friday, 30 March 1928 – a day when possibilities have come flying from out of nowhere. Ya pick up a paper, thought Pagga, see a horse and say that's the one for me!

The result of which is that ya've got three of yar friends, one cart, one horse and yarself out on the roads and headin' for the town of Westport to place yar money and theirs on yar, yar hunch. . . . Clancy'll have me fuckin' life if we don't come up trumps! Jasus, Tipp, if ya're lookin' down at meself from up above I hope ya're not laughin' yar head off. 'Tis yarself I'll blame when they start comin' at me for me pound a flesh!

Ding Dong Brennan's establishment was situated at the north end of town, just off the main street and halfway down a narrow lane. Two rundown cottages with their dividing wall missing provided the punters with sixty square feet of floor space. The sheets of the sporting dailies were pinned to the whitewashed walls, and there was a narrow shelf running the length of the back wall on which to lean as they wrote out on Ding Dong's chits the nags of their choice. The other twenty square feet was walled off by an antiquated pine counter that ran the width of the room. Behind the counter, sitting on barstools, were Ding Dong's two spinster daughters in front of their tills; behind them was the Scribbler's Dais, standing a good foot and a half off the floor. Just above the dais was a blackboard for the results of each race.

It was a drab and damp old ruin of a place, reeking of the stale but still pungent odours of tobacco, bad booze and human piss. Yet for all that, it was the most popular of the three bookie offices that the town of Westport had to offer. The reasons for this were twofold. Not only did Ding Dong Brennan give the best odds, but he was there at hand, ready to pay out, and could take the 6d and the £100 wagers and display his chunky wallet for all to see when the time came for him to cough up. All knew that Brennan wasn't a fly-by-night shyster. His business was his life. He was the first bookie proper to set up shop in the town, and he was still going strong after twenty-five years. Even when the really big longshots came in, the punter could stroll down to the twin cottages any time at his own convenience and Brennan would be waiting behind the counter with the man's winnings in his hands. There was no question of Ding Dong Brennan going out the back door when the happy punters came in the front with their winning chits in their hands.

''Tis the place!' cried Clancy, slightly shaken by the ride and grateful to be on the ground again, as they burst through the open doorway of Brennan's at two o'clock that afternoon.

'It's a fuckin' hovel!' moaned Pagga, looking round the room.

'A right fuckin' dump,' agreed Barra, following on O'Leary's heels.

'I get the feelin' a man could be taken for a ride good and proper in t'is place!' whispered Stallion, looking as though he was unsure as to whether or not he should enter.

Packed bodies squeezed and jostled against each other, with those punters nearest the wooden counter struggling to place their bets with the two ladies who sat aloof on their high chairs in front of their tills. The noise and the barter, the heavy fog of grey tobacco smoke and the undiluted tension of the atmosphere unnerved the four men.

'We can't be in the right place,' insisted Pagga. 'Who ever owns this place hasn't got two fuckin' bob to rub together.'

'This is Brennan's all right!' reassured Clancy. 'And I suggest, fellahs, we push our way forward and place our bet before 'tis too late.' With that he began elbowing a path through the throng, closely followed by Stallion, Barra and Pagga, who kept his hands clenched round the wad of fivers in his left trouser pocket.

'Excuse me, missus.'

De De Brennan, not one of nature's charmers, looked up from her till, giving Milo Clancy's warm smile a scowl in return. 'Yeah?'

'Forty-five pounds to win at a hundred to one on Tipperary Tim for the National, missus,' said Clancy.

'Oh yeah?' De De Brennan didn't so much as blink.

'Oh yeah,' Clancy replied, a little nervously.

'The odds are twenty-five to one.'

'The paper says a hundred.'

'Twenty-five to one,' snapped the prickly spinster. 'All long-shots for the National are twenty-five to one. Place yar bet or stand aside. There's others behind ya!'

'We'll see the fuckin' manager about that!' cried Pagga from behind Clancy's left shoulder.

De De Brennan's beady eyes zoomed in on O'Leary's scowling features. She was about to give him a taste of her famous whip-like tongue, but hesitated seeing the gunflint in the punter's eyes. 'Go down to the end of the counter and ask for Mr Brennan,' she told Clancy.

'Thanks, missus.' Followed by the other three, Clancy shoved his way down the length of the counter.

'Excuse me, sir!' he called to a huge-framed man sitting at a small desk with his back towards him.

'What's yar problem, sonny?' asked Ding Dong Brennan without turning round. His attention was concentrated on the mound of paper and chits before him.

'That fuckin' rap,' Pagga butted in before Clancy had a chance to speak. 'The one with the slit eyes and the face like the back a me cart won't give us the odds we're askin' for!'

Brennan rose slowly from his chair. He was huge.

'That rap ya're referrin' to, sonny, happens to be my daughter,' smiled Ding Dong, planting his vast bulk just two feet from Pagga's startled face.

Even O'Leary was clearly disconcerted, but Milo Clancy stepped in quickly before he had time to grovel an apology. 'This here, Mr Brennan, is Pagga O'Leary,' said Clancy smoothly. 'He's very careless with his mouth, and there's times when I think to meself that the good Lord dished him out a damaged brain.' There was no malice on the bookie's face, only a pleasant smile which served to unnerve Pagga even more. He was ready to make a break for the front door at any sudden movement from behind the counter.

'He certainly lacks manners,' replied Ding Dong.

'Apologize to the man, Pagga,' ordered Clancy.

'I apologize, Mr Brennan,' mumbled O'Leary.

'Louder, Pagga. The man can't hear ya,' urged Clancy.

'I heard him,' smiled Brennan, saving what was left of Pagga's face. 'Now what's yar problem, fellahs?'

'We want to back Tipperary Tim,' said Clancy. 'We want the price in the morning's paper, a hundred to one.'

'That's an outsider. Twenty-five to one is my tops.'

'But the paper states 'tis a hundred to one.'

'Aye, and no doubt ya'll get that price if ya head for Dublin or Limerick, or voyage across the water and place yar bet with the Liverpool bookies. . . . How much do ya want to put on him?'

'Forty-five pounds,' said Pagga, his confidence returning.

'Each way?'

Clancy shook his head. 'No. On the nose.'

'On Tipperary Tim?' exclaimed the bookie. 'Ya can't be

serious, gentlemen. Look, I can see ya're a gaggle a hicks just down off the mountains, so I'll give ya a bita advice. Go study the form and come back to me with somethin' that has a chance a runnin', and I'll see what I can do for ye.'

'If ya're so fired sure that our horse can't win, why won't ya give us a hundred to one and make yarself an easy forty-five quid?' asked Stallion.

'The top odds I give on anythin' is twenty-five to one. I have rules. If I don't stick by them, I'll go under.'

'Well, let yarself be an exception to the rule,' said Stallion. 'For once I'd like to see a bookie take a gamble, a true and proper gamble. Take our money and give us a hundred to one.'

'Fifty. That's it. Take it or leave it.'

'Ya're a dacent man, Mr Brennan, we'll take it,' said Clancy.

'Done,' Brennan smiled back at him. 'Get yarself a chit and write yar bet, and present it to me daughter up there. She'll take care of ya. And by the way,' he added, 'I'd like a word with yarself.'

Pagga saw his pointed finger, and felt a flutter of fear in his stomach as the smile evaporated from the bookie's face. 'Yes, Mr Brennan.'

'What's yar name?' asked Ding Dong with a dangerous look.

'Pagga O'Leary.'

'Well, Pagga O'Leary, when ya get to the counter I want you to apologize to me daughter. Understood?'

'Understood,' repeated O'Leary.

Clancy, Duffy and O'Casey stood near the open door, watching Pagga wait his turn in the queue. They saw him place the bet and exchange a few words with Brennan's gimlet-eyed daughter, but they all found something else to look at the moment he turned to walk back to them.

'Ya got it on, then?' asked Milo, toying with a cigarette butt at his feet.

'Aye.' O'Leary secreted the betting slip in the inside pocket of his overcoat. He could feel their embarrassment for him and cursed himself roundly for what Milo had rightly dubbed 'his careless mouth'.

'You got him at fifty?' asked Barra, looking over Pagga's left shoulder.

'Aye.'

'Pagga,' said Stallion, at last confronting O'Leary's shame-filled face. 'I've always been scared of freaks, especially when they come the size of Ding Dong Brennan. If the shoe had been on my foot, and if he was to tell me to fuck that harridan of a daughter, I'd have done it.'

'Yeah,' grunted O'Leary, eyes looking in a different direction. 'Now, lads, let's change the fuckin' subject. Clancy, ya said the fucker had a wireless. I've looked all around the joint and I'm damned if I can see it.'

'Arrah, Pagga, ya're blind.' Clancy pointed straight ahead. 'Cast yar eyes over the door.'

'It looks just like a wooden box.'

'That's just what it is,' laughed Stallion with relief. 'It's what's inside it that counts.'

'Why isn't the thing talkin' to us then?' asked Duffy.

''Tisn't switched on,' Clancy explained patiently.

'Well, somebody should get that fuckin' shagger over here to turn the fuckin' knobs,' blustered O'Leary, back to his old self.

Duffy smiled. 'Why don't you call him over?'

At a quarter to three, Ding Dong Brennan fiddled with the knobs on the wooden box and the thing crackled into life. A bland, soft voice announced the list of runners for the big race. It sang the praises of the five horses that seemed to have the race sewn up, but as for the rest of the runners, it failed to give any a mention. For a good ten minutes the voice summed up how the race would be run and then it died away. A few seconds later another voice took over. The race was about to begin.

# 8

On the other side of the Irish Sea, on the outskirts of Liverpool, forty-two horses were lining up behind the white tape. Above their heads, remnants of a March storm could still be seen as a mountain of ugly grey moved slowly southeastwards. The rain piddled down and a bone-chilling wind moaned across the flat acres of turf that was Aintree racecourse. Four miles, eight hundred and fifty-six yards of water-sodden terrain lay before the competitors in this year's Grand National. There were thirty fences to be jumped, a good half dozen of them enveloped in heavy mist.

It was two minutes past three. There had been two false starts, and another was clearly on the cards as two of the younger horses showed signs of panicking. But when the starter gave the order for the white flag to be raised, the flag went up, the forty-two runners came under orders, and with a great roar from the crowd the race was on.

Tightly packed, they flew almost as one over the first fence. Those who landed in front shifted the ground as their hooves beat the soft turf. Those behind got the spray of mud, water and grass, and jockeys dug their heads down, tightened the grip on their reins and steadied their mounts for the next obstacle.

At the fourth fence one of the horses (Amberwave – clearly fancied to run well) refused. Way back in the stands thousands of spectators cried out their alarm and disgust. Twenty seconds later their cries filled the air once more: Sprig, winner of the National the year before, came a cropper at the fifth.

The horses now approached Becher's Brook. To the horses it looked an inviting fence. What they saw before them was a hedge, three feet high, with a good lead up to it. What they didn't know was that there was a brook and a huge spread on the other side of it, and a drop of near on seven feet to the ground. They came at it tightly packed. A horse by the name of Koko jumped Becher's first. Its front legs clipped the fringe of the hedge. Koko plus jockey nosedived straight into the brook. Chaos enveloped the entire field. The animals soared and tried to scramble over the deadly barrier, horses and humans mixing in midair and crashing to the ground.

Eight horses, with riders still on their backs, fled like the wind from the savage brook and galloped into the country away from the eyes of the spectators in the stands and into the mists. A fine, deep-chested individual called Billy Barton, which had come all the way from America, led. Over the next couple of fences two of the horses and riders parted company with the diminished pack and crashed to the sodden ground. Only six were left, with the determined American still showing the way. Jockeys and horses peered desperately through the blinding drizzle and mist for the next fence. But the mist that stood right in front of their eyeballs was as thick as peasoup. Suddenly a large, upright hedge materialized. It was the one known as the Chair. They were only ten feet away and it was coming up fast. Frantic jockeys strained to steady their mounts. Two horses left the ground together and collided in the air. Screams of pain penetrated the mists. Three runners jumped cleanly and avoided the rolling horses and their terrified riders, but the last to jump stumbled on landing and the jockey joined his fellows on the ground.

The race was half over and only three horses out of forty-two were still running. Back in the stands the spectators had just spotted the pack emerging from the haze. The American was still showing the way. Five lengths behind him raced Great Span, second favourite for the race and the confident hope of tens of thousands of punters. Fifteen lengths behind, a tired and mud-spattered beast was trying its damnedest to keep the other two in its sights. . . .

Brennan's joint was in uproar. A hundred infuriated punters, including Brennan himself, were cursing and swearing something awful at the voice that crackled down from Ding Dong's radio. For the last five minutes the commentator had been giving them a detailed weather report for the city of Liverpool and its surrounding districts. It cut no straws with them that he had apologized time and again for the poor visibility. All Brennan's clients wanted at that moment was to get their hands on the

126

bastard with the squeaky voice and string him up. Canes and walking sticks walloped at Marconi's pride and joy, and fag butts, snot rags and copies of the *Sporting Daily* were missiled up at its impassive face.

Pagga O'Leary was showing all the signs of a man about to have an epileptic fit. 'Ya shaven bald ballicks you! Ya fucker a ducks! Get yarself a pair a fuckin' glasses and hang 'em on yar arse, for that's where yar fuckin' eyes are at, ya English runt!' he screamed at the top of his voice.

'*. . . and ladies and gentlemen there is still no sign of the runners as we wait for them to turn out of that difficult bend into the straight. . . .*'

'I declare to Jasus!' choked Pagga. 'That cunt is sightless! Sightless! The cunt of a fucker is sightless!'

'*Just a tick! Just a tick, ladies and gentlemen! Yes, yes here they come! They're out of the fog! I can see them! I can see them!*'

A roar of jubilation filled the establishment.

'*I can see two! They're neck and neck! They're neck and neck as they approach the second last fence. I've got my eyes peeled towards that wall of mist, ladies and gentlemen, but unless I'm very much mistaken there are no others left in the National. Hang on. Hang on. Just a minute . . . yes, another has just come into sight. But I can't make him out at the moment. Three horses, three horses, ladies and gentlemen, three out of forty-two are left to fight it out. In the lead by a nose is . . . is . . . it's Great Span! Great Span with, with the American. It's Billy Barton right there at his shoulder. And the third horse, fifteen lengths behind them is . . . it's Tipperary Tim, the outsider! The hundred to one shot! They're at the second last now. Span and the American are rising to it together. They're up and over. No, wait. Wait! Span is down! Great Span is a faller! The pride of America goes on alone but he's tired as he runs for the last. Tipperary Tim is battling on, trying to cut the ground that lies between them. The outsider is gaining. Ten lengths between them now, but Billy Barton is coming to the last. He's at it now! He's up, up . . . he's clipped it, he's stumbling, he's stumbling and he's down! He's down, he's on the floor and here comes the hundred to one shot! He takes the last now. He rises, he's up and he's over! He's the winner! The horse is exhausted but so is the jockey! They've got four hundred and ninety-four yards in front of them. Both are absolutely caked in mud. They can barely manage a trot, but they've nothing to beat. They're coming to post*'

*now. The jockey has dropped his hands. Ten yards! Five yards . . .
he's there, ladies and gentlemen! Tipperary Tim, the one hundred to
one shot, the no-hoper, has won the National! As I look back, I can
see that the American is being remounted. And he's on his way! An
unlucky loser! Victory snatched from his grasp at the very last fence,
but he has the honour of being the only other horse to complete this
gruelling course! The winner! Tipperary Tim! Ridden by the amateur
jockey, Mr Dutton, who is a solicitor by profession so I'm told. The
hundred to one shot!*

'Is he all right?' asked Barra, looking with concern at Pagga's
blood-drained face.

Milo towelled Pagga's face with his handkerchief. 'The poor
bastard has fainted.'

'Give him some air,' ordered Stallion, widening the circle
around the fallen hero.

'He'll be all right.' Milo patted the bleached cheeks.

Pagga's eyes fluttered and opened wide, to see a hundred faces
looking down at him. 'Jasus, I'm in hell!' he croaked.

'Ya only fainted,' Milo reassured him.

'I'm not dead?' asked Pagga, still not convinced.

'Ya're back with us now! It'd take more than a few horses to kill
an old fucker like yarself,' smiled Clancy. 'Tipp won, Pagga. He
won!'

'He did?' asked Pagga, his head just beginning to clear. And
then, as the race came back to him, exclaimed, 'He did, Milo. He
won! He won by a mile!'

Clancy and Stallion helped him to his feet, dusted him off and
checked him over. Brennan appeared with a chair in hand and a
glass of water. Pagga, insisting he was fine, refused the water, but
allowed himself to be coaxed into the chair.

'Give him a minute or two and he'll be fine,' beamed Brennan.

'Ah, sure, 'twas a great strain on the poor ol' devil.' Stallion
spoke with genuine admiration. 'The poor ol' bastard had to force
us at gunpoint to dig our hands into our pockets. He's some man
is O'Leary. Imagine the strain he's been under since he picked up
his newspaper this mornin' plus the fact that he had to stand here
under that fuckin' wireless and listen to every hoofbeat for the
best part a five shaggin' miles!'

'Aye, he deserves yar praise, I'm thinkin',' the bookie agreed.
'It must have taken a whole lota persuasion on his part for ye to

part with forty-five quid to place on an outsider.'

'And thanks to our friend here,' grinned Clancy, 'you owe us a few bob, Mr Brennan.'

'You have the look of a man who thinks he has just taken the devil himself to the cleaners,' grinned Ding Dong.

'Well, ya're about to empty yar pockets and dump over two thousand pounds in small change into our hands.'

'I think ya have been taken to the cleaners, Mr Brennan,' said O'Casey.

'Fellahs.' Brennan's smile never faltered. 'My two daughters have managed to take between them the best part of five thousand quid since my front door opened this mornin'. Look around ye. Do ya see as much as one punter with a smile on his face? Do you see any winnin' chits bein' shoved up me nose? Ye're the only ones holdin' the longshot.'

'Ye bastards can't be beaten. Ya've got the whole racket covered from floor to ceilin',' said Stallion bitterly.

'Well, let's say,' replied Brennan, 'that we're not in this business for charity.'

'Well, we'll not squibble, squawk or go into the pros and cons with the fairness or the unfairness of yar chosen profession, Mr Brennan,' said Clancy. 'We'll just take our winnin's and be on our way if 'tis all the same with yar good self.'

'Over to the counter with ya then, present yar chit and me daughter'll see ya right.' And Brennan returned through the throng to his desk.

'A bastard of a man, I'd say,' said Barra unemotionally.

'Sure, isn't he a bookie, Barra?' Stallion asked, his gaze following Barra's. 'Ya can't get any lower form a life.'

'Ah, for Christ's sake, Stallion,' Clancy interrupted. ''Tis the man's trade. He's payin' us out two thousand quid, ya know. That makes him okay in my book!'

Pagga, his senses almost painfully alert, watched De De Brennan's frosty face as she counted out one hundred and twelve £20 notes and one single tenner onto the counter. Then O'Leary picked up the neatly stacked pile, gave the woman his very best smile, pocketed his winnings, bade her a 'Good afternoon', and walked proudly to the doorway, joined by Barra, Stallion and Milo.

★

At nine o'clock that same evening, Big Mary was sitting by a blazing turf fire in her grandmother's chair. Across from her sat Colin O'Casey. He had his head buried in a comic, and Big Mary was staring into the rising flames. A shadow crossed the kitchen floor. Mary was just in time to see Minno's old black cat disappear under the kitchen table to bed himself down for the night. She watched as the bright emerald eyes looked back at her through the darkness. If the old woman had still been alive the cat would have been in front of the fireplace or snoozing snugly in the warmth of Minno's lap. But a new broom swept the floors now and the emerald eyes that peered out at Big Mary from under the safety of the table were full of suspicion, mistrust and caution.

Big Mary looked back into the flames, and allowed her mind to wander again. This was to have been her first night alone. But it wasn't so, for across from her was another human being, and the loneliness that was to be her constant companion had still not taken up residence in her grandmother's cottage. Another night of reprieve, but she was well aware that, come the morning, O'Casey would collect his son, and she would be alone again waiting for the merciless night to come. She drove her forebodings to the back of her mind and the flickering light from the fine peat fire danced in her eyes. Sure, isn't it the doin's of sin that's sinful and not the thinkin' of the doin's, she asked herself. Sure, 'tis no harm thinkin' and wishin', just as long as ya don't up and do it. But just supposin' Bango Cronin was to say to yarself, 'Go on, Big Mary, I give ya leave to squeeze and cuddle me small-framed arse.' Would ya? Of course I wouldn't. 'Twould be a mortal sin! Beside I don't like the bastard! He's got a big mouth and yar sin'd be on everyone's lips before the day was out. But Stallion O'Casey – now there's a lovely man, a quiet man. I could settle for him. If I were his, I'd work meself to death for him. He could take the whip to me and take the flesh off me bones, and I wouldn't mind. There's Biddy Dannagher, one husband already in the shaggin' earth and another in her bed, and what does she do but complain? Complains, I ask ya! He makes his rightful demands on her and she complains to Father Barry. Oh God in heaven, why can't she drop down dead? Then ya could deliver Tommo Dannagher to me. He'd never have to complain to me, for I'd love him, squeeze him and take his pains from him. 'Tisn't fair, sweet Jasus. I'm large, but I'm as soft and as tender as the next woman. Lay any man on top of me and I swear I'll hold him and never let him go! I know what they say, Lord. I'm the ugliest of women and I'm well outa the marryin' field, but produce the man, sweet Jasus, and I'll carry out all the rules. Ya can't leave me stranded like a barren ol' sow. Why in the blazes did ya put me on this earth if not to carry out me duties? I'll not complain. I'll never swipe and don the trousers. I'll stand behind him. I'll slide between cold sheets and warm our cot before he lays his body next to mine. I'll cool his tea in me own saucer before I bring it to his lips. The other night, Lord, while we were waking Minno, I heard Stallion O'Casey complain to me brother Pagga that his wife had gone and died on him because her child-bearin' hips were too small. If her hips had been that bit larger she would have given birth to a healthy boy and she probably'd have lived. My hips are large. I'm not pretty like she was, but I would have given him a son and the two of us would have watched our own flesh blossom into manhood. Stallion O'Casey would not have had his sorrow, and I'd have been fulfilled. Give me a man before 'tis too late, she silently pleaded. Give me one before I turn sour inside and inflict my poison on those around me.

Colin O'Casey finished his comic, and laid it down on his lap. 'I do declare, but ya're a devil when it comes to the readin', Colin,' said Mary affectionately. 'Will ya take a hot cup a milky cocoa before ya get yar head down?'

'No thanks,' smiled Colin. 'I'm still full to the top from yar fine stew, Big Mary.'

'Well, my grandmother's room is awaitin' yarself. Ya should find it comfy and warm. There's an extra layer a blankets and a hot-water bottle in there, but if ya still find it chilly call out and I'll bring along some more.'

'Thanks, but I'm sure I'll be fine. Are ya not takin' yarself off as well?'

'No, darlin'. I'll stay put for another hour or two. Yar da might turn up, though I doubt it. If they've won on that horse a theirs, then it's a certainty they'll stay put in Westport and drink the pubs dry.'

'And if they've lost, they'll drink Westport dry and Hollymount and Ballinrobe and every other town until the whole of County Mayo is an arid desert.'

'Well, they tell me yar da can do that and stay sober. But my brother, Clancy and Duffy turn into the devil's own clowns once they've swallowed their second pint. 'T'll be yar da that'll have to put them in the cart, and steer Lightning's head in the right direction. He'll have his work cut out, for when Barra Duffy gets drunk he takes it into his small head that his horse is a human being. 'Tis then he goes and fills Lightning's stomach with the same devil's brew that he's been drinkin'. There's no sorrier sight than to see that poor unfortunate beast trying to take herself and her master home after a night out on the tiles.'

'Yar jokin' me, Big Mary,' laughed Colin. 'Mr Duffy loves Lightning. He treats her like a thoroughbred.'

'I'm not joking,' said Mary. 'You should stand in front of me door of a Saturday night and take a look as Duffy's cart comes rollin' by the place. There's Barra asleep in the back of his cart and there's poor Lightning wanderin' all over the road, trippin' over herself as she tries to clear the fog from between her blinkers and get the both of themselves back to their beds. God knows what yar father is goin' to make of it all when he says "giddy-up" to Duffy's bag a bones.'

'Knowin' Da, he'll try and reason with the animal,' Colin said. 'Can't ya just see it! Da havin' a conversation with a drunken horse, with the three of them heaped in the back, and a policeman tappin' him on the shoulder.' Colin doubled over in his chair with laughter.

'And yar da's mouth wide open, lettin' in the night air, as he tries to explain.' Tears of mirth began to stream down Big Mary's face.

'I can just see Da now.' Colin spluttered out the words. 'He'll pull his shoulders back and try to look as upstandin' as the guard and say, "Well, 'tis like this, officer." And that's where he'll stop. His mind'll go blank, and he'll just gawk at the uniform.'

'And my brother Pagga'll jump down off the cart and swear blind in the officer's face that it was Lightning that forced the drink down all their throats!'

'And the guard'll go and arrest poor ol' Lightning.'

'And leave the four of them to pull themselves and the cart all the way home!' said Mary, and laughter overcame her.

They laughed until they were spent. 'Ya're fine company, Colin O'Casey,' said Mary, wiping the tears from her eyes. 'But 'tis the devil I'm thinkin' ya are, makin' me laugh 'til me sides are threatenin' to split at the seams.'

His pale cheeks reddened and his shy blue eyes dropped from her face. 'Ye must be great company for each other, yar da and yarself.'

'Aye. We have some great skits together.'

'He tells me ya're a great man for the stories.'

'I can tell a good cowboy story.'

'Well, ya'll have to collect yar thoughts together and tell me one,' said Mary as the first of the bongs from the clock on the mantelpiece rang out the hour of ten. 'God! 'Tis never the time. Off with ya to yar bed, ya scamer!' cried Big Mary, getting to her feet.

'But how about the story? I tell great stories.'

'Ya little devil. I'm on to yar ways,' smiled Mary. 'Yar da warned me about yar trickery and cunnin'. Off with ya now.'

'Another half hour. Da won't mind, honest he won't.'

'Hop it!' Mary pointed a finger towards her grandmother's bedroom door.

'Okay, okay,' conceded Colin, seeing he was beaten. 'Don't I get a goodnight kiss?'

'Oh, I suppose so.'

Big Mary's heart ached as she watched Colin's crooked little legs take him to bed. 'Goodnight, Colin, sleep well.'

He turned and smiled. 'Goodnight, Big Mary, thanks for havin' me, and thanks for the lovely stew.'

She sat back in the chair and let her eyes dwell on the flames in the hearth and her thoughts on what might have been and her conversation with God. If I had had him, he'd have been firm in body. His legs would have been straight, his chest as clear as a bell. He'd be tall and strong just like all the O'Leary men. But there he is sick and crookedy, and a fool would know by lookin' at the poor creature that he's not long for this world. 'Tis not fair. You made him so by bringing him forth from a woman that had no right to give birth. 'Tis not fair that I should fend for meself and bide the rest a me nights without a man to look after. What has Colin O'Casey ever done to yar great self? What have I done? Go on, tell me, what?

The clock ticked away on the mantelpiece overhead and Big Mary sat with her thoughts, broodings turning darker and more accusing as the night wore on.

★

133

Constable Dysart Kelly left Matt O'Grady's cottage at four o'clock that morning. He had just spent the last three hours drip-feeding the old farmer with glass after glass of whiskey. As Kelly mounted his bike he could hear the old fellah snoring away where he had left him beside the fireplace. Kelly freewheeled down the lane convinced that people only upped and died when he was on duty. O'Grady's son, a navvie working and living in Liverpool, had fallen off his scaffolding at three o'clock that day. Kelly came on duty at ten o'clock that night, and the wire was waiting for him. He had to bike a good two hours to get to the farmer's cottage and now, with a drizzling rain pissing all round him, he had to bike all the way back to his barracks in the town of Westport.

Chin buried in his chest, Kelly pumped grimly at the pedals. A slight incline swept him down a loose-gravelled lane and onto the main road. Lifting his arse off the seat he leaned well forward over the handlebars and tried to get up speed for the hill in front of him. It took him ten minutes of puffing and panting before he reached its summit. There he dismounted and got his wind back, cursing his sergeant roundly for sending him out into the middle of nowhere on such a cruel night.

He walked his bike. The backs of his legs ached and the cheeks of his arse felt raw. He was plodding along with ne'er a house or soul in sight when he heard far-off rumbling in the distance. Half a minute later and the lamp on his bike picked out a horse and cart, approaching at a decent trot. Kelly's attention was focused on the horse. The animal seemed to be making full use of the road. Jasus, he muttered to himself. What the fuck is on here? The beast was zigzagging from one side of the road to the other. 'Hey you! Stop!' called Kelly, taking evasive measures. 'Stop in the name of the law!' The cart kept on coming. 'Oh sweet Jasus!' It suddenly dawned on him that there was no driver. Kelly dropped his bike, and made a lunge forward for the bridle. 'Stop there, girlie! Stop! Stop!' The animal's speed did not slacken, and Kelly had to get the hell out of harm's way as nimbly as he could. The cartwheels sang out a metal requiem as they crushed his abandoned bike. 'Get back here, ya four-legged bastard!' bawled Kelly as his legs found new life: he ran like the wind, roaring as he went. And slowly but surely he gained on the runaway vehicle. 'Stop! Stop, I say! Ya're under arrest!' He was just an arm's length behind now. But Kelly stopped dead in his tracks as a head popped out of the cart and looked straight at him. 'Stop!' screamed Kelly, his voice hoarse.

'What's the matter?' a voice called back at him.

Kelly took up the chase once more. 'Ya're under arrest, ya bastard!'

'Who's under arrest?'

With a last supreme effort, the constable managed to grab hold of the woodwork.

'What's the matter, constable?' asked Stallion wearily.

'Stop this cart at once. You and this fuckin' horse are both under arrest!' panted Kelly.

'I'd stop it if I could, officer. I've been tryin' to stop the fuckin' nag since we left the town a Westport, but that bag a bones has a mind a its own. It's in a hurry to get itself home, I'm thinkin'.'

'Give me a fuckin' hand up!' gasped Kelly as he felt his legs begin to give way.

With much puffing, panting and pulling, O'Casey dragged the half-knackered constable aboard. Kelly slumped like a sack of spuds to the floor.

''Tis a fine bita runnin' ya be doin', sir,' remarked Stallion authoritatively. Kelly's chest heaved as he drank the night air into his aching lungs. 'But if I was you, constable, I'd treat yar legs with a little more kindliness. You don't look as if ya're cut out to run dark unlit roads in the middle of foul, wet nights.'

'Listen, ya bastard! Shift that fuckin' arse of yars, get it up there and bring that poxed animal of yours to a stop!'

'Now that, as I've said to yarself before, I can't do. Lightning is headed for home and she'll not stop 'til she sees the four walls of her shed.'

'Well, by the livin' fuck!' bawled Kelly, struggling to his feet, 'I'll soon put the brakes on the bastard!'

The constable stumbled forward and took the reins in his hand. O'Casey was treated to a litany of abuse as Kelly tugged at the bit. For a full five minutes Kelly fought his duel with the stubborn beast but to no avail. Lightning revved up more power from her batteries and zigzagged on for home.

'I told ya it wasn't any use,' grinned Stallion.

Kelly's face was apoplectic with anger. 'Well, don't just sit there, fuck head! That fuckin' animal of yours is gallopin' now! Do somethin'!'

Stallion rubbed the stiffness from his legs and sat himself down next to Dysart. 'Don't worry, constable,' he said cheerfully. 'She'll have us home and in our beds in no time, especially if she keeps up this gallop.'

The blood rushed to Kelly's gills, and in a voice that filled the night he roared, 'She might very well have ya in yar fuckin' bed before the shaggin' night is over, but my fuckin' bed happens to be twelve miles in the opposite direction!'

'Then ya had better jump off.'

'And break my fuckin' neck? Slow the bastard down!'

'She'll slow down in her own good time, officer. She'll not keep this bita malarkey up for long,' Stallion reassured him reasonably.

Lightning tore them on for another quarter of a mile until her batteries showed signs of running down. She slowed to a trot and then, as if a heavy blanket of fatigue had enveloped her, she pulled up and came to a complete and apparently permanent stop. Kelly leaped down from the cart, figuring the beast would stoke up steam and drag him off again to God-knows-where. Stallion stayed put, lit himself a fag and watched the constable run a check on Lightning.

'This horse of yours isn't sober,' gasped Kelly, his face recoiling from Lightning's breath.

'Ten outa ten for acute observation.'

'She has drink taken!'

'Aye, that she has,' smiled Stallion. 'A bucketful of Westport's finest stout.'

'Then if that's the case I'll have her name and yours, too,' snapped Kelly, his left hand fumbling for his notebook.

'Her name is Lightning.'

'And yours?'

'George Washington.'

'Right!' said Kelly, scribbling the names. 'Ya're both under arrest.'

'But I doubt very much if we'll be accompanying you to the station,' said O'Casey smoothly. 'Lightning has had her little gallop for the night. She'll not move an inch now 'til the dawn comes up. I think she's takin' it into her head to do the sensible thing and sleep it off.'

But Lightning had had her breather. Her head lifted, she saw the road in front of her and, in less time than it would take to pull a pint, she decided that she had best be off again.

'Stop! Stop!' shouted Kelly. 'Stop that horse!'

O'Casey looked back over his shoulder at the struggling, stranded constable. 'Goodnight to yarself, constable,' he called out pleasantly. 'Ya can do yar duty and arrest the both of us when we all meet up at Saint Peter's gate!'

'I'll get ya, Washington!' Kelly's voice was already getting faint. 'I'll get ya and yar bag a bones if 'tis the last thing I do!'

'Did I hear voices?' O'Leary's head popped out from under a sheet of tattered old canvas near the back of the cart.

'Naw, Pagga, ya didn't,' replied Stallion. ''Twas just an officer who couldn't make up his mind whether he wanted a lift or not. Go on back to sleep. Lightning'll have us home soon.'

Half an hour later Lightning stopped at the crossroads. She shook her blinkered head and awaited instructions. Stallion took up the reins and steered her to the left. The rain still piddled down, but it was light and fell like a heavy mist. O'Casey looked up at a pitch-black sky. 'Not a star or moon in sight to show the wanderer home and safely to his bed. Ya're a clever ol' thing, Lightnin' Duffy, and there's no doubtin' that. The stars and the moon can go and die as far as yarself is concerned. As long as ya've got yar nose to guide ya that's all ya care about.' O'Casey looked warmly at the nodding head of the horse. Duffy's nag was confining her gentle trot to the middle of the road. 'Ya'll have yarself a humdinger of a hangover come tomorrow mornin', horse,' grinned O'Casey.

But only two miles from Big Mary's cottage the rain started to bucket down and a hard west wind lent it a biting chill. O'Casey cursed aloud. 'T'is is one fuckin' county I'll be glad to be rid of,' he said to the night. 'Oh ye gods, drive this fuckin' poxed weather from the lands a Mayo. My Colin stares it in the face every day, and mocks it and defies it. Give me my son's faith. Tell me that I shouldn't worry, that this winterland has no intention of claimin' him. Put me frantic soul at rest.'

An hour later and Lightning was bedded down in the old shack at the back of Minno O'Leary's cottage. Milo, Barra and Pagga were cuddled up and sleeping it off in front of Big Mary's fireplace. And Stallion O'Casey was sitting at the table while the woman of the house rustled him up some of her piping hot stew.

'They're a shame on the sweet lands of Mayo,' said Big Mary, ladling her succulent cooking onto his plate.

'Ah, well, Big Mary,' answered Stallion slowly, looking at his three outstretched companions sprawled in front of the fire, 'some men can take all ya wish to pour down their throats and some can't. Some heads swoons and sways under the vapours of the pisons we inflict upon ourselves. My old head is immune to any liquid concotion ya care to throw at me. I guess I'm lucky, that's all.'

'Well, how about a glass of Bridget O'Dea's best to wash down me cookin', then?' smiled Mary.

'Yar cookin' doesn't need washin' down, Big Mary, but I'll take ya up on yar kind offer all the same.'

O'Casey watched her stoop to open the bottom half of her Welsh dresser and retrieve the bottle. God, that's a powerful woman, he thought. I wonder what's she got against men. She should have at least a half dozen babies hangin' from those breasts of hers. His eyes dropped away from her and he concentrated on the stew as she turned around and came back to the table. 'God, Mary, but this is grand! I could eat it 'til it comes out me ears.'

'One a me few skills, Stallion. I can cook.' Mary sat down opposite him and poured two good measures into her finest glasses. 'To Tipperary Tim,' she toasted. 'The horse this time, not the man.'

'To the darlin' horse,' said O'Casey, lifting his glass. The tiredness of his long journey home disappeared as O'Dea's finest slid smoothly down. 'Well, Big Mary, ya're a rich woman. Two hundred and fifty pounds to call yar own. 'Twas shocked indeed I was when Pagga told me he had five quid of your money to place on that four-legged beast. I thought women had more sense.'

'Oh, I have the odd flutter from time to time. But don't get me wrong. 'Tisn't every day Big Mary goes out and lays a fiver on her fancy. But that brother a mine was so fired sure that his hunch had a chance that he bamboozled the money outa me grasp, and was out the front door before I had time to reconsider.'

'What are ya goin' to do with yar windfall?'

'Put it in me tea caddy.'

'Ya're not goin' to give it back to Pagga to reinvest?'

'Like hell I am. It can cover itself with dust can that windfall. I'll not touch a penny 'til I have to.'

'Well, I'll not prise it outa yar grasp, but ya should at least consider lettin' a little of it ride on Bulba's back.'

'No, that I'll not be doin'. Ya're makin' a big mistake if ye think that ye can beat Kusthi's cock. Come June, Tilla Kusthi will be laughin' all the way to the bank and ye'll be all contemplatin' suicide because of yar own stubborn daftness.'

'Well, ya know me feelin's on that subject,' said O'Casey. 'Bulba can't lose.'

'And there isn't a man or a woman in the whole of this world that can persuade ya otherwise,' added Big Mary with a smile. 'Well, I wish ya luck.'

But O'Casey didn't seem to be listening. 'Tell me somethin', Big Mary,' he finally said. 'How is it that the granddaughter of Tipperary Tim isn't married?'

'Eligible men are scarce around these parts.' She looked, but she could see no mockery in his expression. 'The best of them leave as soon as they've saved enough money, for Canada, Australia, America and any other place that can give them a better chance in life.'

'And ya're choosey. What's left isn't right for yarself?'

'Yes, I'm choosey,' said Mary.

'Well, if ya ever pick out a buck for yarself he'll be a very fortunate man indeed. Ya got a lot to offer. Cookin' that can't be surpassed, fine little cottage that's all yours, dacent conversation and the build of body to give him fine healthy sons,' smiled Stallion.

'Ya're a sweet and grand man, Stallion O'Casey,' blushed Big Mary, bringing the glass to her lips.

'Just givin' ya some truth that's rightfully yours, that's all.'

Blushing like a sixteen-year-old, she got up from the table and made a fuss of clearing away O'Casey's empty plate. ''Tis time I was headin' for me bed.'

''Twas dacent indeed of ya to wait up for us.'

'Don't mention it, Stallion. Ya're more than welcome.' Mary kept her back to him as she dumped his plate and the empty glasses into a basin on the lip of the dresser. 'I'm off to me bed.

Ya'll be comfortable by the fire, but if ya need an extra blanket ya'll find some in Colin's room.'

'Goodnight to yarself, Big Mary.'

'Goodnight to yarself, Stallion O'Casey.'

Their eyes met and the smiles fell away from both their faces. 'Ya're a fine big woman,' whispered Stallion.

'And ya're a grand, grand man, Stallion O'Casey.'

Her bedroom door clicked shut. Ya're a fine big woman, he repeated, lighting up a cigarette. But what ya don't need now, Stallion O'Casey, is complications. Ya must use the weeks that are given to ya to prepare Bulba for his moment a truth. With a heavy sigh, he lifted himself out of his chair and laid himself down next to Clancy by the fire. But his mind was restless, moving from thoughts of Colin and the heartless weather, to thoughts of Mary's grand softness and Tipperary Tim.

It was not until dawn that his eyelids dropped and stayed shut, and a dreamless sleep enveloped him.

# 9

Taurus Bulba was strained and nervous as he pecked his way along the mesh fencing nearest the cliffs. He knew that the old hen was following along just behind him, but he gave her little or no regard. The rest of his brood were scattered about the place, pecking and cackling to another rain-sodden day. Only Bulba sensed the tension in the air, and when he reached the end of the fenced wall, he crowed out his worry. Through the mesh wire in front of him was another enclosure, fenced off just like his own but much smaller. It had not been there the day before. It bothered him greatly, so much so that he called out his alarm once more. The old hen shuffled alongside, looked through the wire, turned her head away and pecked back the way she had come. But Bulba stayed put. Every now and again his beak pecked irritably at the mud.

He had been carrying his black mood with very little grace for all of two weeks now, ever since the strangers had come to live in the house. Instead of the man coming through the gate each morning, one of the strangers would appear in his place. It filled him with an unsettling feeling. The eyes that had watched Bulba over the past two weeks were the eyes of a stranger. Every time that Bulba lifted his head, the stranger seemed to be there. And his presence was stifling.

A young, grey-speckled pullet was feeling very adventurous that morning. Three days and three nights of constant rain had washed all the goodness to the surface of the sweet earth at her feet. And inch by inch, she pecked up her way closer to Bulba, whose temper now was razor sharp. Her carelessness dawned on her too late as her beak probed the ground just two inches from Bulba's arse. And then suddenly she was face to face with the indignant cock, who had murder in his eyes. A squawk of fright barely escaped her throat as she watched the cock soar. She stood frozen to the spot, and when Bulba crashed down upon her fledgling body, the air whistled from her tiny lungs. Spite and malice were etched on Bulba's face as he watched the half-flattened creature crawl painfully from beneath his huge weight, and away to safety.

Stallion O'Casey had watched the cock's attack, and noted the way Bulba's deadly talons had folded, sparing the pullet from certain death. He lit a cigarette and waited for Bulba's gaze to focus on him. 'Yeah, Bulba,' said O'Casey aloud as he saw the cock's frame stiffen momentarily. 'Yeah, ya're a sane ol' creature and that's a fact. Ya're a contented bastard, livin' yar life nice and easy lookin' after yours, upholdin' yar dignity and layin' down yar law with true justice and reason. But ya're no good to me that way, Taurus Bulba. I have to get rid of yar sense of fair play. I must tamper with yar reason and yar contented calm if ya're to be any use. I don't suppose ya'll be thankin' me for it but it has to be that way for ya're my ticket outa here.'

'Ya'll be makin' that cock as self-conscious as a naked virgin if way ya keep ogling it, Stallion,' said O'Leary, joining O'Casey at the wire.

'Nonsense. That cock laps up all the attention that's on offer around here.'

'Well, today is his day.'

'Aye,' said O'Casey. 'When Clancy gets back we get down to it.'

'And Bulba gets the very best pickin's from yar brain.'

'But I doubt if he'll be thankin' me for it.'

'But when ya're finished with him he'll be the best rooster in the whole of Ireland, right?'

'Dead right, Pagga.'

'I'm looking forward to seein' yarself at work. They say that the tinkers' ways as to the trainin' of their birds reap them large profits, but that it does very little for their cocks. The story is that the tinkers rob the very souls of their champions. Is that the way it is, Stallion?'

'Cocks don't have souls, Pagga. They're animals, animals that were put on this earth to fight. 'Tis in their blood. My method of trainin' is the tinkers' way. All I do is to turn fighting cocks into murderin' weapons a death. To kill without hesitation or fear, to go in and slash, tear, rip and scissor and to lay their victim low as quickly as possible.'

'Milo has been a bit soft with Bulba. His trainin' has been tender to say the least. He's been pampered and mothered by us all ever since he broke free of his shell.'

'Well, Milo knows what we have to do now,' said Stallion. 'Ya'll not have any qualms about me methods, I hope? It has to be done my way. If we're to sink Kusthi's devil into the earth we're goin' to have to rid Bulba of his quieter ways, send his brain around the bend and drive any of the pet that's left in him from his fightin' carcass. No qualms, Pagga.'

'Qualms! Never a one!' replied O'Leary, managing a half smile. 'After all, he's just a cock. No, Stallion, ya got yarself a free hand as far as meself is concerned. 'Tis just that I was wonderin' how our Barra will take it. He treats that cock as if it were a human being.'

'Barra treats every livin' thing as if it were human,' said O'Casey. 'He feeds that horse of his whiskey. His own pigs that he rears with the sweat of his brow he won't slaughter to fill his belly. He sells 'em but he won't bring himself to take the stabber to their throats. 'Tis time I'm thinkin' that yar Barra grew up and found himself a bita sense.'

Pagga sighed. 'We've been tryin' to make him do that for years.'

Through the mist Duffy's old horse and cart laboured up the steep old coast road towards the gravelled pathway that led to the back door of the cottage. Clancy and Duffy sat hunched against the continuous drizzle.

'Jasus, but they're lookin' like a couple a drowned rats,' said Stallion.

Pagga had already begun to move. 'I'll pop inside and put the kettle on.'

'What kept ya?' smiled Stallion, as Barra brought Lightning to a halt.

'That blasted road. It's got more potholes and puddles on it than a fuckin' sieve,' grumbled Milo, jumping down from the cart.

'That and the fact that we had to haggle with that cunt Connarty Quinlaven for the best part of an hour,' added Barra.

'And what kind of a deal did ya get?'

'Four cocks. A fiver for the lot.' Clancy wiped the rain from his face.

'Not bad.'

'Not for the mangy specimens we got,' snapped Duffy.

'Their quality doesn't matter, Barra.'

'Wait 'til ya have a look at the one we brought home with us.'

Clancy fetched a slatted cage covered with a potato sack from the back of the cart, and with little ceremony placed it on the wet ground. Sinking to his haunches, he said, 'Gentlemen, behold! What yar eyes are about to receive will make them dance with joy.' And whipped away the sacking.

'Jasus wept!' said O'Casey.

The cock was a speckled grey affair, past it in every sense of the word. His fighting beak was stunted, crooked and chipped so badly at its point that as a weapon it was useless. It was clear even to an untrained eye that the bird's left wing had been smashed at least a couple of times during its fighting career, for the frame of the wing sat badly and crooked against the cock's shoulder. His proud chest was bare, devoid of plumage. The pink-white skin showed a lattice work of scar marks, and at least two needed stitching.

'Christ, lads,' said O'Casey. 'I asked for rakes, birds that had seen out the last of their fights, not for an empty bag with a few feathers stuck on it.'

'Correct me if I'm wrong, Stallion,' smiled Clancy, 'but didn't ya tell meself and Barra here to go out and get four cocks that had nuttin' left in them, nuttin' left to offer? Didn't ya instruct us to pick them up for a fiver and not a penny more?'

'But . . . but for Christ's sake, Milo!'

'But shit, Stallion,' Clancy interrupted. 'We did what ya told us to do.'

'But just look at the poor ol' creature.'

'It's healthy.'

'I can verify that fact,' added Barra, presenting the smallest finger on his left hand for O'Casey to inspect. 'The bastard took a fuckin' chunk outa it as I tried to coon him into his box.'

'Well, let's hope he lasts more than a couple a days.' O'Casey rose wearily from his haunches.

'I think he'll hold out a bit,' judged Clancy confidently.

Stallion looked at the scrawny cock and sighed. 'Pagga has got the kettle on. We'll have a cuppa before we start.'

'No,' said Clancy, picking up the cage. 'Let's put him in the new run first. 'T'll only take a minute. Let's see what Bulba makes of him.'

Bulba stood like a statue at the far end of his run, looking at the three of them with fire in his eyes. They had to wait a full minute before he turned his back and resumed his pecking. 'Now!' ordered O'Casey. Clancy lifted the cage door, and the rake strutted forward into the pound.

The speckled grey kept his head down stabbing the earth, relieved to be foraging for the sweet titbits that the soaked ground had to offer. He was completely unaware of what was going on around him. When the quiet of the April morning was shattered by an ear-piercing battlecry, the old cock's head shot up, and panic-stricken eyes swivelled just in time to see Taurus Bulba charge. There was no time to run. The rake dug his claws into the soft earth and prepared to defend himself. As Bulba came within range, he crowed out his own battlecry and sprang forward, his old but powerful legs propelling him off the ground, his damaged wings blasting at the air to meet the young upstart eye to eye and beak to beak. His powerful talons jutted forward ready to gaff and slash. Then the murderous face, powerful splaying wings and snapping beak of his enemy were in his sights. Both birds screamed out their rage as the mesh fencing broke their murderous charge, and they dropped with little dignity to the ground on opposite sides. Bulba landed cleanly, but the rake fell on his side and squawked with pain as his dickity left wing bent back beneath his weight. But he sprang to his feet, brimstone eyes fixed on his enemy, who stood stock still on the other side of the fence. The rake lifted his warlike head and surveyed the towering mesh that separated the combatants. With a maddened crow, he took off, scrawny neck stretched to its fullest and wings flailing the air. But the fence soared with him all the way. His climb died, and seven pounds of flesh dragged him back to earth. The old cock panicked and grabbed out for support. But his talons were trapped in the fencing. With furious cackles tearing from his throat, he hung suspended on the wire, wings flapping helplessly.

Bulba seized his opportunity. He measured the distance and his target. As his climbing head came level with the rake's, Bulba's beak bulleted through the opening in the mesh, but too late. The rake whipped his head back out of harm's way. Had Bulba's beak made contact the old cock would have been minus an eye. Pure rage flooded through the struggling bird on the wire and his crowing echoed round the yard. Bulba fluttered back to the ground, still seething at the speckled grey intruder. Both birds were oblivious as the gate in the new pound opened and the three men came dashing in on the melee.

Milo, Pagga and Stallion sat, mugs of tea in hand, while Barra and O'Casey's young son stood by the open door keeping an eye on the two cocks that were still hell bent on battle.

'What are they doin' now?' asked Pagga.

'Is it deaf ya're?' snapped Barra. 'They're seranadin' each other, whisperin' sweet nothin's in each other's earholes!'

'We'll have to get used to the racket,' said Stallion. 'For the next two weeks. After tha', we'll take the chains off Bulba, spike him up and allow him to kiss the speckled grey.'

'And the reason for chainin' Bulba up in the first place?' asked Clancy.

'To keep him on the ground. That's where his best fightin' is done, ya said so yarself, Milo. We must improve on that fine fightin' quality of his.'

'And what about his soar? We don't neglect that, surely?' interrupted Pagga.

'We'll take care of that later. Kusthi's cock is the best flyer I've ever clapped eyes on. If Bulba tries to match him on stepping into the ring, it'll be over for the lot a us. It's important to do everything right over the next two weeks. This is the groundwork, fellahs. If 'tis not done right the fuckin' house'll fall down.'

Pagga smiled. 'Ya're the boss.'

'That ya are,' agreed Clancy, heaving himself out of his chair.

'We're ready then,' said Pagga, rubbing his hands in anticipation.

'Jasus, ya're in a hurry,' said Stallion. 'I haven't finished me tea yet.'

''Tisn't expensive whiskey ya're holdin' in yar claws. Drain yar mug and let's be havin' ya,' grinned O'Leary.

'Arrah, Pagga, that's what I like to see. Enthusiasm, by the bucketful.'

146

'Best make hay while the sun shines,' Clancy added.

'Sun! What sun?' T'as rained every day since I got to this godforsaken place,' sighed O'Casey, getting to his feet.

'Make way! The wise men cometh,' chanted O'Leary as he led them to the front door, and looking down into little Colin's face he added, 'Are ya goin' to come and watch this genius of a father of yours show us Mayo men the right and proper way to prepare our darlin' cock for the ring?'

'Like hell he is,' said O'Casey abruptly. 'You stay put. Ya can see what goes on from here.'

'Ah, Da! 'Tisn't fair,' moaned Colin.

'Let the mite come with us, Stallion,' pleaded Pagga. 'What harm has a drop of half-baked rain done anybody?'

'When it rains, Colin,' said O'Casey, ignoring Pagga completely. 'When it rains, what happens?'

'I stay put,' mumbled the boy.

'Got it in one.' Stallion's face broke into a smile. 'Stay put, and don't have me take the stick to yar arse.'

'Say a Hail Mary that the rain might stop, then ya can come and watch,' whispered Pagga, as he patted the boy on the head and followed the rest out into the yard.

'Okay, Barra. Go get Bulba and bring him into the new pound,' ordered Clancy, peering through the wire at the old cock still crowing out his challenges to his enemy on the other side of the boundary.

'Now, there goes a man that hasn't had much to say for himself since he took his arse outa bed this mornin',' commented Pagga, as Duffy walked towards the gate of the old pound.

'Leave him be, Pagga,' said Clancy. He could see the seething fury on Barra's face as he opened the gate and stepped into Bulba's domain. 'Kid gloves, Pagga. The whole lota us are goin' to handle our Barra with kid gloves. Do I make myself clear?'

O'Leary caught the look in Clancy's eyes. 'As a bell, Milo. As a bell.'

Pagga O'Leary had the grey-speckled cock secure in his arms. Twenty feet away, Clancy, Duffy and O'Casey were busy preparing Bulba for his ordeal. Clancy had Bulba nestled in his arms while O'Casey appraised the bird with an expert eye. 'He's sound, Milo. Let's get the ball rollin'.'

'Okay, Barra, slip on the corset.'

'I will not,' answered Barra, his chin on his chest, eyes glued to his feet.

'I said, slip on the corset,' repeated Clancy calmly.

'I'll not do it, Milo Clancy. I'll feed Bulba, I'll clean the shit from his roost, I'll handle and fetch him to and fro for yees, but I'll have no part in degradin' our Bulba by trappin' and bindin' down his wings in that foul contraption so as he can be fed to that rooster.' Barra's voice had been calm and steady and he had managed to lift his head from the ground, but Milo Clancy had not lifted his eyes to return his stare.

'I'll do it,' volunteered Stallion.

'Ya'll not,' replied Clancy evenly. 'Barra Duffy is the handler here. 'Tis his job. He'll do it.'

'I won't.' Barra's voice was also quiet.

'Go into the house, Barra. Stay there 'til I come,' Clancy commanded, lifting his head to meet Barra's unflinching eyes. 'Stay put 'til I come.'

'Understood, Milo,' said Barra, and handing the elastic corset to Stallion he turned his back on Clancy and headed for the gate.

'He has a soft and gentle nature, Milo. Go easy on him,' said Stallion.

'He's a fool!' hissed Milo, the fire in his eyes burning into Barra Duffy's retreating back.

'All the same, take it easy with him. Kindness will always get the best results from simple souls with their gentle ways.'

'Come on, Stallion!' Irritation hardened Clancy's voice. 'Get this bird laced up and let's get on with it, for the love a Christ!'

As Milo cooed loving words to his Bulba, O'Casey, with the utmost care, slipped a band of broad elastic over the bird's head and down over his shoulders. A full minute passed with Stallion adjusting and manoeuvring the band into the right position. On O'Casey's instructions, Clancy loosened his hold on the nervous cock and they watched as Bulba tried to free himself of the corset that trapped his wings.

'It's not too tight?' asked Milo with concern.

'No, just right,' reassured Stallion. 'Okay, Milo, off with yarself to the gate and await me instructions.'

Hands on hips, O'Casey stood in the centre of the yard and studied the two men and the birds which they held at the ready. 'Now listen carefully, the both of yees. When I say go, release yar charges but stay exactly in the positions that ye are in now. If ya hear me call out the word "collect", move in straight away, pick up yar cocks and return to yar startin' posts. Is that clearly understood?' They nodded. 'Okay . . . now!'

Taurus Bulba took six lightning strides before he realized his wings were bound. He felt that his inner balance had gone totally haywire and panicked as he tried with all his might to free his wings. On the seventh stride Bulba keeled over on his side like a gutted ship; his fury-filled eyes caught a glimpse of grey-speckled wings descending towards his exposed belly. Instantly alive to the danger, Bulba managed to roll like a ball to his left out of harm's way. The thud of talons biting the soft earth and a crow of frustration smote Bulba's ears as he struggled to his feet. But he had lost sight of his aggressor, who had leaped to the attack once more. Bulba pivoted his body a full half circle, just in time to see the rake's swooshing descent. Using every muscle of his powerful legs, he bolted out of danger. But his fleeing arse was hooked by both talons of the speckled grey. Bulba smelled the stench of impending death but kept his legs pumping forward. And with the old rake crowing on his back, he ran until he stumbled and nosedived into the earth.

'Collect!' shouted Stallion, but there was no need. Pagga and Milo were already sprinting for the centre of the yard.

Clancy's nervous hands tried to soothe their squawking champion, while O'Casey examined Bulba's arse.

'What's the damage?' cried Pagga from the other end of the yard, where he held Bulba's opponent in a vicelike grip.

'Just stay put and keep yar fuckin' mouth shut!' Clancy bawled back at him.

A minute later, Stallion gave the signal once more. Pagga and Clancy released their birds. And soon they were doing minor repairs on Bulba's now very tender posterior.

The third time, Taurus Bulba stayed put on the earth as his master's hands left his body. He stayed put and watched the rake launch into the air for a killing downward swoop. Bulba's body remained as fixed as stone. He seemed to know everything there was to know concerning that one fearful second of time between life and death, to be instinctively aware of its many divisions, fractions and minute subfractions. And so he hopped out of death's way to safety. Yes, he hopped. He didn't flee to the other end of the yard. He simply hopped and turned. The rake's landing was poor, and Bulba was in and on him like a bat out of hell. His beak was like a jack hammer as it pumped and pumped at the old cock's face. His talons slashed and tore like a chainsaw at the rake's exposed undercarriage. He could smell and taste his victory, but seconds away from total triumph hands reached down and dragged him from his prey. Pure indignation and explosive fury engulfed Bulba's entire being, and as the hands lifted him upwards and the smiling face of the man came into his view the cock struck out. A split second later Bulba was dropping back to earth with human flesh pincered in his victorious beak.

By noon, the rain had stopped and the great sheet of light grey cloud that draped the sky from horizon to horizon had vanished, leaving in its place strips of fluffy white which seemed to be stuck to the light blue of the sky. In the new pound, Taurus Bulba pecked at the rich soft earth, while on the other side of the wire his brood cackled nervously among themselves about the morning's events. Now and again, Bulba would lift his head and a stricken crow would hang in the windless air. But the cock's great rage had gone. His peace and harmony had been restored. The intruder had been removed and was no longer in his sights. The fence that barred him from his kith and kin was his only enemy now, and the cock knew it was no use pitting his anger and strength against that towering obstacle. Yet from time to time he would walk the fence from end to end as if seeking out its weakness.

Milo Clancy's kitchen reeked of surgical spirit and iodine. On the wooden table was the speckled grey, and holding the cock fast was Barra Duffy, while Stallion O'Casey worked carefully with needle and thread to stitch together two deep and bloody gashes on the upper part of the cock's right leg. Sitting by the blazing fire on Clancy's best chair was the stricken Pagga, his neck craning up at the rafters. And standing over him was Clancy himself, holding a steaming hot dishcloth to O'Leary's left cheek.

'Clancy! We need a hand here!' cried Stallion as he pierced the needle through the rake's bloody skin.

Clancy abandoned his patient and went to O'Casey's assistance. While Stallion secured the half dozen stiches with a double-barrelled knot, Clancy poured a quarter bottle of iodine into the sewn-up wound. It took all of Barra Duffy's strength to keep the cock fastened to the table. At last O'Casey stepped back to appraise his surgical skills. Apart from the slashed leg, the rake was also sporting a few minor cuts to his underbelly, the crown of his head had a dozen or more peck marks which looked worse than they were because of the spillage of blood. The rake had been to the wars but he was still very much alive.

'Let him go, Barra,' said Stallion at last. Duffy quickly withdrew his hands and stepped back. The cock fought his way to his feet. Gingerly he lifted his damaged leg off the table and arched it back towards his rear, then he placed it solidly on the surface of the table and crowed out his relief.

'Not a bad ol' cock is that,' smiled Stallion as he watched Duffy gather the bird into his arms.

'Bullshit!' Duffy snapped. 'Even with our Bulba bound, chained and served to him on a platter he still couldn't manage to put up a show!'

'Aye, ya're right. I at least expected him to match Bulba on those terms,' conceded O'Casey gently.

But Clancy wasn't interested in comparisons. 'Take the rake out and put him in the old pound, and tell us how Bulba reacts to it all,' he ordered.

Duffy raised his chin with pride. 'They'll be no need. Ya'll hear Bulba's protests from where ya're standin', Milo Clancy,' he replied.

It took a great deal of persuasion to get O'Leary to remove the dishcloth from his wounded face and take a look at himself. Clancy held a mirror in front of Pagga's nose. 'Oh, but yar fuckin' beautiful looks are gone, O'Leary,' he teased. 'The biddies'll never again look in your direction.'

''Tis nuttin' but a small hole,' Stallion consoled him. 'Hardly noticeable to the naked eye.'

'A small hole it might be to yarself, Stallion O'Casey, but to me 'tis a bita me flesh gone missin' and down that fucker's throat!'

'Ah, ya'll live! The bleedin' has stopped. Ya've nuttin' to worry about, man,' Clancy chided him irritably, picking up the iodine.

'Ya can put that fuckin' bottle away, Milo Clancy!' Pagga's

head rammed onto the backrest of the armchair as Clancy leaned in on him.

'Hold him fast!' ordered Clancy. Stallion was quick off the mark. Before Pagga had time to move, he had his shoulders pinned to the backrest, allowing Clancy to pour the remainder of the bottle on O'Leary's wound. Pagga kicked and raged, but Stallion held him fast. 'Are ya okay, Pagga?' he asked, when the struggling had ceased.

'He's okay,' said Clancy with little sympathy in his voice as he put the cork back in the bottle.

'All right, am I?' hissed Pagga through clenched teeth, pure murder in his eyes. 'Where is the king of cunts? Where the fuck is he?'

'Where's who?' asked O'Casey, taken aback as Pagga jumped up out of his chair with the devil's own wrath in his look.

'The cunt Duffy, that's who!' For if it weren't for Barra refusing to do his job, Pagga wouldn't have hurt either his body or his pride.

'Out in the yard.'

'Right!' muttered O'Leary. 'I'm goin' to have that bastard.'

'Pagga,' barked Clancy.

O'Leary turned by the open door and saw Milo calmly strike a match against the brickwork of the fireplace and light his cigarette.

'I'll not pick up the gauntlet this time,' said Clancy icily. 'If ya're goin' out there to settle it with Duffy, I'll go with ya, but only to watch. Ye can bury each other right into the ground but I'll not pull yar bleedin' and broken bodies apart.'

'I don't expect ya to.'

As Clancy and O'Casey stepped out into the yard they were just in time to see the first punch thrown. It was delivered by Pagga's left fist to Duffy's unguarded jaw. Its power jerked Duffy right off his feet and onto his back.

'I'll not interfere,' insisted Milo. 'This time, they have me fuckin' leave to go at it tooth and nail!'

Barra Duffy must have left his brains on the floor when he came up to dance with O'Leary once more. He charged in like a maddened bull and once more Pagga's explosive knuckles blasted into Barra's jaw, knocking him back on his arse. Dragging himself up off the dirt for the second time, Duffy brought a bit more respect for O'Leary's renowned left fist. He circled round his opponent, his own two fists shaped, raised and ready. He had to wait a good twenty seconds before O'Leary let go with his lethal jackhammer. Barra feinted to the left, and swung his right hobnail boot right into Pagga's balls. O'Leary's face went purple before he crunched in agony to the ground, but Barra Duffy wasn't there to see his change of colour. As quick as his legs could carry him, Duffy ran all of twenty yards to the gate of the old pound. Seconds later he was back, brandishing the wooden shaft of a pick axe in both hands. Pagga O'Leary was sitting on his arse, mouth wide open and trying his damnedest to get his lungs to function, while his hands clutched his violated vitals.

Madness in his eyes, Barra Duffy measured his victim and lifted his club. Pagga heard Duffy's berserk roar and hurled his body to one side. The mallet missed him by a whisker.

Duffy stared in astonishment at the dent in the earth where O'Leary's shattered head should have been. But Pagga had his heels replanted on terra firma and was stampeding towards his opponent. With a nifty sidestep, Duffy threw Pagga disastrously off balance. He tried desperately to apply his brakes, but could not avoid a stinging blow to his arse from Duffy's bat. The force of the bullseye rocketed O'Leary nut-first into the mesh fencing of the new pound.

'Give in, ya fucker, or I'll kill ya!' shouted Barra.

'The day I give in to the likes of you, Barra Duffy, will be a long time in the fuckin' comin'!' bellowed O'Leary, scraping himself off the fencing.

'Then on yar feet, cunt, for I'm not finished with ya yet!'

'Get rid of yar cowardly poker first.'

Duffy gave the suggestion a moment's thought and then dashed the club to the ground. Pagga struggled on to his knees, as if the last ounce of strength had been drained from him, and Duffy extended a hand. He knew in that moment that he had made a terrible mistake. Clasping Duffy's paw in a vicelike grip, Pagga shot up like a blob of molten lava from a volcano, smashing his head into Barra's face. It happened so quickly, with such lightning speed and with such savage grace, that Barra never saw the move coming.

A few seconds later it was Pagga O'Leary, blood lust blazing in his eyes, who was standing over the prone body of Barra Duffy with the heavy shaft of wood in his hands. But before he could deliver the *coup de grâce*, Milo Clancy intervened and wrenched the weapon free from his murderous grasp. Stallion O'Casey escorted the bloody victor from the scene of the crime.

A minute later, Barra Duffy's eyes fluttered and opened. The colours of the rainbow danced and waltzed awhile before clearing into a single image of Clancy's expressionless face. 'I lost,' croaked Barra.

'Don't you always, Barra Duffy.'

'I thought you'd step in before we got started.' Duffy eased himself up on to one elbow. 'Why didn't ya stop us, Milo?'

'Because it's time ya grew up, Barra. Ya've had yar head up yar hole long enough. 'Tis time ya pulled it out and away from its cosy warmth and stuck it out into the light of day. We've had enough of yar gentle fuckin' ways and yar puny stomach,' said Clancy.

'And I've had enough of you, Milo,' said Barra, rising to his feet. 'I've had enough of you and Pagga and that fellah, O'Casey. If you don't feel yar stomach turnin' over at the sight of a dumb bird with his wings bound put in against a free-flyin' cock, then 'tis time that Barra Duffy turned his back on ya and found himself a better class a friend.'

'Then get the fuck outa my yard! Get on that cart a yours and hit the road, for ya're of no use to me!'

'That's what I was, then? Of use to you. Nuttin' more than that?'

'That's all,' replied Clancy. 'When yar brain was about yar person ya were a dacent handler to my Bulba, but yar brain turned to jelly the very day we went into partnership with O'Casey. Now ya're fuckin' useless. Ya're a millstone round all our necks, so piss off, Barra, before ya infect us all with yar infantile ways.'

Barra didn't say another word. He turned on his heel, and walked away. And Milo Clancy watched him go.

# 10

One dirty bit of weather after another hit the lands of northern Mayo throughout the first three weeks of April. It was as if March had never made its gloomy mark on that unfortunate land. Young and old alike became cantankerous as each grey, soul-sapping day pushed in only to kick another out. Spirits were low, tempers bad, as hopes of a decent spring vanished. By the third week of April even the most optimistic had resigned themselves to the fact that winter had come to stay.

When the sun did show itself, when it broke through the clouds and shed a little miserly warmth upon their heads on the Sunday morning of the fourth week, everyone shunned its presence, determined not to acknowledge its existence. They knew well that the first man to lift up his head at the miraculous sight would send it packing. That sunlit Sunday died almost unseen, and the night took hold, but the following morning there it was again. They felt its warm effulgence as they rose from their beds. The sweet rays touched their cheeks as the sun climbed over the eastern hills and rose up into clear blue skies. Children and those gone daft in the head lifted their eyes to the heavens, pointed with their fingers and smiled. But the farmers, the shopkeepers, the shepherds on the hill, the milkmaids and all the rest of them knew better. They buried their heads deeper into the shadow, and went about their work with grim faces, determined to hold on to their wintery mood. Four more days passed with clear blue skies, and all but the farmers began to believe in the promise of spring.

Stallion O'Casey was the very last of them to lift his head from out of the ground and acknowledge the fact that spring had finally come to the lands of north Mayo.

It was only when the tenth consecutive day of sunshine arrived and showed definite signs of staying around that Stallion O'Casey was pushed into admitting that spring was finally upon them all. And only then did he hand his son his freedom to explore the sun-blessed day outside Clancy's cottage. However, Stallion had succeeded in keeping a few concessions. Colin had to make his charge for freedom dressed from head to foot in his warmest woollies, a balaclava and a pair of oversized wellington boots that flipped and flopped as his bandy little legs took him across the yard and out onto the open road.

Colin kept running until he felt his frail lungs ache with the strain. When he stopped and looked back, Clancy's cottage was no longer in view. He half expected to see his father come to drag him back indoors. An overwhelming sense of freedom suffused his being. He ripped off his balaclava, threw it high into the air, and set off into the distance. Twenty yards on he did an about turn, ran back, scooped up the balaclava from the road, stuffed it in his coat pocket and dashed forward again, putting as much distance between himself and his father's watchful eyes as possible.


It was well into the afternoon when Colin O'Casey turned up at Big Mary's cottage in the village of Feacledown. He found her in her back yard, bent over the wash tub elbow-deep in suds. 'Mother a Christ!' she exclaimed. 'What in the name of sweet Jasus happened to yarself!' She looked with horror at Colin's bloody nose and his battered left eye that showed all the signs of turning into a real shiner before the day ran out.

'I got into a bit of a fight, Big Mary,' the boy replied somewhat sheepishly.

Grabbing Colin by the scruff of the neck Mary dragged him inside. 'Grace yar puny little backside to that chair!'

Colin sat down at the table, thinking it better to do as he was told until Big Mary calmed down. He kept his mouth shut, offering no excuses or explanations, and watched the large woman pour boiling water from the crock on the fire into an enamel basin.

'Lift yar head, Colin O'Casey.' Wringing a steaming facecloth almost totally dry, she wiped his bloody nose. His head recoiled in pain. 'That'll teach ya,' she said. 'Fightin' indeed, when 'tis clear to all that ya couldn't hold yar own against a fly!' She lifted the facecloth away from his face and stared into his clear blue eyes. 'Is it that I'm to stand here like an eegit all day 'til ya feel like tellin' me what the hell happened to yarself?'

Colin squinted back at her. 'I got into a fight, Big Mary.'

'Ya're pullin' me leg, surely! Who? Who did ya get into a fight with?' she demanded.

'Two boys. I don't know their names.'

'Bully boys were they?'

'I started it,' he answered hurriedly. 'I punched them first.'

'You started it? Is it daft ya are, or is it that ya think ya're a giant of a man like yar da?'

'They called me broken legs.'

'Ya should be able to cope with that, love,' said Mary, the harshness gone from her voice. 'Ya can't afford to raise yar fists every time some brat of a gombeen throws an insult at ya.'

'Why not? Supposin' someone was to call ya fatty, wouldn't you have a go?' He was relieved to see Mary's lips break into a smile. 'Well, I just had to lash out and try an' give those two a lesson. Da has kept me cooped up inside Clancy's cottage for a full month. When he finally let me go t'is mornin' I felt that there was nuttin' I couldn't do. Then just as I was comin' into Feacledown these two sittin' by the side of the road started callin' me broken legs. And because I was feelin' on top a the world I decided to show them the colour of my fists.'

'And?'

'Well, I managed to get one punch in anyway,' admitted Colin, his face beginning to flush. 'But then I got murdered good and proper.'

'Well, ya got one punch in anyway. Ya saved yar dignity.'

''Twasn't much of a punch. When my head is straight on my shoulders, I usually walk away, and if they keep pesterin' me I act the fool, or pretend I'm sicker than I look, but this mornin' I was feelin' great. If it had been a ragin' bull that had called me names I still would have got stuck in.'

''Tis the spring, Colin. It makes us all feel light-headed,' smiled Mary. 'Now, let's try and fix up that eye of yours.'

'Do ya think ya could stop it from blacknin'? If me da sees I've been in a fight, I've had it. He'll never let me go ramblin' again.'

'Let's see what a raw potato can do for it.'

Five minutes later she was sitting opposite him, a mug of tea in her hand, watching him bring spoon after spoon of her best stew to his famished mouth, while his other hand held half a raw potato to his swollen eye. 'And what news do ya bring down with ya from that godforsaken place?'

'From Clancy's?'

'Aye.'

'Did ya hear about the fight, about Pagga and Barra?'

'That's not news, that's ancient history.'

''Twas a good fight though. The best I've ever seen.' Colin pushed aside his empty plate.

'Disgusting and barbaric!' snorted Big Mary. 'Just look at where fightin' has got yarself. Ya're in for another hidin' when yar da sees that face of yours. Anyway, that aside, what about Barra?'

'What about him?'

'Are they copin' without him?'

'They're tryin' to pretend they are, but I don't think they're doing very well.'

'I thought as much.' A malicious grin spread across Big Mary's plump face. 'Milo Clancy will never in a hundred years get by without that man. He's the best handler of the cock that there is to be had around these parts, and that's for sure.'

'Da says if Clancy doesn't swallow his pride and go down to Mr Duffy's cottage and ask him to come back, we'll never be able to get Bulba ready for his big day. Pagga is handler now, but he's no good. Yesterday while he was trying to spur Bulba, he nearly got both his eyes plucked out. Both his hands are covered in tears and scratches and there's a big chunk of flesh missin' from his bottom lip where Bulba ripped him with one of his spurs. Mr Clancy can't even get near the bird at all at all. Every time Bulba sees him coming he charges straight for his face. Me da has done his job all right. He's sent Bulba clear round the bend. Every mornin' it takes them three hours and more to catch him, spike him or bind his wings. Everybody is dead to the ground before the trainin' gets under way.'

'I always thought Milo Clancy to be a clever man. It just goes to prove he's as brainless as the rest of us by riddin' himself of the only man that can handle his bird.'

'I doubt if even Barra can handle Bulba now. He's in a right state, he is.' Finally, Colin took the half of potato from his eye.

Looking hopefully at Big Mary he asked, 'How do I look?'

'Ya'll have a shiner before mornin', I'm afraid.'

'Then 'tis my last day a freedom,' sighed Colin, resigned.

'Never mind about yar eye,' said Big Mary. 'How about you and me goin' around to Barra Duffy's cottage, and tryin' to persuade him back to Milo Clancy's where he belongs? That should please yar da. He'll be so overpowered with joy he just mightn't take any notice of yar shiner.'

Duffy wasn't at home, so they set out on the Boreen Road, and walked a good two hundred yards before they came to Duffy's three fields, fifteen acres in all, that was Barra's tiny holding.

'There he is!' cried Colin.

Barra was sitting with his back against the stone wall he had just spent the last two hours repairing. He spotted them immediately, but didn't move a muscle as they came through the gateway on the far side of the field. Freaks, Barra thought to himself, watching them approach. Two freaks! They should be in a fuckin' circus. When they came within hearing range, he called, 'What is it ya're wantin', Big Mary?'

'Good afternoon to ya, Barra Duffy,' she shouted back, puffing and panting her way up a slight slope towards him.

'What is it ya're wantin'?' Barra gave his sour mood free rein.

'Oh, we just came callin'. Thought we'd stop awhile and have a chat with yarself.'

'I'm a farmer,' snapped Barra. 'I work the daylight hours through to their close. I've no time to be spendin' talkin' to the likes a yarself.'

'Oh, I can see ya're hard at it, Barra Duffy,' Big Mary sniped back. 'I suppose ya're goin' to plough the whole of this field usin' yar arse for a plough.'

'I'm restin' after a hard mornin's graft.'

'And ya haven't got the energy or the good manners to turn yar head a half inch and bid Colin here the time of day.'

Barra's cheeks flushed, but he kept his eyes fixed on Big Mary as he grunted out his 'Good afternoon' to the boy.

'And good afternoon to yarself, Mr Duffy,' said Colin. 'I'm sorry ya lost the fight. I was backin' ya all the way.'

'Who said I lost the fuckin' fight?' Barra glared at the boy, but seeing him take two frightened backward steps, the meanness dropped from his face. 'Well, maybe I did lose it,' he conceded.

'But ya saw for yarself that the fight wasn't fair right from the word go. Pagga O'Leary is a dirty fighter. Ya saw that for yarself, didn't ya?'

Colin nodded in quick agreement.

'And who was it that picked up the pick handle in the first place?' asked Big Mary sweetly.

'That had nuttin' to do with it!'

'How's Lightnin'?' asked Colin hurriedly. There was a crazy picture slickering across Colin's field of vision, of Big Mary and Barra Duffy with fists bared going at it tooth and nail, and Colin was afraid for Barra Duffy's wellbeing.

'She's a bit poorly,' replied Barra, happy to be rescued from Mary O'Leary's tongue. 'One of her legs is actin' up again. Ya'll find her in the stable in the other field. Why don't ya go on over there and take this naggin' excuse of a woman with ya?'

'You go ahead, Colin. I'll follow ya in a few minutes. I just want a word with Barra in private.'

Colin nodded, happy to escape.

'Okay, woman,' said Barra, rising to his feet. 'Whatever ya have to say, say it and clear off. 'Tis painful for any man to have to look at yar ugly ol' face for any longer than is necessary.'

'Ya can look away while I talk if I offend you so,' Mary answered, keeping a tight control on her renowned temper.

'No, I'll gawk at ya if 'tis all the same with yarself,' jeered Barra. 'I've penance to do for me past sins. Forcin' meself to stare at the ugliest woman God ever put on this earth will keep me in good stead with me Maker.'

'Just as long as ya clean yar ears out and listen to what I have to say.'

'Fire away,' Barra sneered, elated to see that his words had struck home.

'Clancy is in the stump,' said Big Mary, coming straight to the point. 'He's in the stump and you've put him there.'

'Then that's fuckin' music to me ears.'

'Bulba has gone mad, madder than Stallion had intended him to be. There isn't one a them up there that can handle that cock.'

'Three cheers for cold justice comin' down hard on the heads of ruthless and savage men.'

'They want ya back.'

'Does Clancy want me back?'

'He does.'

'Then let him come here.'

'And if and when he does?'

'I'll get the greatest of pleasure from tellin' that man to go and fuck himself to death.'

'Then ya're a fool, Barra Duffy. But that bita common knowledge is even known to yarself.'

'Piss off, O'Leary! Take yarself and yar fuckin' insults with ya!'

'Oh, 'twould be easy indeed to turn me back on yarself and not have to gawk at yar bad-tempered mug and listen to the foul language drippin' off yar dirty tongue, but for God only knows why I'm goin' to try and straighten yar brain for ya.'

'Don't ya be doin' me no favours, Big Mary, just piss off outa here and let me get on with me day's work.'

'I'm stayin' put and ya'll listen!' Big Mary folded her Amazon's arms across her chest.

'Ya're trespassin'!' roared Duffy. 'Is it that ya want me to grab ya by yar huge arse and yar barrel neck and drag ya from me sight?'

'If ya think ya can do it, then ya just try. Try, Barra Duffy, and you'll be meetin' up with all yar dead relatives before the day is out.'

Barra Duffy winced as he found himself looking down at her legs that stood solid and fast like oaken stumps buried into the surface of his land.

'Ya'll let me borrow yar ears then?'

'Open yar gobhole, Big Mary. Only make it short and to the fuckin' point!'

'Ya've amassed a powerful lot of enemies over the past week or two, Barra Duffy. 'Tis been written in the heavens for years that you and Pagga would one day have it out, so 'twas no surprise to meselt when ya finally got stuck in. Ya could say Pagga O'Leary was one enemy ya could afford to have. But Clancy! For the love a shit, why did ya have to make an enemy outa Clancy? That was dumb, Barra. That was the dumbest thing ya ever did in the whole of yar life, and if you don't take yar feet out onto the coast road and do it soon, then ya'll be moanin' over yar daftness for the rest of yar days.

'Yarself and himself have lived in each other's pockets for a long time now. Ya've sipped outa each other's glasses, ya've laughed and quarrelled and shared each other's days. The two of yees were one. You've needed Clancy from time to time and he's been there at yar doorstep when he was wanted. But the fact that I'm sure has galled ya most over the years is that Clancy never had need of yourself. He's always been a self-reliant son of a bitch. But now he needs that life-long friend of his. He needs ya, Barra Duffy. He has a chance, just one chance, to heap upon himself a little bita glory, and he can't do it without yar help. But because he's a proud man, ya know and I know he'll never come callin' and askin' ya for yar help. You'll have to go to him. You'll have to do it and soon for if Bulba dies fightin' that tinker's cock, then the two of yees is finished as far as yar friendship is concerned. Maybe after a couple a years of thinkin' things out, you might decide to go knockin' on Milo Clancy's door, but 'tis for damn sure, Barra, when he opens the door you'll find the devil's own face gawkin' out at yarself. He'll present for yar inspection a face full a hate, the likes of which ya have never seen in all yar born days. With shame and regret drippin' from yar person ya'll have to pocket yar pipe of peace and walk the long road back to yar lonely cottage.'

'What ya don't realize, Big Mary, is that Milo Clancy never gave his friendship to me.' Barra's cheeks were tear-stained but his voice was calm and steady. 'I was a fool in his eyes all those years I had thought him to be my friend.'

'That's rubbish!' gasped Big Mary, shocked at Barra's words and surprised by his evident emotion.

''Tis not. Milo Clancy said so himself as he kicked me off his land after me fight with yar brother.'

'Ya poor poor fool, Barra Duffy! Can't ya feel and sense a mouthful of untruth when it hits ya right between the eyes? Oh aye, what Milo told ya was the honest-to-God's truth when he turned ya away from his patch, but the both of yees had the knife out and marked for each other's gullets at the time. Tempers were stokin' hot. For God's sake, Barra, surely even your small brain can see that his words were words of anger, anger and nuttin' else?'

'All I know is that those words left Milo Clancy's fuckin' lips! If a man's ears can't take in a man's words to mean what they say, then I'm thinkin' that it would be far better if the whole world was made up of fuckin' mutes.'

But Mary was not going to be beaten. 'Ah, Barra Duffy, wake up, for the love a Christ! 'Tis time ya took that head of yours out from between the cheeks of yar arse!'

'Ya got the gift of the gab, Mary O'Leary, just like the rest of yar clan. Sure, 'tis grateful I am to be here in yar midst while ya help to straighten out me poor, addled brain! But I refuse on behalf of me civilized nature and upbringin' to degrade my God-given talents by helpin' that bastard O'Casey carry out his heathen experiments on a defenceless cock! That's the reason, the true reason why Barra Duffy will stay put here, on his own land, and never venture forward to Milo Clancy's door ever again!'

'You little green-snotted hypocrite! You shitless excuse of a man!' shouted Big Mary, her face full of contempt. 'Who is it that has embraced the ways of the cock ever since he left his mother's tit? Give me the name of the man that has stroked and enticed every cock that ever came his way before offerin' them up to the slaughter in that low and vile place ye call the sawdust ring? Don't ya ever again give me yar mouthful of holier-than-thou shit. Ya're soaked in the blood of a thousand cocks. Ya're a handler and a fighter of the cocks! Face it, and face also that there never was and never had been rules laid down that protects the cock from the open and lashing spur or the bloody carnage that is surely his lot when his body weakens and age catches up with him. You've got a choice to make, Barra Duffy. Stick to yar cockshit humanity and stand by Bulba, or go back to where ya belong, stand by Milo Clancy and help him win the day over the tinker's devil.'

Duffy kept his mouth shut, unable to look Big Mary in the face. Thinking it better not to press him any further, she held her own tongue. A full minute went by.

'What happened with young Colin?' asked Barra suddenly.

'He got into a bit of a fight with a couple of bullies.'

'That little mite can't afford the luxury of fightin'.'

'That I told him,' replied Mary. 'I thought ya might take the boy off me hands for the rest of the day. I've got a tubful of washin' out in me back yard that needs tendin' to, plus I've got a house to clean.'

'Aye, I'll have him. As long as he doesn't get in me way.'

'And ya'll bring him safely back home to his da well before dark?' asked Mary, keeping her voice normal and matter of fact.

Duffy read what was on her mind, but not out loud. 'Aye, I'll bring him home,' he said quietly.

'I best be off then.'

'Aye. Outa me hair, woman, for God's sake! Let an honest man get on with a day's work.'


Milo Clancy's cottage had always been a well-kept place. The effort put into each morning's sweep and clean was no mean feat. Spinsters with hope in their eyes who stepped through Clancy's front doorway would sigh out their defeat almost at once. The very walls of the place seemed to cry out, 'No woman needed here.'

The cottage continued to look spick and span after the O'Caseys arrived, and even after Pagga and Barra decided to spend their nights beside Clancy's turf fire rather than trudge six miles back to their own abodes. But then came the great bust-up. The house itself fell into chaos. A mountain of dirty dishes apexed, spilled and overflowed from the wash basin on the Welsh dresser. Dirt and dust, bits of half-eaten bread and the stubs from ten packets of cigarettes were strewn all over the kitchen floor. The stench of human sweat, stale food, along with a haze of old tobacco smoke, settled over the three rooms. But fatigue and frustration entered the cottage with Bulba's trainers at the end of each day's stint and no one seemed to notice. The cottage that was once lovingly cared for was a mess and so also were the lives of the people within its walls.

Pagga slouched at the table, a mug of cold tea in hand. It was nearly five o'clock and the afternoon light was beginning to fade from the skies. Clancy's kitchen was beginning to darken, even though the front door of the cottage was wide open. Shouts, screams and roars floated in, but O'Leary was deaf to it all. He had retired shortly after eleven o'clock that morning, sporting a bloody two-inch gash that ran the length of his left palm from one of Bulba's metal spurs. The only thing that lifted his spirits a little was the fact that he would not have to go back and face that devil cock for at least another week.

A scream of sheer anguish pounded in upon O'Leary's brooding thoughts. 'I hope 'tis yarself he's got, Milo Clancy,' muttered Pagga. 'I hope he's ripped yar balls right off.' Seconds later, Milo Clancy came storming into the room, his forehead streaming with blood.

'He got ya then,' Pagga stated coldly, staying put in his chair.

Clancy ignored Pagga's remark and grabbed a bottle of surgical spirit from the table.

'If that stuff gets in yar eyes, Milo Clancy, ya'll know about it,' cautioned Pagga.

'Well, don't just sit there, give us a fuckin' hand, ya bastard!'

'And pray tell me, Milo Clancy, what kind samaritan gave me a helpin' hand t'is mornin' as I dragged meself back to yar kitchen? What gentle soul tended to my wounds?'

'Get yar arse off that chair, O'Leary!' The blood from the crimson spurline had started to drip down into Milo's eyes.

'Arrah, hold yar whist.' Pagga grabbed a grubby piece of sheeting from the table, took the bottle of spirits from Clancy, edged him into a chair and administered his own kind of first aid. 'Milo,' he said tentatively, 'we have to stop and take stock. We can't go on like this.'

'What the fuck do you suggest?' Clancy winced as Pagga dabbed gingerly at the wound.

'We stop and think awhile.'

'We can't stop. We're runnin' a month behind with the trainin'.'

'Then get Barra back!'

'Get t'is into yar head, O'Leary. That cunt is out! He stays out! If he was to come beggin' I still wouldn't have the bastard back!'

'Subject closed,' sighed Pagga as he saw the fire in Clancy's eyes.

Stallion stomped into the room and plonked himself down in Clancy's best chair. 'How is he?' he asked. His eyes were already closing as he heard O'Leary answer, 'He'll live.'

'Great,' replied Stallion and a few seconds later was sound asleep.

When Colin returned from his day of rambling, his father was still asleep by the fire.

'Sufferin' Nora! What the hell happened to yarself?' cried Pagga, jumping up out of his chair.

'I fell,' replied Colin.

'Against whose fist?'

''Tis a beauty,' said Clancy admiringly.

'Is he back then?' croaked Stallion, trying to pull himself together. He wiped a hand over his weary face and squinted at his son. With a start he was on his feet. 'Mother a Christ! What happened to ya?'

Colin took an involuntary backward step towards the doorway. 'I fell, Da.'

'Fell, me arse!' Swaddling his son's tiny face in his palms, he inspected the damage. 'Who did that to ya?'

'I got into a fight. There was two of them.'

'Who were they?'

'I don't know. Honest, I don't.'

'Then that's it, me lad. Ya're housebound from now on. No more gallivantin' for you.'

'Arrah, Stallion, and isn't yourself the walkin' saint, to be sure,' chided Pagga. 'Didn't ya never get yarself into the odd scrap way back in yar long-distant youth?'

'Keep out of this, Pagga,' warned Stallion. 'Do ya get me drift, Colin? Ya're housebound. Understood?'

'Understood,' replied Colin miserably.

'We'll get Milo here to give ya a few boxin' lessons,' smiled Pagga. 'Sure isn't he a great man with his fists. Aren't ya, Milo?'

'That I am,' agreed Clancy.

'Mr Clancy,' said Colin with great deliberation. 'Barra Duffy is out in yar front yard. Ya might be wantin' to show him the wonders of yar fists, but I'm thinkin' he's come to see you.'

'In the yard, ya say?'

'Ya'll treat him gently, won't ya?' asked Colin, but Clancy was already through the door.

'Stay put, Pagga,' said Stallion as he saw O'Leary head after Clancy. 'Ya'll only complicate things. Best stay put.'

Clancy walked quietly across the yard towards Bulba's pound. He stopped for a moment and searched the pockets of his jacket for a stray butt, found one, lit it and stood in silence, looking through the mesh fencing at Barra Duffy who was down on his haunches inspecting Bulba's isolated coop. Duffy got slowly to his feet and came over to Clancy.

'How are ya, Milo?'

'Not bad. And yarself?' replied Milo evenly.

'I could be worse.'

'Ya've seen our Bulba?'

'I have.'

'And?'

'Ya've succeeded. That's what ya wanted isn't it? To drive him clean out of his skull.' Despite his resolution, Duffy could not contain his anger.

'That was the idea.'

'But ya've got a problem.'

'Aye, we've got a problem. We can't handle him. But we'll get him to his peak with or without ya.'

'But 'twould be much earlier if ya had me. Right?'

'Right.'

'Okay, then. Ya've got me services.'

'And O'Casey still gets a free hand?'

'Yes.' Duffy looked back at Bulba's coop, that was now veiled in almost total darkness, slowly shaking his head. 'By the fuck, but you, O'Leary and that bastard O'Casey didn't half do a job on him.'

'It had to be done. You know that. If Bulba is to fight and beat Kusthi's devil, then he needs to be armed with Stallion's knowledge. You know that.'

Duffy brushed his eyes with his sleeve. ''T'll be hard going. From what Colin has told me Bulba has tasted all yar flesh. Big Mary says that her brother is minus a bottom lip.'

''Tis almost true. And as for meself, Bulba all but took the eyes outa me head this afternoon. Ya'll have to tread carefully with him if ya're to remain in one piece.'

'Ya don't have to tell me my business,' snapped Barra, turning his back on the fence.

'How about a cuppa then?' suggested Clancy with a half smile coming to his lips.

An hour later Duffy and O'Casey were locked in deep discussion at Clancy's table. Pagga was snoozing quietly by the fire in Milo's best armchair, while Clancy himself and young Colin were going through the cottage with bucket, mop and broom.

''Tisn't a matter of correctin' any of Bulba's faults, Barra,' Stallion was saying. 'That cock doesn't have any.' Duffy's face was expressionless. 'The thing is that Kusthi's cock has got stuff inside of his head that our Bulba doesn't have. What we've got to do is stuff the stuff that makes the tinker's cock great into Bulba's head, and do it fast. But we don't have that much time. Now here's the situation. Ya'll notice all this when ya see Bulba fight come tomorrow mornin'. Already we've managed to change his pattern of fightin'. When Bulba faces his victim now he stays put on the ground and lets the other bird do the soarin'. Bulba watches him climb and ducks outa harm's way as his victim starts to swoop down on him.'

'But what about his soarin'? Ya'll not neglect that, I hope.'

'No.' O'Casey could not ignore the concern on Duffy's face. Keep him sweet, keep him interested, he thought to himself. Don't give him time to think how much he hates ya. 'Gettin' the best of his soarin' will be easy now that ya're back amongst us,' he continued. 'It's a matter of "firing", and you know all about that.'

'And I'll be handlin' that cock mornin', noon and night right up to the grand day?'

'Aye,' said Stallion cautiously, noticing the calculating look that lit up Duffy's eyes.

'Then pray tell me, Stallion O'Casey, who's goin' to handle Bulba come the great day?'

'I don't understand yar meanin'.'

'Oh, ya don't, don't ya?' mocked Duffy. 'What I'm meanin' is that if I'm handlin' him all the way up to the fuckin' day, then isn't it a fact that by then I'll have only stumps for hands and two bloody sockets for eyes? Won't me poor ol' face be just a mask of torn flesh?'

'Come off it, Barra,' said Stallion, relaxing again. 'Ya're known as the best handler the west of Ireland has to offer. Can't ya see that the tension has gone outa the lot of us now? For don't we know that ya'll find a way outa this mountainous problem that we've created for ourselves?'

'Oh, 'tis glad I am to hear ya admit as much as that,' said Barra. 'What ya're sayin' is, you maddened Bulba, and now ya can't handle him. Let me ask ya somethin', then.' Duffy leaned forward, eyes ablaze. 'If ya screw up a cock's brain in order to teach him new tricks, and then ya find ya can't handle him, what's the point of it all?'

O'Casey leaned forward too. 'Barra, the honest-to-God's truth to yarself,' he said with all the sincerity at his command, 'is that

Bulba is unique. There isn't another cock like him in the world. Now because of me and me trainin' he's mad, but 'tis a special, deadly madness the likes of which I've never seen in all of me born days. He's a killer now. Anything that comes within his range is fair game. 'Tis more than my knowledge can deal with.'

'Can ya halt yar training for a day or two?'

'What for?' asked O'Casey with suspicion.

'I'm goin' to need to make meself some gloves for me hands, somethin' to guard me face, and I want to study the murderous movements that you and Clancy have instilled in him.'

'Two days then,' agreed O'Casey, and breathed a sigh of relief.

# I I

It was a shock to everyone when young Colin fell ill. Winter was already dead and buried: the black and deadly winds of March and early April were gone, and it was the middle of a perfect May. The skies were clear, the air was warm and what breezes there were were light and gentle.

But on the second Monday of that month Colin O'Casey rose from his bed, trying to disguise a runny nose, a nagging headache and a pair of lungs that sang and wheezed as they drew in the morning air. It was a relief to find that the men of the house were already out tending to the training of Taurus Bulba. The lad stayed put in the kitchen for the rest of the morning, willing with all his might to rid himself of the demon cold that had invaded his poor body. On the stroke of one the men came through the doorway, and half a minute later Colin O'Casey was back in bed.

That was on Monday. All day Tuesday Stallion nursed his boy, and on Wednesday Big Mary came up from the village to take up her post by Colin's bedside. She kept watch along with Stallion right through the seemingly interminable night, and when dawn finally came the gloom that had hung over Clancy's cottage since Colin fell ill seemed to have lifted with the dark. Big Mary could only lower her head and blush into her bib as Stallion O'Casey sang her praises. The choir of little devils in his son's chest had died to a mere murmur, the little blobs of hard, yellowish phlegm that had been coughed up for the best part of three days were no more. The sheen of a sweat that had clung like a piece of fine silk over Colin's forehead was gone, and all because of Mary's gentle care.

Big Mary stayed on through the day, nursing her charge, going through Clancy's cottage with broom and mop, and hauling every morsel of food she could find out of his larder. There was just about enough beef to make a decent stew. At noon four very hungry men slumped down at her table; half an hour later they were gone, leaving behind well-scraped plates, four empty porter jugs and the lingering smell of their pipes. She cleaned up, checked on a sleeping Colin, and then she retired to the comfort of Clancy's best armchair.

The clock was chiming three when she opened her eyes again. Yawning, she stretched her vast frame, and then got up to have a look at Colin. Ten seconds later she came dashing out of his bedroom, heading for the yard.

Clancy had Barra Duffy's horse shackled and was on his way before another five minutes had time to pass. Big Mary, Stallion, Pagga and Barra were with Colin. The boy's chest rose and fell agonizingly as he tried to inhale the life-giving air around him. His frail lungs sang with the effort of it all. Sweat shone from his forehead and had saturated the pillow that supported his head. Mary could only dab away at his drenched forehead and Stallion O'Casey could only look down at his son's terror-filled eyes and watch. It was too much for Barra, and so he had fled the room to keep watch outside for Clancy.

Four o'clock came and still there was no sign of Milo. When Duffy returned to the darkened room, his legs all but gave way at the scene before him. Big Mary swaddled young Colin's head in her arms while the lad spewed blood from his trembling mouth into a basin that Pagga O'Leary was holding just under his chin. Stallion himself was to the left of the bed, seated on a chair, his elbows resting on his knees, his supporting arms and open palms cradling the whole of his face.

'Get back out there!' hissed Mary through clenched teeth. 'Get back out and keep yar eyes on the road and shout the very minute Clancy comes inta yar view!'

At ten minutes past five Duffy's horse and cart finally rolled into the yard. It had hardly come to a complete stop before Barra Duffy was dragging the august and slightly indignant Dr Flynn down off the cart.

'Ya're finished as a horse, Lightnin' Duffy,' sighed Clancy, stroking the nag's sweat-covered flank. 'Ya'll never crank up another little burst of yar famous and well-renowned speed, even if ya were to step back into yar youthful years. Sorry ol' fellah, it had to be done. Ya're here to serve and by Jasus that ya did today.'


Duffy's ten-year-old mare died in the wee hours of the morning. Her eyes were wide open and glazed by melancholy as well as by death. Barra Duffy stood in the centre of the doorway staring down at his old companion, surprised at his own calmness and at the absence of his tears. 'You best bury it,' he thought out loud, stunned as his words reached his own ears. 'Tis Lightnin' that's dead, he chided himself. A dacent and kinder horse ya couldn't wish to have! But still the grief and sorrow wouldn't come. Mother a Christ, he thought to himself. You've become no better than one of 'em! His eyes left the dead animal as a sigh left his lips. Best get a shovel and bury it, he said to no one. Best get it done soon.

He buried Lightning with Clancy's help. After they had filled in the hole, they stood for a moment with bowed heads.

'She wasn't a bad ol' horse, as far as horses go,' said Barra.

'Didn't she take us all the way to Westport so we could put our money on the winner of the National?' asked Clancy.

'And in good time, too.'

'Aye, as far as horses go, she was one a the best. If there's a place in God's heaven for the beasts of the field, then 'tis for sure that Lightnin's right in the middle of it.'

'Aye, ya're right there.'

''Tis sorry I am, Barra,' said Clancy, not raising his head to face his friend's eyes. 'Lightnin' would be havin' her breakfast now except for me.'

'Arrah, don't be goin' on about it, Milo.' Duffy wiped his sweat-streaked brow. 'It had to be done. It's not your fault, it had to be done.'

'Aye,' agreed Clancy. 'But I'm thinkin' now that it was all for nought.'

For the first time in minutes, Duffy's eyes came away from the grave. 'Are ya sayin' young Colin'll die?'

Milo leaned on his shovel and gazed into the distance. 'Ah, Barra, don't ya recognize that Black Angel when he comes callin'? Wasn't his bloody visitin' card the clearest ya've ever laid eyes on in a month a Sundays?'

'But isn't that Dr Flynn comin' back? Didn't he say he'd be back sometime tonight? That's a good sign, isn't it? He hasn't given up hope.'

'Ah, wake up will ya! The only reason that bastard'll be callin' on us is to sign the fuckin' certificate.'

Only when Milo had disappeared into the cottage did Duffy lower his head and say a quick, silent prayer over Lightning's final resting place. Then he too headed back to the house, but as he reached Clancy's back door he suddenly stopped. Fuck it, he decided. I can't go back in there. Not now. One death a day is enough for any man. He headed around the back to the coops. When he got to the mesh fencing he found O'Leary throwing Clancy's birds their morning feed. Before he could retrace his steps he heard Pagga call out. Barra, hands deep in his pockets, walked towards the old pound. He stopped by the wire and watched Pagga approach from the centre of the yard.

'Ya buried her, then?' said Pagga gently.

'We did.'

''Tis powerful sorry I am.'

'For who?' asked Barra. 'For me or for me horse?'

'For your sad loss and for yar Lightnin's sad passin'.'

'Be Jasus!' snorted Barra, beginning to feel like himself again. 'Is it a soul that yarself is gettin' after all these years? Jasus, but it took ya a long time to find it! Is it consideration and thoughtfulness that's comin' to yarself at last? Is it that ya're now admittin', after all this time, that the other beasts apart from us humans have a right to some consideration, and an admission that they are part of God's domain as well? This is a bloody miracle I'm witnessin'.'

'Arrah, give over, Barra,' grumbled Pagga. 'I'll not pick a fight with ya. Not today anyway. We should be holdin' each other up now, not tearin' each other apart. Leave off, for Christ's sake, man, with yar daftness and zip up that mouth a yours with yar talk of yar dead and mistreated animals. Inside Clancy's cottage one of yar own species is preparin' to head for his Maker. Think about him, man. He's one of yar own kind. Think about him and the sorrow and upheaval that his passin' will bring to the lot of us.'

'How come I get this feelin' that the grief that's pourin' outa yours and Clancy's heart is for yar own selfish interests, and not for Stallion O'Casey's dyin' son at all?'

'What is that daft brain of yours on about now?'

'Nuttin', nuttin' at all.' Duffy turned away.

'Where are ya off to?' Pagga called to Duffy's retreating back.

'To the village.'

'Ya can't do that. Ya're needed here.' But Barra's step didn't falter or hesitate. 'What time will ya be back?' Duffy raised his hand in a blind wave and disappeared from his view. 'Bastard!' hissed O'Leary.

Darkness had brushed away the last traces of twilight and a soft, warm May night embraced the tiny cottage.

Clancy and Pagga were bowed over the table with mugs of tea in hand. By the fireside sat Big Mary, her elbows resting on her stout thighs, the open palms of her hands supporting her ample chin and her eyes looking down at the grey ash of the turf in the hearth. The kitchen was silent. When heads turned towards the closed door of Colin's bedroom they did so furtively. Now and again Mary would tiptoe across to the door and place an ear against the woodwork. 'Anythin' happenin'?' Clancy and Pagga would whisper. And Big Mary would shake her head. It had been like that ever since the doctor came.

Suddenly, the bedroom door opened and Dr Patrick Flynn walked quietly in, his head lowered and his eyes dulled.

'Oh no! No sweet Jasus, no!' cried Big Mary aloud, her head bowed in defeat.

'I'm sorry, Mary O'Leary,' Flynn said softly. 'I did all I could. The little mite has passed on, into the arms of Christ. And if the truth be told, he's better off there.'

Tears filled Mary's eyes. 'Ya did yar best, Doctor.'

Flynn put one hand on her sturdy shoulder. 'Dry yar tears, Mary. Ya're needed in there now. There's a man in there that needs comfortin'.'

She dried her face and brushed past Flynn and through the bedroom door. The doctor stayed put, warming himself in front of Clancy's fireplace.

'There's cunts and there's fuckers, there's murderers and there's men that are as black as the night itself,' said a voice from behind him. 'But the whole lot a them are saints compared to the men that make up yar fuckin' profession!'

Flynn blinked and turned around. 'Good evenin' to ya, Pagga O'Leary,' he said, managing a half-hearted smile.

'And a pox on you, ya cunt!'

'Take no notice of this mad ol' soul, Dr Flynn,' Clancy intervened. 'Come, sit down and join us and I'll pour ya out a cuppa. Ya look shagged out.'

'Yar offer I'll gladly accept, Milo Clancy,' smiled Flynn, pulling up a chair.

'Is it thick ya are, or stupid, Flynn?' hissed Pagga. 'I pay insult to yarself and yar profession, and you just sit there with yar cowardly face away from me. Is it gutless ya are as well as everythin' else?'

The doctor gratefully accepted the mug of lukewarm tea from Clancy's hand and drank it down. He took out a packet of cigarettes from his pocket and lit one. They watched as he took his first, deep drag and exhaled with a profound sigh. 'If I was to get steamed up at yar insults, dear Pagga,' said Flynn, 'if I was to get steamed up enough to get up off this chair and beat the livin' daylights outa ya, I'd have to admit that I was twice if not thrice as thick as yarself! For wouldn't it have to be that I would have to patch up yar wounds and put ya back together again? So, I'll hold on to me temper if 'tis all the same with yarself. Besides, I've got used to yar sweet endearments over the years. They come at me every time we have occasion to meet, and the fact of the matter is, Pagga, they go in one ear and out the other.'

'Then ya're double the cunt, Flynn! It goes to prove that yar conscience is paper thin. I suppose when ya leave this cottage tonight, ya'll go home to ya bed and sleep soundly, ya bloody murderer!'

'Aye, I'll sleep soundly, Pagga, for I did what I could. I tried to save that child's life. But I'm no Christ and I can't work miracles. I also did my best for yar grandfather. Though he was fast approaching his century I tried to keep him here on this earth for you.'

'And ya failed there too.'

'Yes, I failed there too.' Flynn rubbed his haggard face.

'Of course ya failed,' sneered O'Leary. 'And still, after every failure, ye come out from the dead man's room and look into the faces of the livin' and wring yar hands and say the same old thing,

"I did me best, I did me best." And we the livin', bein' thick and stupid, smile at yar ugly face though our hearts are breakin' and say, "Well, ya did yar best doctor, ya did yar best." Cunts! The whole fuckin' lota yees! Ye write yarselfs out yar certificates that none but yarselfs can read and set yarselfs up on altars above the rest of us. Ye practise yar chicanery and we let ya! Jasus, but ya've a lot to answer for, come the Day of Judgement.' O'Leary stood up with fist clenched, glaring down at Flynn's balding crown. Clancy got ready to intercede, but there was no need. As quickly as he'd begun, Pagga turned his back on the table and stormed out of the door.

'I wouldn't be takin' much notice of Pagga's mad spoutin's, Doctor. He's a bit upset,' said Clancy.

'I'm not too sure if Pagga isn't spoutin' a whole lot a truth in his own daft way,' sighed Flynn, taking another long drag on his cigarette.

'The man holds a dagger in his paw whenever one a ye fellahs come into his sights. If ya want the truth of it all, Pagga O'Leary is scared witless about dyin' himself.'

'No, the man's right. We've set ourselves up as priests who can do no wrong. And when we fail, we make sure ya turn yar eyes from us and blame yar gods.' Flynn groaned his way out of the chair. 'Well, I must be off. I have a bed to go to and 'tis glad I'll be when I finally crawl into it.'

Clancy rose too. 'Ya'll not have another cup of tea? Sorry I can't offer ya somethin' proper, but I'm all out.'

'Ah, don't worry about that. What I need is me bed and a few dacent hours of rest.'

Clancy saw the doctor safely to his trap and watched him out on the coast road until he was swallowed up by the night. The bedroom door opened just as he returned to the cottage and Clancy looked into Big Mary's tear-stained face. 'How's he takin' it?' he whispered. She said nothing, but stepped to one side, indicating with a nod of her head that he should enter.

When Pagga and Barra came in half an hour later, they found Mary seated in Clancy's chair by the fireplace.

'Ya can feel Death's presence comin' out at ya from the very walls,' remarked O'Leary, stopping just inside the doorway, sniffing the air as if looking for Death's source.

'Aye,' Barra agreed. 'The very air is thick with it.'

Mary's eyes were empty and her voice was almost inaudible. 'Ye best go in the both of yees and pay yar respects.'

'Ya're sure 'tis okay?' Pagga's voice betrayed his fear. 'After all, we must let Stallion have a little bita time to grieve his sorrow quietly and alone.'

'Clancy is in there,' Big Mary replied, staring at the black hearth. 'If the sight of a dead child frightens the two of yees so much, ye can always hide behind Milo Clancy's broad shoulders. But get yarselves in there now and get it over with. Another ten minutes and I'll be in there myself to prepare the mite for his final journey.'

At midnight, Clancy, Pagga, Barra and Big Mary sat down to a late supper. In the spare bedroom Stallion O'Casey was sitting by the bedside of his dead son, keeping watch over him as the night travelled on. The whole of the cottage was in silence, yet no one slept. Not until the silver-grey light of dawn sneaked its way through the darkness were the sounds of life heard.

Bleary, sleep-filled eyes turned as the bedroom door opened. Big Mary rose from her chair and went to the man's aid. She steered him towards Clancy's best chair by the fire and sat him down. Then off she went to make breakfast for them all.

'Stallion!' whispered Clancy. Stallion looked round at him, but his face was hollow and devoid of life. 'Stallion! There's arrangements to be made.'

'Arrangements,' O'Casey repeated, like a man in a trance. 'Arrangements.'

'Aye. Colin has to be seen to now,' said Clancy. 'The burial arrangements have to be got under way. But don't worry yar head about it, we'll see to that.'

O'Casey frowned and shook his head. 'I was right about the priest, Milo, wasn't I?'

'About the priest?'

'Aye. The last thing a dyin' boy wants to see is a black-vested priest lookin' down at him. It would have frightened him to death.'

'Aye, ya're right there, Stallion. The last thing yar boy needed was a priest.'

'What sins would a ten-year-old boy have to confess? What use would he have for those holy oils that they'd plaster his body with? Wasn't my boy as pure as the angels in heaven?'

'When ya're thirteen years old, Stallion, ya're as pure as the freshly fallen snow. Yar Colin is in heaven now. We can rest assured on that.'

'Aye,' Stallion sighed wearily. 'Aye, he's in heaven, if there is one. But if there isn't . . . then he's in the great void, floatin' around somewhere.'

'There's a heaven,' said Milo confidently. 'There's a heaven and your Colin is right in the middle of it this very night.'

'I'll take yar word on it,' said Stallion, a weak smile touching the corners of his mouth.

'Well, gettin' back to reality, Stallion,' pressed Milo, 'the fact of the matter is, arrangements have to be made for yar Colin to be buried.'

'Aye.' O'Casey laughed bitterly. 'Ya can let those black-frocked men of the cloth through yar doors now and spout their witchery and nonsense over the body of my dead Colin. They can't harm him now.'


They laid Colin O'Casey's remains to rest in Drumcliff cemetery on the outskirts of the village of Feacledown two days later. It was a simple service, carried out under the bluest of skies on a sweltering morning. When the service was finished, Clancy took Stallion to Sullivan's pub in the village, and for the rest of the day they drank to the lad's memory. It wasn't until the wee hours of the following day that both men placed their boots on the coast road and headed back to home. After ten hours wrapped in stupified sleep, O'Casey was on the coast road again, bound for Sullivan's pub. Clancy stayed behind. When the day died and Sullivan closed his doors, Stallion found himself on the coast road once more. Eight more days passed: Stallion was always on the coast road by noon at the latest, and the stars were always glittering above his head when he returned to Clancy's again.

It was twelve days since they had given Colin O'Casey's body to the ground. In the front yard, Barra and Pagga were working Bulba, slowly but surely bringing the mad cock to a peak of fitness. But Clancy knew that the cock was only half-schooled. The rest of the knowledge was inside O'Casey's head. It was coming up to noon and O'Casey was in bed and dead to the world.

Milo had a hundred words in his head, all formed into sentences, his thoughts were clear, his head was ready, and what had to be said to O'Casey's face would be said as soon as O'Casey walked through the bedroom door. But when Stallion O'Casey did come through the bedroom door the only words that left Milo's lips were a whispered, 'Good mornin', Stallion, how're ya feelin'?' Maybe O'Casey didn't hear Milo's concerned greeting, and maybe he did, but he kept walking. Four strides took him across Clancy's floor and out into the light of day. Milo bounded out of his chair after him, but stopped silently in the doorway and let O'Casey walk on down his path, through the gateway, and onto the coast road and out of his sight.

Pat Sullivan shut his doors on the stroke of eleven that night, and Stallion O'Casey found himself on the street once more, with five miles of walking in front of him before he reached the warmth of his bed. But O'Casey was in no hurry, and leaned up against the stained-glass window of Sullivan's establishment to watch the drunks depart. He envied them their staggered walk, their booze-filled songs, their careless speech and their well-doused, childlike, drunken brains. For twelve days he had tried to woo his own brain into that selfsame condition. But try as he might, he never came even close. The only thing that Pat Sullivan's booze ever did was to give him a mother of a hangover.

He patted the pocket of his jacket to reassure himself that he had his lifesaver for the long journey home. His half bottle of Powers was there. Halfway down the street, a dog scrounging for a midnight snack in an overturned dustbin lifted its head on hearing the clomp of hobnail boots on the cobbled stone. The dog wagged his tail at the lonesome figure, but received no friendly pat in reply.

As Stallion reached the end of the village, he passed a young couple, arms linked, heads touching, returning to civilization after their night of courting out there in the bogs. 'Evenin' to yarself. A fine night,' saluted the young buck. The lass said nothing but gave Stallion a shy but friendly smile.

'A grand night indeed,' replied Stallion. He watched them out of sight, then took the nightcap from his pocket and drained half its contents. He stared bleakly at the pitch-black road. Give yarself one good reason why ya should go back there, Stallion O'Casey, he told himself. Isn't Milo Clancy's ol' shack the most soul-decayin' spot that ya ever clapped eyes on? Isn't it where yar darlin' boy . . . Stallion raised his head to the star-filled sky. 'Are ya up there, ya ol' bastard?' he cried aloud to the firmament. 'If ya are, and ya're listenin', then listen well, for 'tis Stallion O'Casey that's addressin' ya! A thirteen-year-ol' boy, a cripple with a paper chest went through yar fuckin' doors two weeks back! Keep yar eyes peeled for him! Do ya hear me, ya ol' shagger? Keep those all-seein' eyes of yours open for my boy. He's small in frame, delicate, insignificant, ya might say. Ya're the mother of a cunt that took him from me! He's yours now! He's your responsibility! Seein' as I don't stand a ghost of a chance of gettin' past yar fuckin' doors when my time comes, and seein' as how I'll never lay eyes on me darlin' again, then 'tis you that's got the fuckin' job whether ya like it or not! So take care of him, ya king of shits! Ya murderer of cripples! Ya widow-maker! Ya famine-maker you!' O'Casey's howling rent the night air, until his throat ached with the effort and his heart was nearly stopped with the pain.

The mournful bells of the village church peeled in the midnight hour. 'Jasus! Holy and Divine Jasus, help me! If ya love me, help me!' Stallion's cry died in his throat. The village was in darkness, except for a light in Big Mary's window. He took two strides to her doorstep, but there he hesitated for all of twenty seconds before tapping quietly at the woodwork. His eyes caught a movement behind the curtained window, then the bolt was drawn back.

'Good evenin' to ya, Big Mary.'

'And to yarself, Stallion O'Casey,' Mary O'Leary replied.

'I saw a light in yar window. 'Tis late that ya're up.' Stallion hovered awkwardly, intimidated by her blank face and the arms folded tightly against her chest.

'It's lucky I'm up though, isn't it? Otherwise wouldn't I have had to get outa me warm bed to answer the door to yarself? Did ya not hear Saint Columba's bells bring in the midnight hour? Why aren't ya in bed, Stallion O'Casey?'

'Aye, I heard the bells, Big Mary, and their peals went right through me. Right down into me very soul, rippin' its very fibres to shreds.'

'What do ya want, Stallion?' Mary asked flatly.

Stallion O'Casey stared into her expressionless eyes. 'Comfortin'.'

She opened the door wide. 'Ya best come in then,' she said.

From her seat by the fire, she watched him dip into a bowlful of mashed potatoes doused with a quarter pint of cream. From the way he attacked her spuds, she guessed he hadn't taken food for at least twenty-four hours. He looked to her like a mad man that had just walked in off the bogs, after a lifetime of courting the bleak winds and the slate-grey rains. His face was stretched and taunt. There was at least four days of stubble carpeting his jowls, and the eyes in his head were as lifeless as two stones.

'That was grand, Mary. Just grand.'

'Arrah, 'twas nuttin' at all,' replied Mary. 'Ya should have let me cook ya somethin' with a bit more substance.'

'No. That did the trick. Just what the doctor ordered,' smiled Stallion.

'Well, at least it brought a smile back to yar face.'

'Even the sourest and the most miserable of men have to smile when they come in contact with yar fair and lovely self, Big Mary. Isn't the whole of yar mass forever glowing with the finest of warmth, sensitivity and buckets of pure understandin'?'

'Ah! Now I can see ya're comin' back to yarself,' Mary smiled back at him. 'When ya start spoutin' yar flattery and yar blarney at me, sure 'tis then I know ya're on the mend.'

'I don't think I'll ever be properly mended again, Big Mary.' The smile froze on Stallion's face. 'I'm not the same man any more. The whole of me insides is tellin' me that. Me heart is tickin' sure enough, and me lungs are still takin' in air, but I'm not really alive. I'm just goin' through the motions. I'm as dead as me darlin' boy that lays under the sods this very night.'

'Give yarself more time, Stallion. It takes time. Don't be impatient.'

Stallion buried his face in his hands and she heard him softly sobbing. When he finally raised his tear-stained face, she beckoned him over to join her by the fireside.

'I'm not a woman that keeps her company with the black nights. I'm usually in me bed and asleep well before nine most nights. But these past two weeks I've put me backside down in this chair as soon as the light starts to die out from the skies. And here I've stayed put, Stallion, night in and night out, waitin', waitin' and worryin'. . . . Waitin' for you. Waitin' to hear yar hobnail boots click on the cobbles outside me door. 'Tis then I know that Sullivan has shut his doors, and that there is nuttin' else left for you but to head for yar bed. As soon as yar boots are past my door and beyond me hearin', I know all is well. I walk with yarself right throughout that last hour, and me eyes keep watchin' till ya're tucked up and sleepin' soundly. 'Tis only then I can rest.'

'Yar heart was made and fashioned by the finest goldsmiths God could muster together, Big Mary,' said Stallion quietly, watching the flames that licked and played against the backplate of the chimney. 'When they poured that gold, Mary, they made sure it was pure, the purest they could find. 'Tis a heart of the purest gold ya have got for yarself, and 'tis glad I am to be able to bask in its shimmering light.'

'Ya can gather to yarself a fine collection of words when ya have a mind to, Stallion. You put me in mind of the great seanachie, O'Dowd himself.'

'The seanachie gives out those words because 'tis his trade, his livin'. But that I'm sayin' to yar lovely self I mean,' replied Stallion, looking into her gentle face. . . . The same ache that had gripped his heart when the bells of Saint Columba's tolled just an hour before gripped his heart once more. 'Oh, Jasus, Big Mary, but I'm lonely! I'm the loneliest man that God ever shoved onto this planet! I need yar softness, woman!'

She took his hard calloused hands in hers and held them tight. 'Oh my darlin', darlin', darlin' man!' she whispered, her eyes beginning to moisten. 'What softness can ya possibly get from meself? 'Tis forty years of arid, dry livin' ya're lookin' at, Stallion O'Casey. Me lips have never known the touch of a man's cheeks. I've never gone before any man to warm the sheets of his bed. I'm forty, and given a few more years me brain will cease to bother about the secrets and doin's that go on behind bedroom doors. I'm anxiously awaitin' for that time to come, when me heart will content itself with just tickin'. 'Tis peace I'm lookin' for now, Stallion. I can't be givin' ya the . . . the comfortin' ya're requirin' of me.'

'Oh Mary! Is it daft or heartless ya are? Ya don't have the right at all at all to don the old woman's shawl! Ya're in yar prime, woman. And there ya are spittin' in the face of life. Ya have no right to do that. Here's meself, Stallion O'Casey. God's own cruel sledgehammer has come right down outa the heavens and dealt me the most vile of blows, crushing to smithereens me poor ol' skull, smashin' me poor ol' heart into the tiniest of pieces and yet me eyes are alive this night. They're alive and lookin' across to the fairness of yar own sweet self. Dead though Stallion O'Casey may be, his eyes, God bless the both of them, have still the good sense to see and recognize beauty when it comes into their view. So don't ya dare tell me vision to go and pack its bags. Ya're a woman, Big Mary, in yar prime and ripe as the red, red berries of autumn! Ya have no right to lay down and dry up when the well stands before ya with plenty of water in it.' Stallion eased himself out of his chair. 'Stand up, me darlin', lovely woman! Stand up and bring yar grand and lovely face with ya.' He raised her to her feet. 'Look and take heed at the only two things that are alive and kickin' within me! Me eyes, Mary O'Leary! Can ya not see how they cry out to ya? Can't ya understand what they're tryin' to tell ya? Do what God has built ya for, Big Mary! Give succour and comfort to us that are dead!'

His tears fell freely now. She pressed her head to his chest and heard the thumping of his troubled heart, and she felt his broad strong arms wrap round her waist. . . .


The front door of the cottage was open wide and streaming shafts of sunlight carried on the early morning air cast their swords of light on the flagstone flooring of the kitchen.

The best of the late Minno O'Leary's Delft was to be found adorning the breakfast table. A turf fire was ticking over nicely in the hearth. Half a dozen potato cakes sizzled on the cast-iron plate that had been swung into position over the flames. A blackened kettle hanging from a snake-like hook snorted steam.

Big Mary filled her wash basin with the contents of the kettle. She dropped a cake of carbolic into the boiling water. With one of her best towels over her shoulder and the basin held tight in her two hands, she walked towards the open doorway of the bedroom. She hesitated momentarily in front of the doorway, coughed, and then stepped into the room. Half a minute later she was back preparing breakfast. She scooped her potato cakes off the fire plate and onto her best platter. She filled her best teapot and gave it pride of place in the centre of her neatly laid table, and then she sat herself down with her eyes facing the open doorway of the bedroom and waited.

With the open palm of her left hand she brushed the crown of her head in a vain attempt to tidy the renegade strands of wild hair that helped to form her cow's lick. She pinched and squeezed the flesh of her ample cheeks, succeeding in making her rose-coloured features even redder. Then she heard the scrape of his boots, and her hands disappeared beneath the table where they hugged the flesh that made up her ample thighs. 'Ya're up then,' smiled Mary as he appeared in the doorway.

'I am.'

'Then come sit yarself down. 'Tis potato cakes and tea that's on offer.'

'Why have ya got yar front door wide open?' asked Stallion, staying put.

'To let a bita God's own light inta the place on this grand mornin'.'

'Well shut it, Mary, will ya, or ya'll have the whole a the bloody village gawkin' in at us.'

'And why should I?' said Mary, the smile dying the death on her lips. 'I carry no shame, Stallion O'Casey. You might, but I do not! What we did was grand and lovely. As far as meself is concerned it was the most beautiful thing that ever happened, and if Father Barry tells me that the act is vile and sinful, then 'tis my back I'll turn on him, him and his bloody church!'

'Whist, will ya, woman!' O'Casey slammed and bolted the front door before Big Mary had time to protest. 'God almighty, Mary,' he said. 'It's okay to say what ya say to yarself, or to yar nearest and dearest. But ya don't go around broadcastin' yar utterances to the four bloody winds!'

'Is it a new and different O'Casey I'm lookin' at this morning'?' asked Mary, a hint of an impish smile touching the corner of her lips. 'Ya look like a frightened little schoolboy, Stallion. Who is it ya're frightened for?'

'You and yar reputation, woman!'

''Tis a bit late to be thinkin' about that now, isn't it?' laughed

Mary. 'Come on. Get yar legs over to this table and sit yarself down.'

She poured his tea for him and buttered his cakes. She watched him devour his breakfast, and as she poured him out a third cup of tea she asked, 'Is there more than four ways?'

'Four ways? Four ways a what?'

'Of doin' it,' said Mary coyly.

'Ah, sufferin' Jasus!' groaned Stallion. 'Not at the table, Mary! Not while we're eatin', for the love a God!'

'I'm only askin'. I'm only askin' a question that needs answerin', that's all. I don't know about these things, do I?'

'Ya're mockin' me, aren't ya? Go on, ya brazen hussy, admit it, ya're havin' yarself a skit at poor ol' O'Casey's expense.'

'I'm sorry, Stallion,' laughed Mary. 'You were askin' for it. You must admit that surely. The daylight is upon ya now, and because the daylight is upon ya, ya zip up the fly of yar pants, ya close the blinds around me grandma's four poster, and ya pretend there was never such a night. Ya're just behavin' like the rest of them, I suppose. But me, well, what I'd like to do is to go down to Saint Columba's church, step up to the altar and declare for the whole world to hear the wonderous things that ya did for me last night. . . . Don't worry, Stallion, no need to worry. I'll stay put.'

'If ya're tellin' me I'm made a the same stuff as the rest of them, ya're wrong! 'Twas only yar reputation I was thinkin' of. You have standin' in the parish, being the granddaughter of the great Tipp himself.'

'To hell with me standin'.'

'Don't knock standin',' said Stallion. 'Standin' is somethin' worth havin'. Now, to get down to brass tacks,' O'Casey continued as he ran a hand through his uncombed hair. 'Who do I go to? Who do I talk to?'

'About what?'

'About yarself and meself.'

'If I'm gettin' yar drift, if I'm thinkin' what I think yar thinkin', then ya've no one to see but me own self.'

'Then 'tis you I'm seein' then.'

'And 'tis me that's sittin' here waitin' for ya to make a bita sense.'

'Well, will ya?'

'Will I what?'

185

'Marry me.'

'Why?'

''Cause ya're a fine big woman, Mary O'Leary. 'Cause ya saved me from goin' under, and 'cause I'm gettin' this feelin' that I still might go under if ya're not around to buoy me up.'

'I'll gladly be yar buoy, Stallion O'Casey. For 'tis the most darlin' of men ya are, and 'tis glad I'll be to honour and serve ya.'

'Then 'tis settled,' stated Stallion solemnly. 'Any chance of another cup of yar grand tea?'

# 12

Pagga O'Leary's horse and cart were packed outside Clancy's cottage, loaded with all the paraphernalia that would be needed for the long journey in front of them. Milo checked the ropes that kept the great load secure, while Barra Duffy shut up the cottage. He bolted the back door, made sure all the windows were shut tight and that the ashes in the hearth were doused good and proper.

'Safe and secure, is it?' asked Milo, checking the harnessing on O'Leary's old nag.

'As the Bank of Ireland itself,' Barra assured him. He clambered into the cart and picked up the brand new slatted cage that rested at his feet, cooing endearments to the bird that was jailed within. Bulba crowed his rage-filled hate at Duffy's face and flapped his wings helplessly. With a sigh Barra returned the cage to the floor of the cart. 'Sad the day is, Taurus Bulba, when ya turn yar spite and anger on yar own handler. 'Tis cracked indeed that ya are.'

'What are ya whisperin' about?' snapped Clancy as he jumped up onto the duckboard.

'Just havin' a few words with our Bulba.'

'We haven't forgotten anything?'

'Nope.'

'Then 'tis away we are,' said Clancy, and flicked the reins down lightly on the horse's flank.

The sun was barely up. The slight breeze breathing in from the glass-like ocean kept hold of its night-time chill. The sky was one great expanse of the palest blue. Mingled with the aromatic whiff of seaweed and bitter-whipped salts were the hidden smells of morning – faint, perhaps, but they were there, perched on the still air. The faint but unmistakable scent of the reckless young sparrow who had flirted with the June moon and the smell of the old seahawk whose talons had clasped the little sparrow's breast. All the happenings of the night mingled in the early morning air and were wafted over the steep-riding cliffs to drift and disperse inland.

The metal rims of the cartwheels creaked and groaned and ached as they rolled along the old coast road. O'Leary's horse clip-clopped at a steady trot, and Milo Clancy gazed vacantly at the nag's hindquarters as they rose and fell in a steady and unchanging rhythm. Barra Duffy was sprawled in the back against a sack of spuds.

Jasus, sighed Barra quietly to himself. Who the hell knows when I'll next see this old road again? This road has been part and parcel of me very existence since I crawled away from me mother's tits. Only the Almighty knows when we shall return from this damn pox of a journey. 'Tis the bloody unforeseen that gives me the shakes! Didn't the unforeseen take the three of us by the hand and introduce us to that cunt of a man, Stallion O'Casey? Didn't it make us bring him back with us to our own homes so as he could torment us with his high-falutin' dreams of grandeur? A year ago O'Leary, Clancy and meself were just ordinary gombeens livin' out our simple lives as the good Lord had intended. Now look at us. All of us changed men. Chasin' the very stars themselves. And where are the lot of us bound for on this fine June mornin'? Back to the very source of all our woe and grief.

All our bad luck, all the troubles that have come down upon our heads haven't taught us a blessed thing. Didn't the Christ himself intervene on our behalf? Didn't he take away from O'Casey his only son, to show that damn man the errors of his wicked ways? Didn't he try to knock the mountain of greed out of his pitch-black soul? But did he learn his lesson? Not a bit of it. Look at what that bollocks of a cunt did, went and married one of our very own. Jasus, there'll be no gettin' rid a him now. Anything he dreams up, Clancy'll go along with, and what Clancy goes along with the rest of us will have to put up with. The bastard has poisoned us all. Bulba stirred in his cage. And you too, me darlin'. Duffy lifted the cage onto his lap, and the cock crowed out his rage and pecked at the wooden slats, trying to get at his handler. He's infected us all and you more than most, Taurus Bulba. He's taken yar own tiny brain and dipped it into the fires of hell itself.

★

188

Pagga O'Leary was on his knees in front of a well-stacked turf fire toasting some bread when Clancy and Duffy walked in on him. 'Top a the mornin' to yees,' he said.

'Big day,' greeted Clancy in turn.

'For all of us,' replied Pagga, getting off his knees with a platter stacked high with toast. 'How's yarself, Barra?'

'Fair to middlin'.'

'And our darlin' cock?'

'Prime condition.'

'That's what I like to hear.' O'Leary's eyes fairly twinkled. 'Well, come sit yarselfs down. 'Tis chef O'Leary that provides breakfast for yees t'is mornin'.'

'And where's the two paragons of love sublime?' Clancy drew up a chair and sat himself down at Pagga's badly laid table.

'Give ya a million guesses.'

'Ah, I see!' nodded Clancy. 'Ya'd be thinkin', Barra, wouldn't ya, that our friend Pagga here'd be in deepest mournin' for the loss of his sister to our friend O'Casey? Eh? After all, don't ya remember how Pagga used to go on about how Big Mary was his pride and joy and how he'd cut down any man who'd so much as dare look at her?'

'Be Jasus, Clancy, ya're in a right fuckin' joyful mood, aren't ya?' Pagga's face hardened.

'Well, 'tis a grand mornin'. Our long-awaited journey commences. The world is lookin' good for me. And it definitely looks good for you, now that Big Mary has finally gaffed her salmon and taken him to her bed. It looks good for Stallion too, for he seems to be in love with his entrapment. It's lookin' good for us all.'

'And if you stop yar mickey-takin', it would look all the better.'

'Right,' said Clancy. 'No more mickey-takin'. Now what's for breakfast?'

'What ya sees in front of yees.'

'Toast and a pot of tea?'

'Well, if 'tis finer grub ya're after, Clancy, ya'll have to go in the bedroom and prise those two lovers apart.'

'I don't have a crowbar.'

'That's what ya'd need an' all!'

'Ya're not complainin', Pagga, are ya?'

'The devil I am!' laughed Pagga, as he lifted the teapot and filled three mugs to the brim.

'Ya landed on yar feet and ya landed laughin', didn't ya, Pagga?' Duffy bit into a slice of hot buttered toast.

'That I did, Barra. Now it's your turn.'

'Turn for what?'

'For the gods to smile kindly on ya.' O'Leary's smile was sincere and his tone disarming.

'The gods don't need to do any favours for Barra Duffy,' said Milo. 'Barra's in clover right up to the neck. He'll be a rich man the same as the rest of us when we see the tinker's cock to its final resting place. Isn't that right, Barra? Ya're in clover and happy with it.'

'I'm not complainin', if that's what ya're on about, Milo.'

'Mornin' to yees all!'

The three of them turned to discover Stallion at the doorway in his nightshirt.

'Up and with the livin' at last,' grinned Pagga. 'Come draw up a chair and join us. Ya look like a man sorely in need of some rest.'

'Is it my imagination when I say that ya've been gettin' through a whole lota sleep these past few weeks?' asked Clancy.

'It's yar infantile imagination,' snapped O'Casey.

'Arrah, stop takin' the mickey outa the poor man,' said O'Leary. 'Doesn't he need all the rest he can get now that he's takin' on new responsibilities?'

'Responsibilities. Is that what it is, Pagga?' grinned Clancy.

O'Casey threw Milo a look that made it clear the joke was wearing a bit thin. He managed to fill a mug from the teapot without further harassment but he was only halfway to the bedroom before Clancy struck up with a few bars from 'Oh, how we danced on the night we were wed'.

Pagga waited for the bedroom door to click shut before he opened his mouth. 'Imagine that, though. Takin' breakfast to yar wife in bed.'

'It's called love, Pagga. Don't worry, it's a condition that soon wears off.'

'The sooner the better. Bloody disgustin'. A sane man traipsin' out here in his nightshirt to fetch tea for his missus.'

'Terrible. Just terrible.'

O'Casey emerged once more and joined the three of them at the table. Clancy waited until Stallion brought his mug of tea to his lips before asking, 'Big Mary not feelin' too well, then?'

'She's feelin' a bit tired, that's all,' frowned Stallion.

There was nothing he could do but watch Clancy and O'Leary break their sides. Even the 'forever gloom' Duffy was sporting a grin and a half.

The bedroom door opened then and Mrs Mary O'Casey came in upon them all.

'The dead arose and appeared to many!' choked Clancy.

'Top o' the mornin' to ya, Milo.'

'Sure, 'tis a healthy flush ya've got about yar cheeks this mornin', Mary, to be sure!' said Clancy, as Mary pulled up a chair.

'I've heard ya take the mickey outa my man all mornin', Milo Clancy.' Big Mary's eyes were cold and threatening. 'He's too good and kind a man to be givin' ya a wallopin', but ya're now lookin' at his better half, and I'm a different kettle a fish altogether. Another word, another half ounce of yar half-baked wit and I'll lay ya flat. Do ya get me meanin', Mr Clancy?'

'Loud and clear, Big Mary,' replied Clancy, the smile on his face dying the death.

'It's Mrs O'Casey to you. That or Mary. Big Mary is out!' Her eyes raked the table. 'Do ye all get me meanin'?'

Everyone nodded. Even her lesser half.


The clock in the tower of Saint Columba's church was ringing in the hour of noon as the two horses and carts made their way up the village street of Feacledown. All the inhabitants of the village were at their front doors to see them off. Some of them ran to the leading cart to push money into the hands of Pagga O'Leary to invest for them in that faraway place they would never see. But the women had their eyes trained on the duckboard of the trailing cart, appraising the woman who sat erect, head held high, eyes staring at the road ahead.

A mile outside the village they came to a stop. All got down. Stallion O'Casey opened wide the wrought-iron gates to the little village cemetery and walked through into the tiny graveyard.

Colin O'Casey's grave was at the top of the knoll that made up Drumcliff cemetery. All it was was a mound of upturned soil. But the summer grass had sprouted over the brown earth. Big Mary led them through a decade of the Rosary as they knelt on the greening earth, their thoughts their own. Only Stallion remained standing, watching them from some distance away.

Big Mary eased herself off her knees. The men blessed themselves, stood up, and followed her down the slope to the waiting O'Casey. 'I think 'tis best we tell them now, love,' said O'Casey, looking at his wife.

'Whatever ya say.' Mary took hold of his arm. 'Pagga,' she said, 'we're not comin' back.'

'What do ya mean?'

'We're not comin' back here to live.'

'Back to yar own place is it, Stallion?' asked Pagga.

'America,' said Stallion. 'Win or lose, we're off and makin' for the New World. I'm sellin' my own patch and leavin' this godforsaken bitch of a country for good.'

'Then 'tis all the very best a luck to ya.' Clancy extended a hand.

'Thank ya, Milo.' O'Casey shook hands with him warmly.

''Tis sorry a thousand times over I'll be with yar partin',' said Pagga to his sister.

'Am I to believe a word a that, Pagga O'Leary?'

'Believe me, sister, I'll be sorry,' mumbled Pagga into the open neckline of his shirt.

'I'll believe ya, Pagga O'Leary, 'cause ya're my brother and I love ya. I left a cottage back there. It's yours, though what ya'll do with two cottages, God knows. But it's yours to do what ya want with.'

'Thank ya, Mary,' said Pagga, head bowed.

Sensing Pagga's embarrassment, Stallion came to the rescue. 'And what about you?' he said to Duffy. 'No doubt ya'll be glad to see the back of me?'

'I can't say I'll be broken-hearted,' stated Duffy frankly. 'But I'll tell ya somethin' for nuttin' though. All the cocks in Ireland'll be crowin' their heads off with pure joy as soon as they see yar boat upon the waters.'


Aggie Carney came to life a second after her maid stopped rapping on her bedroom door. 'In ya come!' she shouted, yanking the top of the eiderdown up over her head. She heard the bedroom door open, stayed motionless while the maid crossed the bedroom floor, and heard the breakfast tray clink down on the bedside table. 'A little less noise, if ya please, Kathleen.' A cheerful 'Good mornin', Mrs Carney,' was the response. There was a swish and scrape as the curtains were drawn back. Aggie waited patiently until the bedroom door clicked shut. Then cautiously she exposed her face, to confront a bright, delicate early morning light. She found herself thinking aloud. 'The eve!' she said out loud. Today is the eve of the big day. The biggest day in yar life, Aggie Carney! She gritted her teeth and frowned. For the love a God, Aggie Carney, she chided herself, be normal for once. Switch off the grey matter! Be like everybody else and keep yar brain dopey and relaxed, until ya at least have had yar breakfast! She punched and puffed the pillows, and reached out for her tea.

Having drained the cup, she relaxed and allowed her brain to restart its motors. Every room at the White Willow was booked. She had upped the price five times and had found every one of the cockfighting fraternity only too willing to pay. Six of her poorer rooms she had turned into dormitories. Four beds to a room. Twenty-four beds in all. Five pounds a bed per night was her asking price and she was full up twenty-four hours after the offer was made. The only rooms going free in the hotel were for her own special guests, Stallion O'Casey and company. This thought irked her calculating brain a little, but she erased it, knowing there was little to be done. Decisions had to be made. Five extra barstaff were needed. She tallied up the cost and decided two would do.

The ringing clatter of empty beer barrels just outside her bedroom window interrupted her train of thought. Her pot man was at work. The White Willow was coming to life. It was time to get dressed.

An hour later, breakfast was being served in the large but overcrowded dining room. Three waitresses shuffled back and forth under the hawkish eye of Aggie herself. Everything was going smoothly. Her decision, reached three mornings before, to make do with just the three of them had been the right one. She was just about to check on her overworked cook when her own personal maid appeared.

'What is it Kathleen?' snapped Aggie. 'Why aren't ya upstairs on the beds?'

'Sergeant Hassit to see ya, ma'am,' Kathleen snapped back, lifting her head just that bit higher.

Aggie's eyes narrowed. 'What's he want?'

'Search me! He's in the bar if ya want to see him.'

'But the bar is closed.'

'That's where he is.'

'Off with ya and tell him I'll be along in a minute.' The sting had gone out of Aggie's voice. Her brow was furrowing and her brain was on the go. Now what in the blazes does that bastard want? I saw him right only a month ago. Don't ask daft questions, she scolded herself. The bastard's palm is itchy again. It's opening up just like the bulbs a May. Someone ought to chop it off!

Tim Hassit was sitting at the bar, peering through the gloom at the army of bottles that were ranked in straight lines all the way along the glass shelves. The whole place looked strange and different to him. This was his favourite watering hole, where his pints of refreshment were cheerfully administered, mostly free of charge. It was seldom, if ever, that Sergeant Tim Hassit had to dig into the depths of his trouser pockets.

As his eyes roamed the bar, he sighed deeply at the sheer sadness of it all. There was less than a month of drinking left to him in this most pleasant of drinking establishments. Two weeks more and the day of retirement was on him. He had picked himself out a rich widow at the start of the year, courted her and married her. She would be taking him away from all this, to spend his twilight days in the fair city of Derry itself. There was a fine house waiting with a good few acres of land to potter around in, if he felt so inclined. But parting from a community that he had served for the last fifteen years still held an ocean of sadness for him. The drawn curtains around Aggie Carney's bar, the tables and chairs standing empty on the rich carpeted floor, and the morose, church-like silence heightened his sense of melancholy.

'Ya look as if someone has gone and robbed yar cop shop, Tim.'

'Ah 'tis yarself, Aggie darlin'. Top a the mornin' to ya.' Hassit turned to see Aggie's broadest of smiles lighting up her cheery

194

morning face. He had given her his very best shots over the years, tried his damnedest to lure her in the direction of the altar, but to little avail. Pity, he now thought sadly to himself. If only I'd succeeded, I'd never have had to leave this place.

'And what brings ya here at this hour a the mornin'?' asked Aggie, as she climbed onto one of the high stools.

'Well,' smiled Hassit, 'I'm here with grand news for yarself. Ya know I'm bein' put out to grass in a matter of a few short weeks.'

'That I do, and 'tis sorry for every man, woman and child in this parish we are that we'll be losin' ya. Isn't the whole town askin' themselves who the big nobs in Dublin are goin' to replace ya with?'

'Well, ya can rest easy in yar bed tonight, for I'm here to tell yarself that the fellah that's comin' here to step into me very own boots is none other than the grand Pascal Shannon himself. That's the good news I've come to yar door with this fine mornin'.'

'Pascal Shannon? I'm sorry, Tim, but he doesn't ring any bells with me.'

'And why should he? After all, ya've never clapped eyes on the man. He's been poundin' the beat way down south in the county of Kerry for the past twenty years. But 'tis meself that knows him, and 'tis me, after a lot a hard work and the pullin' of strings, that has got him for ya. When they gave me me stripes I was based in Tralee, and the youngest little scut there was our man Shannon. Sure, didn't I teach the lad everything he knows? He has meself to thank for his grand standin' now. When I go out to pasture he'll step in here and take over, and ya don't have to worry about a thing for he's as grand as meself if not grander. He understands the way things are here. Upholds the law when it needs upholdin', but he's by no means a stickler to its letter. He understands that people have to make a livin'. He has an eye for a good-lookin' cock, just like everybody else around here. Sure, the man will even put a few bob down to see one fight, that's if the fight is worth watchin'. A grand man, Aggie, in every sense of the word, and 'tis me, Tim Hassit, that's found him for you. It took a lota phone calls, a lota ringin' up the Dublin headquarters to get the big boys to move on it and to get our man Shannon transferred here. A lota hours a hard graft to pull the strings, a hell of a lot. . . .'

Aggie's eyes sparkled with gratitude and her smile was warm and full, but inside she was fuming. Hassit was into her for a big bite. The big cockfight was just one day away, the biggest that the parish had ever seen. It was known by all that she would make a bundle, and Hassit was asking for his share. That it would be his last gave her little satisfaction. Shannon, whoever he was, would slip easily into Hassit's own boots, and doubtless, knowing the form, would soon come calling on her. It was the way things were.

'I'm grateful to ya, Tim,' she said, 'that ya put yarself out for all of us, and you with all the responsibility of looking after the whole of the parish and keepin' the blackguards from our doors.'

'Think nuttin' of it, Aggie.'

'Can I get ya a short?'

''Tis a bit early in the day for me,' protested Hassit, making himself comfortable on his seat.

A quarter of an hour later, with her morning smile wearing a bit thin, Aggie waved the sergeant back to his beat. He walked off with a spring in his step, and with one hundred of her hard-earned pound notes in his pocket.


As the morning progressed the town came to life. Shutters were taken down from shop windows and doors flung open. Far-sighted housewives did their shopping early, knowing that for a good two hours the streets would be almost deserted except for the shopkeepers waiting on their doorsteps. The pubs of the town also settled down to those two hours of forced calm, with only the barmaids keeping vigilance behind their counters, polishing their trays of glasses and waiting for the storm to break. Noon came and was ten minutes gone before the first horse and cart was seen arriving on the south side of the town. Doors opened on every street, and heads craned out to see a half-starved piebald horse carting his master and missus and four snotty-nosed kids. The horse pulled up in the middle of the town's square. And a crowd quickly gathered to watch the hawker and his family set up their stall. It was the signal for things to happen. Half an hour later and the little town square was packed solid with hawkers and their rickety stalls. By three o'clock all the roads into the town were jammed with horses and carts, cars, tinkers' caravans and travellers-a-foot. The hustle and bustle as the pilgrims poured in lasted well into the latter stages of the afternoon, but as the bells of the two churches rang in the hour of six the streets were finally cleared and the relentless clamour died down. The town was full to bursting.

Twilight didn't encroach on the late June skies until well after nine, and it was only as the first shades of night dispelled the day that two very decorative gypsy caravans were spotted coming in off the old southeast road. Immediately, the pubs and hotels emptied themselves of their patrons. The whole town spilled back onto the streets, lining the kerbs to watch the cortège go by. Little girls, attracted by the beautiful paintwork on the sides of the caravans, skipped along gaily behind, while little boys, gog-eyed at the four midnight-black horses that pulled the vans, flanked the wondrous animals on either side to provide an escort through town. The grown-ups fell in behind the children and the procession continued. The drivers finally reined in their horses at the main entrance to the White Willow Hotel and the landlady, Aggie Carney herself, was there to greet them. Mothers tried to hush their excited children as they watched the drivers dismount. Several seconds passed before they all saw what they had been so long waiting for. . . . A canopy was pulled back and a man stepped out into the night air. He stood for a moment on the duckboard, his face hidden in shadow. He passed down some kind of parcel to the driver and then got down himself. The lights from the White Willow Hotel finally trapped the man's face in their glare. The silence was almost audible. Then someone in the crowd started to applaud. It was taken up at once by the rest and a gusto of cheering broke. Aggie Carney stepped forward with the most gracious of smiles adorning her face. 'Tilla, ya ol' rogue,' she cried, ''tis a welcome sight ya are for these eyes of mine!'

'It's not yar own sweet self, Aggie darlin', is it?' The old man inclined his wrinkled face at an odd angle, revealing that he had only one eye. The left was just a black patch of lacquered cardboard.

''Tis meself and none else, ya old scamer,' beamed Aggie.

'And ya've got some accommodation ready for me and me boys, I hope?'

'The field out back is all ready for ya and yar troop. But if ya'd care to consider a bed in me own best room, ya've only to say the word.'

'Room! Ha!' scoffed the old tinker. 'Unhealthy, unairy and downright tubercular.'

'Well, a drink in me bar before ya settle down for the night,' pressed Aggie.

'No thanks. Meself and me brood better hit the hay. We've had a long journey.' His drivers on either side of him, Tilla Kusthi led the way to Aggie Carney's field. And the crowd dispersed as quickly as it had arrived.

Half an hour before midnight, Stallion O'Casey and his party came in off the west road. There was no one to greet them.

# 13

He slid the blankets down off his chest and, with infinite care, eased himself out of bed and onto the carpeted floor. Standing by the window he lit his first fag of the day and looked out onto Aggie Carney's back yard. Dozens of empty beer crates were stacked with some care one on top of the other all along the streetside wall. Beyond, in Aggie Carney's half acre of field, Tilla Kusthi's two gaily coloured caravans sparkled in the early morning rays of the sun. The four horses were nose deep in grass, grazing contentedly under the blue of the sky. Nothing else stirred. He doused the butt in the ashtray and stood stock still as his wife stirred in her sleep. He waited for her gentle snoring to resume before he tiptoed for the door.

Five minutes later he returned, a cup of tea in each hand. He tapped her softly on the shoulder.

'Mornin', darlin'. What time is it?' asked Mary, drowsily reaching for her tea.

'Comin' up to seven,' replied Stallion, and wandered back to the window.

'There's a man down there in that field that can make or break us this day.'

'Bulba'll see him off. Don't fret, me darlin'.'

'I hope so, my pet. I hope so, for all our sakes.'

'There was a time when ya were full of confidence. When the word "no" wasn't allowed to walk in yar presence.'

'I was me own god then. I was me own creator and maker.'

'And what are ya now?'

'A man like the rest of yees with big ideas, a pocketful of hope and fuck all else!'

'Ya can't let the lads hear ya talk like that.'

'Don't worry. I'm a great actor. Besides, I've hope and buckets a faith in our Taurus. It's Kusthi I'm not so sure of.' Stallion walked over to the bed and planted a kiss on his wife's lips.

'Well, we'll beat him,' said Mary. 'We'll rob him of his confidence, tear down his faith and bury his proud cock in total defeat.'

'That's the spirit! Jasus, Mary, as I keep tellin' yarself, ya're my salvation! Let's get dressed, get those lazy bastards next door out and off their arses and go bury this day in a mountain of glory.'

Three of the White Willow barstaff helped their boss onto the counter of the bar. Reassured that there was no fear of her toppling over, they stepped back out of the limelight and waited with the hundreds of others gathered there for Aggie Carney to open up and address them all.

Hands on her ample hips, she surveyed the expectant throng, and then her stern lips parted in a generous smile. 'To the lot a yees, welcome! The heartiest a welcomes to yees all! Now let me begin by sayin' . . .'

'Hang on a minute there, Aggie Carney!' cried a voice from the floor.

'What is it, Pat Slattery?' Aggie looked daggers at the small-framed man in the centre of the crowd.

'Is it true,' asked Slattery, undaunted by the towering figure of the proprietress, 'is it true ya're askin' us all to fork out a pound each for the privilege of goin' through yar barn doors tonight?'

'It is,' said Aggie firmly. 'Ye are about to witness the greatest cockfight ever to take place in these parts. It's cost me a pretty penny to stage the proceedings here, as well ya all know. However, Mr Slattery, if ya object so strongly ya needn't bother showin' up. I'm sure ya presence will not be missed.' Slattery's bravado evaporated in an instant. 'Now if I can continue . . . .' No one else would dare interrupt her now. 'There are twelve fights tonight. The climax of which is that between Mr Tilla Kusthi's cock, Satan the First, and Mr Milo Clancy's Taurus Bulba. The judge for all twelve fights is Mr John Barrett. Most of yees won't have heard of the man. He comes from Limerick, is as neutral as stone itself, and that's all there is to say about him. He's been vetted by all the participants in the contests and found to be honest, pure and true, and a lover of the cock. Without further ado, I'll now bring on the main contenders of this evening's events. Gentlemen, from the lands of west Mayo may I please present . . .'

The parlour door opened and out walked Barra Duffy with Taurus Bulba encased tightly in his arms. They were followed by Clancy, O'Leary and O'Casey. A pathway opened up for them and, with Barra in the lead, they walked right into the heart of Aggie's bar. The patrons of the White Willow closed in around them. All eyes were on Bulba. Those that had seen him before swore to each other that the cock had doubled his weight and size. Others, who had believed that the tinker's cock had no equal, had second thoughts as they watched Bulba struggle and fret in his presenter's arms. Questions came raining down upon Duffy's head. Why was he wearing protective gloves? Why was the bird hooded?

From the vantage point of her high counter, Aggie stamped her foot on the woodwork, and reluctantly heads turned away from the hooded bird and towards her. 'Gentlemen! The cock! The cock known by all to have come from Satan's own loins! The one and only . . . Satan the First!'

Eyes swivelled again towards her parlour. Framed in the doorway stood Declan Mango Kusthi, with Satan the First held gently under his left arm. Roars and cheers reverberated round the bar. Tilla Kusthi's youngest son stepped proudly forward and a circle cleared for him. Mango lifted his bird sky high. Satan responded to the occasion and lifted all their hearts with a blood-chilling crow. Towering above their heads, blacker than the blackest night, yellow pincered beak agape, he crowed on and on. The whole of his body was bulging muscle on bone. His wings' purity of line as they slammed the air brought chilling draughts of air upon the uplifted faces.

Then, from the other end of the room, Satan's call was answered, and the cockfighting fraternity's ears were entertained as another bloodcurdling crow rang out, doubling the intensity of the barbaric aria. The whole bar exploded with shouts and cheers of encouragement.

The birds and their handlers withdrew, and the punters settled down to debate, haggle and place their bets on the fight of fights.

Everyone knew Carney's bar was the place to spend the day. With Aggie's ale in their glasses each man sat back and allowed the grand proceedings to unfold right in front of his very eyes.

Eleven o'clock it was when Condour Kusthi rolled up to the front door of the White Willow in a spanking brand new Model-T Ford. Imported all the way from America itself, the car attracted nearly as much attention as the great man himself. An army of fans followed Kusthi's eldest son into the clogged bar and witnessed the introductions as Aggie presented Condour Kusthi to Milo Clancy. The two men stood pinned against the bar, exchanging pleasantries. Ten minutes later, in came the king himself, Tilla Kusthi. With much pushing and shoving, a pathway was cleared. Condour had not seen his father for the best part of six weeks, and embraced him warmly. And Clancy took the opportunity to study the man who was reputed to have the finest fighting bird in the whole of Ireland. Short he was, couldn't be more than five and a half feet. A man who kissed his eighties goodbye at least five summers ago, Clancy reckoned. Tilla Kusthi wore every one of his years badly. His head was as bald as an egg, and the winds on the many roads he travelled had carved a cruel harshness into his worn and tired features. The black lacquered patch that adorned his empty left socket seemed like a natural part and parcel of the tinker's appearance. Kusthi reminded him a bit of the old seanachie, O'Dowd. O'Dowd, as everyone knew, was close to death, and so too, thought Clancy, was the tinker before him.

'Da, I'd like ya to meet Mr Milo Clancy, owner of the cock Taurus Bulba. Milo, my father, Tilla Kusthi.'

''Tis glad I am at last to be meetin' ya, sir,' said Clancy, extending his hand.

'Likewise,' replied Kusthi, with a faint, toothless smile. 'I understand you have a cock!'

'A cock I have!' smiled Clancy.

'A good one?'

'None better.'

'None?'

'None.'

'Then I'm in for a bad night,' sighed the old tinker in mock despair.

'I'm afraid so,' smiled Milo in sympathy.

202

''Tis a whole year I've been travelling the length and breadth of this country, guiding my Satan through his last few fights. He's seen off three very fine birds. Now there's yours. Your bird is the very last, before I finally send my cock out to his well-deserved pasture of retirement. But, as I see it, ya're tellin' meself my cock won't come through, that he'll die in the embrace of yar Bulba's talons.'

'I'm afraid so, Tilla,' said Clancy.


One of Aggie Carney's maids brought a tray of sandwiches and half a dozen bottles of stout up to Milo Clancy's room at four o'clock that afternoon. It was Barra Duffy who answered the door and took the tray. An hour later, the stout was gone but the sandwiches were still on the plate.

Bulba was in his cage on the mattress with Barra Duffy beside him. Clancy was staring blankly out of the window, chain-smoking. O'Leary was elsewhere putting their money to work. O'Casey and his wife were downstairs in Aggie's parlour, sitting down to one of her famous high teas.

The room was hot and the air heavy, and the sultry afternoon seemed like it would never end. A car backfired somewhere, and Bulba was momentarily unsettled. 'Anythin' happenin' out there in that field?' asked Duffy absentmindedly, forgetting he had asked the question as soon as the words had left his lips. It was hot; beads of sweat glistened on his forehead. The room reeked of stale tobacco and the odour of human bodies.

Ten minutes later Pagga came back, bringing a brief injection of artificial energy. All their money was down. Pagga had got odds of six to one and better. His part of the job was done. The rest was up to Bulba now. Pagga revelled in their warm praise, but the humidity of the soul-sapping afternoon soon imposed a weary silence once more.

At seven o'clock, they were joined by Stallion and Mary. The room buzzed up once more but only for a little while. When Stallion asked with an exaggeratedly cheery voice if Duffy could take Bulba down off the bed so as he could stretch his legs he was told in no uncertain terms to 'Fuck off!'

★

The June sun had burned the land dry. It had also succeeded in baking to boiling point the vast expanse of corrugated roof that covered Carney's infinity of a barn. When the evening came, with no hint of a breeze, the mercury inside was touching 115 degrees, and threatening to climb higher as the heat and sweat from over two thousand bodies rose in a haze towards the rafters.

A crescendo of noise battered the walls of the barn as the eleventh fight of the evening died the death, with the two blood-soaked cockerels dead and spattered in bits all over the sawdust ring. It had been a poor affair. They had gone for each other's throats from the word go and the sweltering heat had soon drained their sap. It was a crude, clawing, pecking match from then on, until the victor struck home with a lucky spur. A second after it had nailed its victim it keeled over, dead from heart failure, exhaustion or both.

That fight was forgotten. Thirty-eight bookies proper were pinned against the walls of the barn as hundreds of crazed punters came rushing at them to get the last of their money down on the cock of their choice. An entire half hour went by and still the bets were being shouted and signalled. The let up only came when the master of ceremonies made his entrance through the main door-way. An almighty roar went up. Behind the master came Taurus Bulba clamped tight in the arms of his minder. A step behind strode Bulba's trainer and presenter, Milo Clancy. Ten paces behind came the champion cock, Satan the First, at ease in the arms of his minder, Mango Kusthi. Behind Mango came the king himself. The roaring continued unabated as the procession marched towards the ring; it was a further ten minutes before the master of ceremonies could make himself heard. The introductions were made with much pomp. The handlers drenched their fighters' heads for the last time with water-filled sponges. The ballyhoo died down almost to a hum as the cocks were handed to the presenters, who then entered the wire doors from opposite sides of the ring.

'Gentlemen, present yar birds.' Clancy and the tinker swung their birds towards each other. Beak met beak, and two pairs of spurred claws lashed out. The presenters withdrew their fighters at once. 'Very good, gentlemen. Yar birds show signs of doin' battle this night. They're a credit to ya both. Let's pray for a good fight. Gentlemen! Retire to yar stations!'

The master of ceremonies withdrew from the ring. Kusthi and Clancy walked the longest road of their lives to their dropping points. They stopped, turned, and a second later Tilla Kusthi, with a nod of his head, gave the all clear. Clancy responded in kind, and together both men let their birds flutter down onto the sawdust floor, and left the ring.

Immediately, Satan took three lightning strides and, his black wings beating, climbed for the heights. Bulba stayed where he was. Legs arched, spurs glinting, eyes trained on the target below him, Satan hovered seven feet above the ring. Then he dropped, true as a stone.

Bulba waited, coiled like a spring, until the last fraction of a second, before shooting out of harm's way. The claws of Satan managed only to catch a few talonfuls of air. Helter-skelter Bulba tore in on the descending cock, legs pumping like pistons. But the tinker's bird hit the sawdust with perfect balance. With razor-sharp reflexes he braced himself for the attack. Clancy's Bulba cannoned into him with the power of a bullet, but Satan stood firm. There was an explosion of feathers. Beak, spurs, talons and the brute power of their bodies all whirred into action. They slashed, tore and gouged, beaks aiming for a score on the vulnerable eye, spurs and talons aiming for other vital targets of underbelly and chest. But only the most perfect arrowed downward swoops could bring the slits of steel home to rest in those elusive regions. Yet breast to breast they stayed for three murderous minutes, giving no quarter.

For the first time in his fighting career the tinker's cock was on the sawdust, battling for his life. His prowess was in the air, but the challenger continued to crowd him, confining him to the ground. But suddenly, Satan's pincered beak struck home into Bulba's chest. It hacked into the sparse flesh on the chest bone and it hooked! It hooked and gaffed there and when the beak withdrew it came away with a supper of meat. The blood oozed out through Bulba's rich plumage, and the shocked Taurus darted backwards.

Satan zoomed up into the air again. Below him the target was running. Satan's legs arched to the required length and he dive-bombed. A hoot of pure elation poured from his throat as his spurs caught Bulba's retreating back. But he failed to topple his prey. So swift was the challenger's mad burst for safety that the spurs of his opponent were dragged along with him. The tinker's cock screeched his rage and fear as he lost his balance. For a good two feet, Satan was scraped along on his back, until his frantic spurs tore themselves free.

The length of his back in shreds, but free at last from those slits of steel, Bulba rocketed into the wire wall. He bounced back off it like a rubber ball and collapsed in a bloody heap. There he stayed, on his right side, trying to drag the putrid air into his aching lungs. A crimson river flowed freely through his open beak. Sheer exhaustion and total despair enveloped him. His blood-clogged nostrils sensed the chill wind of death itself come to claim his remains. He lifted his bloody head to face it, and saw his black enemy soaring for the heights in order to deliver the *coup de grâce*. Bulba drove the fear from his heart. Emitting a crazed crow, he struggled to his feet. A standing bounce of pure muscle propelled him off the ground. His wings beat the air and he was climbing, but the tinker's cock was already into his swoop. The two fighters collided eighteen inches above the earth in a volcano of feathers. The force of Satan's descent knocked his opponent to the floor. But the cock's talons never made contact with Bulba's flesh, and in a flash he had regained his feet.

It was only Stallion O'Casey who could see into the workings of Bulba's brain at this moment. He knew instinctively that if he let Satan take to the air the battle would soon be over for him. An unholy fury deluged Bulba's brain as he fought for a dominant position in the ring. It cost him plenty to get there. One of Satan's deadly spurs had done terrible damage to Bulba's left thigh. The cruel beak of his opponent had ripped a good four inches of muscled flesh on the shoulder of his right wing. But the tide was turning for Clancy's cock. The fight was into its fifteenth minute. It had been the longest fight in Satan's history, and even his enormous strength was beginning to wane. The heat, flies and dust that clung to his proud velvety plumage seemed to weigh him down. The upstart enemy, forever pressing with wings at full splay, blocked his retreats, and prevented Satan from taking up any position for a calculated attack.

It took another five minutes of brutal head-to-head confrontation before Bulba had backed and bullied his aggressor from the centre of the ring to the wire wall. In doing so, he had also managed to sink a spur into the soft underbelly of his prey. It was a lucky back-kick. But it had done lethal work, and Bulba could at last smell blood other than this own. He redoubled his efforts. With his wings at full stretch he mantled himself over the tinker's cock and his bloody beak rammed home with the force of a jackhammer. Satan fought back desperately, but he was trapped against the wire. The stubbed comb on his head was in shreds and was spurting jets of blood in a constant stream into his eyes. The lights were fast going out for the tinker's bird. Terror in the face of death helped Satan dig out one last almighty effort, and he made a bid for freedom and the air. As he sprang his face came level with his aggressor's. Bulba's beak shot out and plucked the left eye straight out of Satan's head. With an ear-splitting squawk the tinker's bird shot up into the air. Clancy's cock echoed the cry, and took off in hot pursuit.

They met four feet above the ground. Legs, talons and spurs engaged. The tinker's cock was blind. Not even a foggy haze could be seen through his one remaining eye, but his maddened senses were on key. Bulba's spurs shot out and sank home in the lower part of Satan's belly. An instant later Satan's right spur took root, lodging itself at the base of Bulba's neck. The spur came out. The birds separated and both plummeted to the ground.

The spectators were on their feet, baying on the fighters. Five seconds passed and there was no movement inside the wired arena. But then the whole barn erupted in cheering as one of the cocks staggered to his feet.

Taurus Bulba faltered and almost toppled over on to his face, but somehow he regained his balance. Blood, almost black in colour, oozed slowly through a matchhead hole on the right side of his neck. But his head was held high, and he made his painful way towards his enemy. He fell, and the crowd held their breath.

With his remaining strength and indomitable courage, Bulba forced himself upright. He climbed on to the bloody carcass and dug his talons into Satan's flesh. The tinker's bird did not rise up to do battle with him. Bulba lifted his head to the rafters . . . .

Standing over the two of them the master of ceremonies gave the dead flag to Satan the First.

Taurus Bulba looked long and hard at those rafters. Then he opened his bloody beak and crowed out to the heavens themselves his mighty victory. Something burst within the bird's throat a few seconds later, and a river of blood spurted through the wound on his neck. Clancy's Bulba collapsed in a heap, his mighty wings splaying in his death spasm to cover the valiant dead foe that lay beneath him.

Barra Duffy, his face pressed up against the wire, watched Clancy and Condour Kusthi burst in to retrieve their dead birds. He turned his back on the arena as they lifted the dead carcasses skyward for the benefit and jubilation of the crowd, walking away from the deafening melee with tears streaming down his face.

As he cleared the great doors of the barn he lifted his face to the night sky to drink in the air, but there wasn't a breath to be had. The night itself was as dead as the two fighters he had left behind him. His stomach heaved as he saw again Satan's spur enter Bulba's throat. Helplessly, he vomited up through his dry, strained throat.

Three hours later and the bar of the White Willow was alive with song, good fellowship and celebration. Aggie's stout was flowing from all four pumps as the fraternity charged their glasses time and time again to the valiant birds who had enriched their lives with the finest display of cockfighting that had been seen in anyone's lifetime. The night was passing, but it would never be forgotten by those who had stood under the roof of Carney's barn. The day would be remembered for ever – 26 June 1928.

The Mayo men were much sought after that night. Clancy, Pagga, O'Casey and his wife were kept nailed against Aggie's counter as the wee hours of the morning started to slip away. It wasn't until well past three before Milo managed to break away from amongst the huge arc of admirers that surrounded him. He craved their indulgence, declaring that his bladder was in dire need of emptying. Reluctantly they let him go.

In Aggie's foyer he turned left and ran up the stairs to the second floor. A few seconds later he was tapping on his own door. There was no answer. He waited a few seconds before turning the knob. 'I thought you were in bed,' said Clancy with a smile. But Barry Duffy was very much dressed. He was standing on the far side of the bed, a fistful of clothes in his hand, and his travelling sack half full on the mattress. 'I thought you were in bed,' Clancy repeated, as he watched Duffy stuff the last of his clothes away. But Barra ignored him completely.

208

'Ya're feelin' better then?'

Barra lifted his head and looked at Milo for the first time since he entered the room. 'Yeah. I'm feelin' better.' Duffy's voice was crisp, but the anger had already left his eyes as he added, 'A few hours' kip does wonders for a dickety stomach. Don't ya agree?'

Clancy didn't like Duffy's smile. 'Where are ya goin'?' he asked.

'Home,' smiled Barra broadly as he picked the sack up off the bed. 'Home where I belong.' He walked towards the frowning Clancy.

'Ya're goin' to walk all the way back to Mayo, are ya?' sneered Milo, his stance menacing as he blocked Duffy's path to the landing outside.

Duffy halted a hair's breadth away from Milo's nose. His voice matter of fact, his manner as still as the night itself, he said, 'If ya don't move aside I'll kill ya. Ya might do some damage to meself but ya'll end up dead and bleeding on that there carpet. Move aside like the good chap that I know ya aren't.' Clancy stepped aside and it wasn't until Duffy had left the bedroom that he called out, 'You forgot somethin', Barra.'

Duffy stopped. 'What did I forget, Milo?'

Clancy took the wad of notes from his inside pocket and held it in the air. He smiled as he saw the conflicting emotions fight it out on Barra's face, and his smile spread from cheek to cheek as Duffy stepped forward and took the money. 'How easily we all kid ourselves, eh Barra? Every man jack of us a hypocrite, but some more than others.' Duffy did not reply as he stuffed the wad into the back pocket of his trousers. 'I'll see ya when I get back then,' said Clancy.

'You set foot on my land, you darken the doors of my cottage and yar lips'll taste the mouth of me da's shotgun. Stay clear of me, Milo. For yar own sake stay outa me path.' Duffy's voice wasn't threatening; it was pleading, and that same cold chill of ice ran the length of Milo Clancy's back as he watched Barra turn from him and go out of his sights.


Four days later two horses and carts came out from behind the back of the White Willow Hotel.

With Stallion's nag leading the way, the wheels groaned and clanked over the surface of the sloping road as they came on down into the twon proper. But apart from the lament of the wheels no other sound could be heard. Right up the main street they went and not a soul was in sight. Pub doors were shut, blinds were drawn on cottage windows, even the bell in the steeple of the town's church was silent and had no intention of ringing out until another hour had come and gone. No one was about to lift an arm and wave a hand in a final farewell for the little group who had come and conquered all.

''Tis the burner of a day for travellin' and that's for sure,' said O'Casey. 'But then 'tis best to be up and at it before the sting a the heat sucks the steam outa horse and man. Don't ya agree, me darlin'?' But his wife was dozing. Stallion turned his head around towards the trailing cart and found Pagga in much the same condition; his chin down into his chest while his nag took the road as it came, following her nose. Milo was nowhere in sight.

Another good mile went under the wheels of the carts before the Cross came into Stallion's sights. 'Take yar head out from between yar cheeks, Pagga!' cried O'Casey as he slapped the reins down on the horse's flanks. 'The partin' of the ways is a hundred yards to our front.' Then looking across to the other cart and O'Leary's downcast head, O'Casey said, 'Crossroads have an awful lot to answer for, Pagga. They're for ever sendin' friends and lovers in opposite directions.'

'Sure, the same can be said a railway stations and bus depots too. Sure if places a departure had souls, then wouldn't it be the devil himself that would be for havin' them, havin' them in his own black burnin' bog to torment the life outa the damned?' snapped Pagga, his chin on his chest and his eyes resting on the flanks of his horse.

'There'll be a Christmas card in yar letterbox every year, Pagga,' smiled Mary, willing him to lift his head to meet her gaze.

''Tis thinkin' I am that I'll be missin' the both of yees,' whispered Pagga. 'America, Mary! It isn't a land that lets go of its Irish. What happens when the time comes and the two of yees go forward to yar God? Who'll wake yees? Who'll sing the sad songs over yar deathbeds?'

''Tis best ya summon the dead to life, Pagga, so as we can say our farewells before bein' off,' suggested O'Casey kindly.

'Leave us alone, O'Leary,' roared Clancy, as he felt Pagga's knuckles rap against his very tender forehead. 'I'm not a well man.'

'Rise up outa yar tomb, Milo Clancy, and be sayin' yar goodbyes to these two lovebirds here.'

Eyes still shut tight, Clancy got off his back and onto his knees and shuffled himself forward to the left-hand side of the cart. 'Where in the name a God am I, Stallion O'Casey? We're not at the Cross yet, are we?' asked Milo as his sore head strained to get its bearings.

'Aye, we're there!' growled Pagga. 'And 'tis been an hour we've been waitin' for yarself to come to.'

'Well, Milo, we're off,' said Stallion. 'This is it!'

'America bound,' smiled Clancy. 'Ambitions about to be fulfilled, hey, Stallion?'

'Well, things turned out differently than planned, didn't they, Milo? God or the devil had intentions right from the start.'

'Come on,' snapped Pagga. 'We best be hittin' the fuckin' road!'

Milo kept his eyes on O'Casey's face as he came off his knees and settled back down into the cart. 'Take care a yarselfs, the both of yees,' he said softly. But he couldn't manage to muster even the ghost of a smile as he added, 'Let that new country of yours be good for ye and may the good Christ bring ye children by the score . . . . Start makin' tracks, Pagga!'

The cart moved forward on into the west road, Pagga looked back over his left shoulder. His sister was standing up on the cart waving her arms in a last farewell. She was smiling, a warm, soft but sad smile.


'Well, we've had a hell of a fuckin' year,' said Pagga as they turned towards home. ''Tis a wonder us two kept our sanity.'

'The reason we're not both as mad as Barra,' said Clancy, looking into the horizon, 'is because we've got ambition.'

'To go forward, searchin' the length and breadth of Ireland lookin' for another Bulba or another hen that can produce one for us, you mean?' asked Pagga.

'Yep,' smiled Clancy with real relish. 'Come the spring we'll set out and see if this land a ours isn't hidin' another Bulba in some forgotten back yard.'

O'Leary smiled straight ahead. 'And if there's one we'll find it.'

Three weeks later and two workmen took down the sign that hung over the main door of the White Willow Hotel. They put up a brightly painted new one in its place. Aggie Carney's establishment had changed its name . . . the new sign read, 'THE TWO COCKS'. Just inside the door in the foyer, high up on the wall behind the reception desk, a large glass case had been mounted. Inside the casing two stuffed birds stood facing each other. One was a rich velvet, midnight black, and the other had a plumage of the purest copper. Their stance was placid if not peaceful. Their faces were dull and lifeless, and their eyes without expression. Underneath the glass box was a sheet of flattened brass, and embossed on its surface were these few words:

TAURUS BULBA – SATAN THE FIRST
26 JUNE 1928
BULBA THE VICTOR